Crysis: Escalation

Also by Gavin Smith from Gollancz:

Veteran
War in Heaven
The Age of Scorpio

Crysis: Escalation

GAVIN SMITH

GOLLANCZ

LONDON

© 2013 Crytek GmbH. Crytek, Crysis and the main
characters are registered trademarks or trademarks
of Crytek GmbH in the US, EU and other territories. 2013

The right of Gavin G. Smith to be identified as the author
of this work has been asserted by him in accordance with
the Copyright, Designs and Patents Act 1988.

First published in Great Britain in 2013 by Gollancz
An imprint of the Orion Publishing Group
Orion House, 5 Upper St Martin's Lane, London WC2H 9EA
An Hachette UK Company

A CIP catalogue record for this book is available
from the British Library

ISBN 978 0 575 11570 5

1 3 5 7 9 10 8 6 4 2

Typeset by Input Data Services Ltd, Bridgwater, Somerset

Printed in Great Britain by Clays Ltd, St Ives plc

The Orion Publishing Group's policy is to use papers that
are natural, renewable and recyclable products and made
from wood grown in sustainable forests. The logging and
manufacturing processes are expected to conform to the
environmental regulations of the country of origin.

www.gavingsmith.com
www.orionbooks.co.uk

To Dyanne & Tobias Heason and the Saturday Club
who taught me some of the things within these pages.

ACKNOWLEDGEMENTS

Thanks to Michael Read, Tim Partlett, Steven Bender and Rasmus Hoejengaard at Crytek for their support, ideas, contributions and hospitality in Frankfurt. Thanks also to Guy Perkins at EA, and Steven Hall, Richard Morgan and Peter Watts.

Particular thanks to a very patient and diplomatic editor, Marcus Gipps. And to Chris Edwards and Cat Halsworth, the former for help with research, the latter for putting up with the research (we were playing video games).

Chance – Part 1

Airfield, CELL cobalt mining support depot, upper Podkamennaya Tunguska River, Krasnoyarsk Krai, Siberia, Russian Federation, 2025

Walker tried to blink away the tears. Many of the other CELL "security personnel" wouldn't make the call to their partners before a big op. They felt it was bad luck. Before CELL Walker had been in 2 Para, running patrols into the LCZ during some of the worst of the London troubles. He had seen the people who made the calls and the people who didn't get killed in equal number. He wanted it fixed and strong in his mind why he had to survive each op.

'I know I shouldn't, I know you just need to hear that we love you and miss you. I know anything else just messes with your head, but we need you back.' Carlotta was crying and, sensing her mother's distress Elsa, just six months old, started crying as well.

Walker squeezed his eyes closed, a tear running down his cheek. Outside the comms booth there was a long queue of hard men and women waiting their turn to use the Macronet portal, despite the shitty reception and the constantly frizzing images. That didn't matter, this was his two minutes, nobody would get in his face about that. Just like nobody would comment on the tears. It was the unspoken rule. They'd all be the same.

Walker's eyes opened as his girlfriend and child shimmered momentarily and then solidified.

'I'm due leave soon and I'll be back ...' his Birmingham accent was still thick, despite years away from the West Midlands of Britain.

'Do you know when your tenure's up?' Carlotta asked. Walker had effectively been drafted into CELL for non-payment of their energy bill. He'd been labouring when they invited him to "work debt free", but they certainly had uses for a skill set learnt in the British army. His biggest fear had been that he'd end up fighting the Ceph in New York or some other infection area, but at least that seemed to be all over bar the clean up now.

'I don't know,' he answered truthfully. His superiors acted cagey every time he asked about it. How much debt had they run up, he wondered? Walker had thought that they had always lived a reasonably frugal existence.

There was a discreet tap on the door. The red counter above the booth had run down to zero, but nobody was going to be a dick about it unless he really took the piss.

'Baby, I've got to go ...' he started.

'You're scared ...'

2

'I'm always scared, I miss you, both of you, but they give us drugs for the fear ...'

'I don't want to hear that. This one's different, isn't it?'

The Macronet link cut. The words: Predicted Operational Security Breach appeared in red floating letters where the poor quality image of his wife and child had been moments before.

'It's just routine, baby,' Walker lied to the warning message. *Why's that a high-resolution image but my girlfriend and kid aren't?* Walker wondered, inanely, unable to process anything else. There was another more urgent knock at the plastic door of the booth. Walker took a moment to wipe away the tears and then, red-eyed, head down, he stepped out of the booth.

'Sorry man,' he mumbled and made his way through the queue towards the exit.

He pulled down the patch on the arm of his fatigues between the straps for his body armour. He took the first syringe, let the smart needle guide itself to a vein, and he injected the good stuff in. He thought of it as getting his game face on. GABA, trycilics, the military grade stims that he had sworn off when he left the paras. He started to experience the artificial feeling of power coursing through his veins. He knew it was artificial because he knew the contrast between being up on the combat drugs one moment and then coming back down to Earth the hard way a moment later. When you found yourself wearing your squadmate's internal organs as outerwear. He still embraced the high. Locked the final flickering image of Carlotta and Elsa away. That image was for when he needed to fight harder, just to live.

He pulled his glove off with his teeth. Pressed his thumb against the needle. The weapons rack accepted his DNA and released the Scarab assault rifle to him. He checked the weapon and took as much spare ammunition as he felt he could get away with and headed out onto the airstrip to join his squad.

Outside, under the harsh sodium glare of the floodlights, the second heavy-lift aircraft was unloading APCs. More heavily armed and armoured CELL security personnel filed down the aircraft loading ramp into the freezing Siberian night. Whatever it was, CELL were going in heavy. *Maybe it is another Ceph incursion after all,* Walker thought. His fear of the aliens was suppressed under a sheen of narcotic courage as he joined his squad.

'Your head in this game?' his squad's new CO asked as she checked her Jackal combat shotgun. The African-American woman had a strong New York accent. She wore a helmet, and a fleece cap under that, but Walker knew that her head was shaved down to the bone and he'd noticed that her ears and noses had holes in them from multiple piercings that had clearly been removed.

'Locked and loaded, LT,' Walker said, with a confidence the drugs were almost making him feel.

'Outstanding,' his new lieutenant said.

Rovesky Township, upper Podkamennaya Tunguska River, Krasnoyarsk Krai, Siberia, Russian Federation, 2025

'I hate it when it gets in your eye,' Eda said in her native German.

'You're just going to have to woman up, I'm afraid,' Klaus told her, and then he sighed theatrically and mimed wiping his eye clean.

There was giggling from some of the other prostitutes present who spoke German. It wasn't voyeurism, Prophet told himself as he listened to the translation of their conversation. No, it *was*, he admitted, but it had nothing to do with the sex in the brothel below his attic hidey-hole. He just about knew all the prostitutes' stock responses now. It was their lives. He knew that Klaus was jealous of Vladimir's cheekbones. He knew that Eda was still young enough to dream of a Pygmalion scenario. He knew who was secretly pregnant. Who were lovers. He heard their Macronet calls to their friends and family back home, the lies they told them, the tears after.

It wasn't the bad old days of the slaving sex trafficking rings. Natasha's House of Pleasure was registered and unionised and Prophet wouldn't be surprised if he could trace ownership of the brothel back to CELL. They seemed to own everything else these days and the township existed to service their cobalt mine. Though Prophet was convinced that it was a front to continue their scientific investigation of the Tunguska Crater.

However, thousands of years of social stigma against those who rented their bodies out for the enjoyment of others wasn't going to be wiped away in a moment.

It was life that he listened to, spied on. It was something that the nanosuit had effectively cut him off from.

He didn't think that conditions were great for the workers in the brothel, but what he found was that no matter how bad things got, even if a miner went "thatch" on one of them due to too many productivity enhancing drugs, there was always humour present. In that they were like soldiers. He had almost intervened the last time a client had gone "thatch" – fortunately the security had got there before the John had cut the guy too badly.

Still, he knew this was a distraction. The brothel, the coming down off the roofs to walk the frozen streets late-at-night. Looking through windows at people having lives, scraping by in this brave new economy. Somehow, when he saw people huddled around the glow of the Macronet feeds, like they would give warmth, all the stories seemed to be about the CELL Corporation these days. Crynet Enforcement & Local Logistics. Somehow the security consultant company – or mercenaries, to give them their older name – that had so badly bungled the Ceph incursion in New York had managed to pretend competence long enough to re-invent itself as an energy company. It was a rebirth worthy of a particularly corrupt phoenix, he mused.

'I know what you're doing,' Psycho said from his corner of the loft. The other nanosuited soldier had been watching a feed from the Macronet on a portable screen. Something about CELL launching a satellite network to complement the work they had been doing to turn the ruins of New York into a vast facility for energy generation.

There was only Psycho left of his nanosuited team, Prophet mused. They'd all left him now. All gone their own way, died or been captured by CELL. Or just lost faith in the mission. Cupcake, Bandit, Fire Dragon and Lazy Dane, who had been getting weirder and weirder. Eighteen months of hitting Ceph incursion sites. Auckland, Wuhan, Tokyo, then, on his own, the last one beneath St. Petersburg. That was when even he had to admit he was forgetting what he was. *What I once was*, he corrected himself. And now only loyal Michael Sykes remained with him. Psycho, who'd rather nail his left bollock to the ground and crawl away from it than let a "mate" down. But Psycho didn't understand, none of them had, it wasn't a job, it wasn't mercenary work, it wasn't about loyalty to friends, and, sadly, it wasn't about fucking over CELL. *It's about survival, pure and simple, us versus them, a very old equation*, Prophet thought.

'You're listening in on your little whore-house soap opera, aren't you?' Psycho said. The tone in his voice said that he was out to needle Prophet. Prophet tried to ignore him.

'What? You don't want to talk to me? I'm pretty much the only other carbon-based life form you've got any contact with these days!' Prophet continued trying to ignore him and Psycho lapsed into silence. And then let out a short, humourless laugh. 'I'm sorry that you can't nip downstairs for a quickie.'

'I don't want to be wasting time here either,' Prophet all but growled. 'Did you think this would be easy?' He stood up and looked around the room. It was a large spacious attic, with exposed wooden beams. The building that contained the brothel had been built from locally quarried stone during one of Siberia's gold rushes. It sat on the corner of a junction in the township. Nobody had ever quite got around to laying down a proper road and currently the streets were frozen mud. Prophet glanced out the window. He could see the glow of the garish neon sign reflected in the gently falling snow.

'You're not just wasting time, mate, you've lost the plot.'

This is where he brings up St. Petersburg, Prophet thought. He'd heard this song before.

'You were out of control in St. Petersburg, you know you were. It was the last straw for Fire Dragon.'

Prophet knew that Psycho was right. The thing was, he had only realised it in retrospect. At the time it had all seemed to make sense. They were the bad guys. He had needed access to the Ceph tech. He needed information and he needed to upgrade the armour. He had to be strong enough for when they finally found what he was looking for.

'And what's with the Ceph tech? I know it won the day in New York but it's changing you, mate. Turning you into …'

'One of them?'

'I was going to say something else.'

'When did you get so soft?'

Psycho's eyes narrowed dangerously.

'Careful,' the British soldier said quietly.

'We're fighting a war. I'm not human now. I am something else. You need to get used to that. If becoming one of them is what it takes ...' Psycho was just staring at him. 'What do you want from me, Psycho?' Prophet asked.

'Something to say that we're on the right track. Any evidence at all that it's actually real.'

'Tunguska was where Hargreave and Rasch originally encountered ...'

'I know.'

'It has to be here.'

Psycho sighed and leant back against the wall, the top half of his nanosuited body disappearing into shadow.

'We need to be thorough this time ... take our time, search everything ...'

'There's no intel, Prophet. We're running missions based on wishful thinking now.'

Prophet whipped round to glare at the British soldier, the suit automatically running firing solutions and reflowing into a combat-ready configuration. All Psycho saw was the inhuman face of the nanosuit's helmet. He knew his own suit was sending out identification signals. What worried him more than anything was that he was now sure that the face under the visor probably wasn't much more human than the alien-looking suit.

'After all this you don't trust me? It's there. It's got to be there.'

'You said that in Wuhan, Auckland, St. Petersburg. It doesn't exist, Prophet. I think you know that. You need to wake up.'

Prophet was across the attic, forgetting that he had to be careful of people hearing his steps in the brothel below. He stood over Psycho.

'No, there's a threat ... the Ceph.'

'Are dead, understand?' Psycho said evenly, looking up at Prophet. 'There are no more aliens. We fought and won that war. The world has moved on but you've got stuck, mate.'

'You don't know what I've seen ...' Prophet was leaning down over Psycho now.

'Where?' Psycho demanded. 'In your head?'

'They were visions,' but even Prophet realised this sounded weak.

'What? Put there by an alien?' Psycho said more softly now. 'Reliable source, then. Prophet, we're in uncharted territory. Fused with these suits, interfacing with alien technology, suffering from combat stress and we really have killed a lot of people. We've killed like gods ...'

Prophet straightened up.

'You think I'm mad.'

Psycho stood up to face his friend.

'How could we not be struggling? Think of the things we've done, what you, especially, have been through.'

'You don't trust me anymore?'

'Prophet, mate, you know I'd follow you to the ends of the Earth …' Psycho laughed and held up his hands. 'Because we're here, now. I'll push bullets at what you tell me to, but it's been eighteen months and not a sign.'

Prophet leant in close to Psycho. Psycho didn't shift. He just looked back at the helmeted face.

'The thing is, I know. I know what's coming. I can't un-see it.'

'Can you hear yourself?' Psycho asked sadly. Prophet turned and walked away from the other nanosuited soldier.

'So what do we do now? Become mercenaries? Go to work as guns for hire like you were when I found you in Mexico? Or do I just turn myself into a VA clinic for psych evaluation?'

'I think you … we've been so obsessed with hunting for this thing that we've not been watching what's going on. The world is being bought.'

'CELL?' Prophet asked, failing to keep the scorn out of his voice. Psycho nodded. 'And you think I'm obsessed.'

'At least they're fucking real!' Psycho snapped. 'All I see is greedy corporate bastards taking over the world, killing anyone who gets in the way, and it scares the shit out of me.'

'What difference does it make who's in charge? That's human politics.' Psycho stared at him.

'You cold bastard,' Psycho said and turned to head back to his gear in the corner. Prophet grabbed him.

'Psycho, wait …'

Psycho turned on him.

'No, you fucking wait. Taking your call sign a bit seriously these days, aren't you? We should be fighting the bastards who are actively fucking us and the rest of humanity. Not that you're still one of us! We shouldn't be chasing some mythical alpha-ceph! With these suits we have a chance.' There was passion in what Psycho was saying that Prophet had not heard from the other man in a long time, if ever. The suit's analysis of Psycho's voice showed him that this was something that he truly believed in.

'How do you fight a company? What? Do you want to go into the board room and start laying fire down?' Prophet demanded.

'If that's what it takes,' Psycho said firmly. Prophet checked the voice analysis again. Psycho was telling the truth. 'Let's go back to New York, finish what you started. Let's tear the heart out of CELL and shove it down their fucking throats.'

It was tempting. Not because Prophet believed like Psycho did. He really didn't care who was in charge. It was tempting because it sounded like a life. As harsh, violent and short as it might be, it sounded like something a human would do. But he knew that the images of what he had been shown, the future, would never stop playing through his head.

'CELL aren't the mission ...' Prophet started.

'You were always a good little boy weren't you, Prophet? Did what Hargreave told you after they got you out of that little jam. Has it occurred to you that they've done something to you, in the suit, that makes you not want to go after CELL, to do as your told, behave?'

Prophet was across the room. He had Psycho by the neck and lifted the other man up. He started squeezing.

'Do you know what they did to me!?' he screamed, but as quickly as the rage had come it was gone. He dropped Psycho.

'Nobody puts their fucking hands on me!' Psycho raged, his suit flowing and preparing for battle. Prophet could see the Londoner was seconds away from going for him.

'Psycho, I ...'

Something changed. It took a moment for Prophet to work out what. There was something different in the rhythm of the town. It had just got quieter. He cycled through various comm frequencies. Nothing. Even the company that handled the policing in Rovesky had gone quiet.

Dead lips smiled. A rictus grin. They were learning. Mainly about comms discipline, it would seem. He could hear engine noises now, the suit sorting, separating and analysing the sounds. Images of the vehicles making the noise started to appear in his Heads-Up Display, effectively playing across his vision.

'What?'

'Here's your chance,' Prophet all but whispered.

Both of them heard the fire door battered open with a sound-dampened pneumatic ram several floors below. They heard boots on the stairs.

Psycho picked up his gauss rifle, quickly checking it.

Time to send the message, Prophet thought. Every Macronet-connected comms device in Natasha's House of Pleasure started chiming urgently as it received a priority text: *You don't know me, but I know you. Something very bad is about to happen. You all need to leave, now.*

Even if they believed the message Prophet knew that there wasn't going to be enough time for them to evac. It was going to go badly for the prostitutes, the regulars, the overseers and the door staff he'd been living vicariously through for the last days. CELL wanted their toys back and in his case they wanted what was left of the corpse in it out, regardless of who was driving the corpse's head.

He stood up and started walking towards the skylight at the front of the building. It overlooked the junction of frozen muddy streets in front of the brothel. Cold blue light flooded the attic. The suit's visor darkened to compensate. Prophet could hear the roar of the VTOL keeping pace with him as he walked, its searchlight shining through the other skylights.

He should stealth now, he knew, Psycho already had, but before it started he just wanted them to see what they were dealing with. He wanted to know how frightened they were.

'Here, Prophet, ever seen Butch Cassidy and the Sundance Kid?' Psycho asked over the suits' comms.

He reached the skylight at the front of the building. He looked down onto the frozen streets. Perhaps he'd underestimated just how much CELL wanted the suit back, he thought. The street outside was full. APCs, Bulldogs, Armoured Security Vehicles, at least four VTOLs in the air, slowly circling him, and a lot of soldiers. The HUD was showing a ridiculously target-rich environment and all the weapons he could register, from SMGs to vehicle cannons to missiles, were pointed at the attic.

The glass broke as Prophet stepped through the sky-light onto the ledge outside the attic. More searchlights stabbed up at him, fixing him in their glare as his visor darkened further. He could hear amplified voices shouting at them. He found it absurd that for some reason their instructions were repeated in Russian.

Prophet took a long, slow look at the CELL forces. Then he started to move ...

The Cult

Department of Antioquia, Northern Columbia, 2019, Operation Scarface (Joint Columbian, US and UK anti-Drugs Operation)

There's a first time for everything. He remembered his first gunfight. He had been frightened but he had got through it; his training had overcome the fear. What was he trying to prove here? The thought flew through his head. Along with: *I should have used the .45.*

Cutting a throat isn't a smooth slice, Barnes knew, you really had to do some sawing. As he'd emerged from the undergrowth the mercenary had started to turn. In the old days the *Medellin* and *Cali* cartels had used British, US and Israeli ex-military to train their people. This new breed of cartel used Eastern European mercenaries, many of them ex-*Spetsnaz*, both to train their own gunmen and to augment their forces.

As Barnes wrapped himself around the man and took him to the ground to control his movement and started to saw at the throat he realised that the man really could fight. The mercenary knew what to do in this situation, how to counter it, and knew that he desperately wanted to live. In short, Barnes' silent takedown was not going nearly as well as he'd hoped.

Artery, artery, starve the brain of blood, windpipe, stop him crying out. Clamp down tight, stop fingers from getting in the way of the blade. He was all but riding the man around the small clearing overlooking the Ferranto Valley and making enough noise to warn people in Bogotá that somebody was being murdered.

The cartel mercenary stopped moving. Lieutenant Laurence Barnes, 1st Special Forces Operational Detachment-Delta, did not stop sawing, not until he was positive that the mercenary was good and dead. He sagged, covered in sweat, fighting for breath, his right arm coated in blood up to the elbow. It was his second mistake of the day.

The second mercenary moved quietly out of the jungle, assault rifle at the ready. The expression on his face didn't even change as he took in the scene. The barrel of the mercenary's rifle swung towards Barnes as he frantically reached for his sidearm. Barnes knew he was not going to be quick enough. The cartel gunman had him cold. The mercenary's face seemed to distort, crumple in on itself. Then again, as the second near-silent round took him in the face. The hydrostatic shock popped the top of the mercenary's head off. His ruined face became red and he hit the ground.

Thank you Earl, Barnes thought. He heard what sounded like two coughs from the nearby trees as at least one other cartel gunman died due to suppressed gunfire. He'd told himself that he'd use the knife instead of the suppressed Heckler & Koch Mk 23 .45 automatic because of the chance of the muzzle flash warning other nearby elements of the Antioquia Cartel and their FARC allies' military forces. If he was honest, an element of using the knife had been because he wanted to bust his knife-kill cherry, and that came from a new lieutenant in Delta Force wanting the respect of his people. Particularly as he'd come from 82nd Airborne and not Special Forces or the Rangers, as was more normal for Delta Force. It was a silly game to play at this level, he admonished himself.

He rolled the mercenary off and got back in the game. He wiped his blade on the corpse and sheathed it. Kneeling down he brought the M4 CQB carbine up, accidentally smearing the blood of his victim on the underslung 40mm M203 grenade launcher. He checked it quickly to make sure it hadn't been damaged in the struggle, but as far as he could tell it hadn't.

Chavez appeared out of the treeline. She had her Mk 23 held steady in both hands, the suppressor attached to the barrel. Judging from where she had emerged it had been her shots Barnes had heard. Chavez was probably average size for a woman but to Barnes she looked tiny. She looked too small for her load-out but she never seemed to have any problems keeping up. She was one of the few women in the special forces community. Barnes knew that she would have had to work hard for acceptance, both as a woman and as a

USAF combat air-controller. Combat Air Controllers were attached to special forces units like Delta and the Navy's SEALs to coordinate air support for their operations. In Afghanistan and Iraq there had been grouching from special forces units about whether or not the Combat Air Controllers were trained to their standards and could keep up. Chavez, from what Barnes had seen, was completely accepted by D Squadron's recce/sniper troop, certainly more so than he was, judging by his current performance.

'What's up LT? I think you nearly cut his head off.' T, short for Thomas, never Tom or Tommy, appeared next to Barnes. Barnes glanced at the sergeant, but there was no reproach or judgement in the SAW gunner/medic's eyes. Maybe some concern. He was the oldest of the four operators, in theory Barnes's 2IC, but Barnes was happy to defer to the senior NCO on operational matters whilst he played catch-up. Barnes had found the sergeant both friendly, which was sometimes unusual in the SF community, and a consummate professional. T had originally served with 1st Special Forces before transferring to Delta. He never talked about his mother, but Barnes knew his father still worked for the Department of Agriculture's Forest Service in Montana's Oxbow Quadrangle near the Idaho/Canadian border.

'Chavez and I took down another two in the trees. Earl got that one,' T nodded at the second dead gunman in the clearing, 'and he's covering us on overwatch back there,' T nodded at some higher ground back in the treeline. Barnes just nodded. T was unscrewing his Mk 23's suppressor and holstering the weapon. He readied his M249 Special Purpose Weapon, the special forces variant of the army's M249 Squad Automatic Weapon.

T knelt down by the mercenary that Barnes had killed. He opened the man's mouth with his gloved fingers and inspected his teeth.

'Yep, definitely Eastern European, you can tell by the dental work.' He glanced down at Barnes's blood-stained arm. 'You'll need to wash that off or the flies'll gather.'

They were on the edge of a steep cliff some four hundred feet up, overlooking the narrow, cliff-lined, Ferranto valley. The whole area was home to the Antioquia Cartel, the heirs of the Medellin Cartel's territory and violent legacy. They operated in northern Columbia's Antioquia Department, an area that was largely controlled by FARC guerrillas since their 2011 offensive. This made it difficult for the Columbian government to police the area.

The cartel, however, had overextended itself when it blew up an airliner to kill the new Columbian Minister for Defence. The Minister had been in the pocket of the Norte del Valle cartel and their right-wing AUC guerrilla allies further to the south. The airliner had been American and had been in British airspace, en route to London from Bogotá, when it had exploded. The US and UK governments had exerted pressure on the Columbian government to allow boots on the ground in Northern Columbia to "assist" the Columbian Military's efforts to deal with the cartel and FARC. Conspiracy theorists were already blaming the CIA for the bombing of the airliner, claiming that they wanted to use it as an excuse to eliminate a left-wing threat on America's doorstep. Barnes had heard the theory, and felt that the theorists vastly underestimated how much the US government didn't want to be involved in a South American Vietnam-style fiasco.

Barnes moved towards a small stream on the edge of the clearing to wash the blood off. T grabbed his arm.

'Someone might see the blood in the water downstream. Use the water in your canteen and then refill it in the stream.'

Barnes nodded and followed T's suggestion, adding a couple of water purification tablets to his canteen. He also decided that he'd made his last mistake of the day and, if he had his way, the last mistake on Operation Scarface.

Barnes crawled to the cliff edge. Chavez had established contact with the USAF liaison at Joint Special Operations Command in Medellin City. T was watching their back.

'Do you want to lase and I'll call it in, LT?' Chavez asked during a lull in her radio conversation. Barnes nodded. He used the scope on the M4 to look down into the valley at their target. Their target had once been a ranch house. Now it was a heavily fortified compound belonging to Diego Ramiraz, the Antioquia Cartel's chief enforcer and thought to be the mastermind behind the airliner bombing. He was also believed to be directly or indirectly responsible for the deaths of over five thousand people in gang violence, bombings and assassinations worldwide.

'This is going to be fun. Just like fucking Afghanistan.' Chavez was always angry and pretty foul-mouthed. She talked street but Barnes knew that she came from a respectable middle-class family who lived in Harlem. He could, however, see her problem. When Barnes had first looked at maps and satellite imagery of the area he had thought that the Ferranto Valley was a suicidal place for Ramiraz to use as a base. He thought that the cartel enforcer and his people had basically trapped themselves in there. However, the compound was all but built under a rocky outcrop in the valley's opposite cliff wall. That and the narrowness of the valley meant that it was going to very difficult to hit with airstrikes. It would be even more difficult if the rumours that intel had picked up on, about a bunker complex within the cliff side itself, were true.

Barnes removed the boxy laser designator from his webbing and got ready to "paint" the compound. The compound itself was a hive of activity, with trucks and four-by-fours laden with heavily armed mercenaries coming and going. The Ferranto Valley might have seemed like a trap for Ramiraz but if this didn't work then the American, British and Columbian forces would have to go in there the hard way, and then it was going to be a vicious fight.

'Two fast movers inbound,' Chavez told him. Barnes

just nodded. 'This is Venom two-four to Vulture leader: okay stud, listen to me carefully,' She was talking to the pilot of the lead FB-22 Wyvern fighter-bombers. New in service, they were derived from F22 Raptor air superiority fighters. 'You got to come in low and slow, you hear me? Get tight in on the deck or this shit just isn't going to work, over.' Barnes couldn't hear the response but he had heard that a lot of the alpha-male jet jockeys didn't appreciate Chavez's style of forward observation. Chavez couldn't care less. After all, they weren't down here in the shit with them.

They heard the fighter-bombers before they saw them. The thunder of their approach echoed down the valley. Barnes caught a glimpse of them banking hard and then dropping altitude as they headed down into the valley. He turned his attention back to lasing the compound. The beam from the designator was mostly invisible except for where it touched the compound's main building

'Too fast,' Chavez muttered under her breath. 'Attack run aborted.'

Barnes turned to look up the valley. He could see the missile contrail against the blue of the sky. Both Wyverns were climbing at ninety degrees. Burning hard, outdistancing the missile easily. It looked like it was raining chaff and countermeasures as the missile detonated far from the two fighters.

'Stinger?' Barnes asked. Chavez nodded.

'Venom two-four to Vulture two. That wasn't a fucking SAM emplacement, it was a peasant with a tube.

Now get fucking back here and finish the fucking job, over.' Barnes knew that she would get reprimanded for that. He'd do what he could to shield her. '*Pindago* asshole, how fucking difficult is it to deliver smart munitions?'

'Take it easy, Chavez,' T said quietly from behind them.

'I'm going to find this *puta* and beat his bitch-ass to death with his own joystick.' She went quiet, listening to incoming comms. She handed Barnes the handset for the sat-uplink. 'They want to speak to you.'

Barnes took the handset and listened.

'Venom leader to Broadsword Actual, received and understood.' He passed the handset back to Chavez and then depressed the send button on his tac radio so that Earl would hear what he had to say as well. 'Okay, the mission's scrubbed ...'

'Pussies ...' Chavez muttered. Barnes gave her a look to let her know that was enough. He knew she felt that the air force had let them down but she was going to have to deal quietly.

'We've been re-tasked. We're exposed here, so we're heading five klicks in country and I'll brief you there. Earl, you're leading the way.'

Barnes took a moment to check the map whilst Chavez and T kept a lookout. He gave Earl a grid reference and the three of them headed into the rainforest. Somewhere ahead of them Earl was leading the way.

Joint Special Operations Command for Operation Scarface, Medellin.

Major Harold Winterman was staring at the newcomer like he'd just tracked dog shit into his command post. He turned back to look at the order he had just received from the Joint Chiefs of Staff and looked at *that* like he was holding dog shit.

Winterman's people knew him to be a consummate professional. He had to be, to be entrusted with command of all special operations on Operation Scarface. They had never seen their commanding officer so close to losing his temper. They also had the feeling that his temper would be something to behold.

The focus of Winterman's ire was stood in front of him in some crisply-pressed, new-looking jungle fatigues, but the man carried himself like he was more than capable of handling himself, and the way he'd spoken to Major Winterman suggested he'd better be.

'Who or what the fuck is CELL?' Winterman demanded.

'Crynet Enforcement and Local Logistics,' the tall, brown-haired, well-built man told him, 'part of Hargreave Rasch.'

'You're military contractors?' Winterman asked, barely containing himself. The man in the new fatigues nodded. 'Then what. The. Fuck. Are you doing? Coming into my CP and giving me orders?' Winterman was thinking about having this person shot. Actually, he was thinking about shooting him himself and then having the guards that had let him into his CP shot.

'I'm not. The Joint Chiefs, that would be your employers, are. They are also commanding you to extend me every possible courtesy. In effect, I am in command here.'

'I'm not sure that's my reading of the orders ...' Winterman started angrily.

'I don't give a fuck.' The newcomer snapped. There was a sharp intake of breath from Winterman's people. Winterman actually took a step forward, as did the Delta operator who had been assigned to him as close protection. 'You don't like your orders, remove yourself from the CP and go and have a cry somewhere. We've measured cocks, mine's bigger. Now, are we getting on with the matter at hand or do I have you arrested for disobeying a direct order?'

Winterman was shaking with fury. He badly wanted to hurt this man. Nobody had spoken to him like that since he'd been a junior officer. The vein on his forehead was pulsing with barely controlled rage.

'I know you, don't I?' Winterman managed. He had definitely seen the man somewhere before, probably Iraq at a guess.

'I've got no time for you special forces cowboys, but you're the best I've got for the job in hand. My name is Commander Lockhart. You can call me "Sir".' He turned and gestured to a group of civilians who had been standing by the entrance to the CP and gestured for them to enter. The Rangers on guard halted them and then turned to look at Winterman. Reluctantly, the Major nodded and they were allowed in.

The five civilians were looking around for a place to set up their equipment but every inch of the CP seemed busy and in use and none of the military personal were very interested in helping out the newcomers.

Winterman, slowly mastering his anger, leant against one of the desks.

'You've just scrubbed a mission that could have significantly aided our operation, not to mention the fact that you've wasted a lot of man-hours and resources and spoiled the air force's opportunity to actually contribute.' Winterman glanced angrily at the air force liaison officer, who looked away quickly. 'This had better be good.'

'I don't give a fuck about Operation Scarface, and neither does anybody else in this room until I say otherwise. Venom got a camera with them?'

'Yes,' Winterman said through gritted teeth.

One of the civilians, a sweaty, balding, piggy-like man with glasses, whose very presence in his CP offended Winterman, gave Lockhart a piece of paper and handed him a tablet. Lockhart studied the tablet, looking less than pleased, shook his head and handed it back to the piggy-looking man. Lockhart handed the CP's communications officer the piece of paper.

'Task Venom to head to these coordinates. I want them to shoot footage and transmit it to me and me only. The freqs are on the paper. Understood?' The communications officer turned to look at Winterman. Lockhart did the same.

'I want to know what you're doing with my men,' the Major told the military contractor.

'No, actually, you don't.' He seemed to be giving the situation some thought. He glanced down at the comms officer and then back to Winterman. 'I will have you arrested if you do not follow my order. You will be court martialed for disobeying a direct order from the Joint Chiefs of Staff. That is assuming that you are still a serving officer in the United States Army.'

Winterman's face was a mask of barely controlled rage as he turned to the communications officer and gave her the nod.

'Ooo, hark at the pair on this one,' a decidedly not-American voice said. Lockhart peered into the corner of the tent where the voice had come from. He saw a squat, heavily-built man with a shaved head lean-ing back on a chair, his combat boots up on a folding table. Lockhart looked at the Major. Winterman just shrugged. Along with a reluctant USAF, the British liaison had been Winterman's biggest pain in the arse. The Major was reasonably sure that the SAS had inflicted the obnoxious cockney on him out of spite. They seemed to take a particular pleasure in wind-ing up US special forces personnel. At least this time they weren't rolling homemade bombs made from cola bottles into tents and showering the sleeping operators with soda.

'Name and rank, soldier,' Lockhart commanded. The British soldier shook his head apologetically.

'I'm sorry mate, that's classified and, unlike your

man here,' he pointed at the Major, 'I'm not under the command of your Joint Chiefs of Staff.'

Winterman was gratified that the SAS trooper was even-handed with his obnoxiousness. Lockhart glared at the British soldier. The British soldier met the glare and just smiled.

'Get the fuck out of my CP,' Lockhart growled.

''Fraid I can't do that either. See, my orders has me here, and I'm a good boy.'

Lockhart took a deep breath. Now it was his turn to try and control his anger. He turned to the ranking NCO of the Ranger security detail that was guarding the tent.

'Have this man escorted out of the CP. If he resists shoot him.'

The British soldier just laughed. The Ranger sergeant didn't seem particularly interested in escorting the SAS trooper anywhere. He looked over at the Major.

'I tell you what, why don't I escort me-self out. Save anyone getting hurt straining themselves. I'll go back and tell my boss-man that I've failed in my mission, God knows what he'll say. I'll probably get a proper bollocking. Mebbe even get "court martialed".' There was some laughter from around the CP. Even Winterman had to suppress a smile.

The British soldier got up and headed towards the tent's entrance. He paused right in front of Lockhart.

'You should bring your toy soldiers and come over and visit us. Try your cock measuring bullshit there, see how far you get.' Lockhart said nothing; he just stared down at the smaller man, his nostrils flaring in anger. The British soldier turned and headed out of the CP, nodding to Winterman on the way out. *Well, it's as close as any of that lot ever get to a salute I suppose,* the Major thought.

***

Barnes was sure it was CIA. The re-tasking the mission, shooting footage and transmitting it, encrypted, to new freqs stank of them, as did the paper-thin mission brief and distinct lack of intel.

The three of them were deep in the rainforest now, in theory far away from anywhere useful, in a bid to avoid cartel gunmen and FARC guerrilla fighters. Chavez and T were keeping a watch out. Earl was still hidden. Barnes was studying the map.

'That it?' T asked despite himself. Barnes felt like apologising to the rest of the patrol, the briefing had been so light.

'Uh huh,' Barnes mumbled quietly. Both of them were too professional to call bullshit on their new orders.

'This is bullshit,' Chavez muttered. 'Is there even anything there?'

'A plantation and a small village. I guess they work the plantation.'

'Coca?' T asked.

'No,' Barnes muttered. 'That's the weird thing, according to intel it's one of the few remaining coffee plantations in the area.'

'Maybe the administration is finally getting tough on caffeine?' Chavez suggested. T chuckled.

'Okay that's enough, Chavez,' T told the combat aircraft controller. 'FARC?'

'In theory they control the area but there's nothing there for them. Maybe a cache, arms or drugs, but it's not a good place. The transport links are for shit,' Barnes told the sergeant. He could tell the more experienced operator was having serious misgivings about this mission.

'It'll be a walk into nothing, T, you know that. We're just chasing ghosts for the Company,' Chavez told the sergeant.

'Earl, you know where we're going?' T asked over the tac radio.

'Sure.' Even with just the one word over the tac radio it was easy to pick up the laconic sniper's thick Missouri accent. The sniper came from rural folks who when the double dip hit and the bottom fell out of farming turned to cooking crystal meth. Earl had chosen to join the Rangers instead. T had told Barnes that Earl was such a good sniper because he made every shot like his next meal was relying on it.

T looked at Barnes. It was a courtesy, nothing more. Barnes nodded.

'Okay Earl, lead us out of here. We don't want to see you.' The Missouri sniper didn't answer. T and Earl had been working together for a long time now. They waited for a couple of minutes and then Barnes took point, Chavez the tail, as the three of them headed into the jungle trusting that Earl was in there ahead of them.

***

Lockhart didn't like being this close to Dr Asher. As an ex-marine he was disgusted that anyone could let themselves go physically as much as the other man had. He also thought that the scientist smelled of milk gone off and the hotter the clime, the worse he smelled. Lockhart was at a loss to explain the stench. His disgust had been further magnified when he'd seen Asher's personnel file and read about some of the fat man's proclivities. Unfortunately, the doctor had made himself indispensible to Hargreave-Rasch Biomedical, CELL's parent company. A microbiologist by training, Asher had cross-trained in enough disciplines to become very useful to the biomedical multi-national when it came to situations like this one.

Lockhart was looking over the scientist's shoulder at satellite thermographic imagery of the suspected incursion area. There was a surprising amount of blue on the laptop screen for a plantation in the middle of a rainforest, even at this elevation.

'I don't like that we're not using CELL personnel for the reconnaissance,' Asher said. He had a pronounced and educated English accent that Lockhart thought sounded whiny.

'You've noticed there's a full scale military operation underway here?' he muttered. He hated explaining the intricacies of military thinking to dumb-ass civilians. 'We didn't have time to get clearance for that kind of operation but it's being worked on at the highest levels at the moment. Had we gone in now, we would have ended up getting shot at by both sides.' Lockhart left unsaid that the Delta team would be better at this than CELL personnel. As much as he was loath to admit it, the CELL special operations team weren't capable of operating at this level. Yet. 'If they find anything then we'll be putting boots on the ground.'

'Oh, they'll find something,' Asher said, somehow managing to sound patronising and whiny at the same time. 'Even a man of your limited "education" must realise that those heat readings aren't right, not to mention the tectonic activity we've seen.'

Lockhart turned from the laptop's screen to stare at the scientist. Asher was oblivious to Lockhart's look of utter hatred. He had no idea how close he had come to having his neck snapped.

Lockhart straightened up and turned around, eager to be away from the repellent little man. He turned around to find Major Winterman staring at him. Lockhart couldn't make out the expression on the JCOS commander's face.

***

'Well, hell.' Earl's accent made 'hell' sound like 'hail' in the earpiece of Barnes' tac radio. Barnes signalled for them to halt. The three of them went to cover, making sure they could see as much of the surrounding area in all directions as the thick rainforest would allow them. Barnes noticed that it had gotten cold. Despite the altitude he was still surprised to see his own breath mist.

'What you got, Earl?' T asked over the tac radio. The experienced Delta operator was perturbed to hear the normally emotionless sniper express surprise.

'Ice,' Earl said. Barnes assumed he'd misheard, or it was an acronym he was unfamiliar with.

'Say again, over,' T instructed over the tac net.

'Naw, you heard me right T.'

'LT?' This time T was genuinely looking to Barnes for guidance.

'Earl, we're moving up to check it out, find a position to overwatch us.' The sniper didn't answer. Barnes glanced over at Chavez and T. T had his game face back on but Chavez was looking unsure. It wasn't an expression he was used to seeing amongst operators.

***

He had known what to expect. He had been briefed on it, but it had still come as a surprise to him. They were receiving grainy footage over the satellite uplink shot by Senior Airman Chavez. Asher was looking at Lockhart with a smug impression on his face. The rainforest was frozen. Everything was encased in ice.

'So, commander? Freak weather, perhaps?'

'I want proof.'

'You'll end up with some illiterate monkey with a

gun knowing far more than they should. I'm telling you the ice is the by-product of an energy release. They have initialised a piece of their tech here.'

'And you've seen this before?' Lockhart demanded, knowing the answer. Asher sighed.

'Nobody alive today has ever seen this before,' he said, as if explaining something very simple to a particularly stupid child.

'I'm sending them in.'

Asher just sighed and shook his head.

***

'Understood, out.' Barnes clipped the sat uplink's hand piece back onto the main unit at the top of Chavez's pack. 'We're to make our way to the village.'

'We are wearing entirely the wrong sort of fatigues for this bullshit,' Chavez muttered, looking around at the winter wonderland the rainforest had become. It was freezing here, and the thin tropical fatigues they had on were doing little to keep them warm. There was no snow, just ice. The air was surprisingly dry, as if the moisture in the air had coalesced into the ice that encased the jungle. To Barnes' mind, when he saw the plants, flowers, fruit and trees in the ice it made him think that a god had chosen to preserve this little bit of rainforest. The ice was like a prism when the sun caught it. Very little of it had started melting yet. It was quite beautiful, if very, very strange.

'Layer up if you've got anything with you,' Barnes

told them. Chavez and T had already put sunglasses on to combat the glare.

'Earl's ghillie suit's going to be worse than useless,' T told the lieutenant. Barnes nodded.

'Earl, sorry to cramp your style but fold in with us.'

Two of them kept watch whilst the other layered up. Barnes had a fleece top and a fleece-lined hat with him that he was thankful for. A little while later Earl warned them over the tac radio that he was about to appear and then did so. The tall, rangy sniper's ghillie suit made him look like a living part of the jungle. Amongst the ice it just made him very conspicuous and he removed it whilst the others kept watch.

'Okay, we don't know what the fuck's going on, so let's assume the worst,' Barnes told the other three members of the patrol. 'Earl, you're on point but don't run away from us, T you're tail.'

'Rules of engagement?' T asked.

'No change but let's err on the side of caution, yeah?' Chavez and T agreed, Earl said nothing, which Barnes took as assent.

They advanced though the frozen jungle in a diamond formation with Earl at the point. Every so often the sniper would point at an area that they would use as an initial fall-back point in the event of a contact.

There were few clouds in the bright blue sky above them and the sun was causing them problems with the glare, despite their sunglasses. As it heated the ice they could hear a steady dripping noise as it started to melt.

***

There was no cover. Barnes had rarely felt so exposed. Anywhere they went in the icescape they stuck out like a sore thumb. *This must be Earl's worst nightmare,* Barnes mused. They were on a dirt track. One side of the road was frozen rainforest, on the other side of the road were frozen, cultivated *coffea arabica.* The small, spiky trees must have been part of the plantation, Barnes guessed. The trees had flowered before they were encased in the ice. All around them now the sun was heating the ice and it was dripping, making the ground more and more treacherous underfoot.

Ahead of them Earl stopped by a bend in the track. He was looking up at something. He gestured to a fall-back point and then moved ahead.

Barnes and the others, weapons at the ready, followed the sniper round the corner. Barnes looked up and froze for a moment. Earl had gone to ground and was covering up the road.

'Want me to go ahead and check it out LT?' Earl asked over the tac radio.

'Negative. We stick together.' *Because this is just getting weirder and weirder,* Barnes left unsaid as he looked up at the strange structure towering over the frozen trees ahead of them.

It was some kind of spire but the architecture was all wrong. There was something organic about it. The spire looked like it was made of cracked, blackened, seamed, diseased bone. Circular blade/drill-like mechanisms spotted the body of the strange twisted spire like technological flowers. Barnes swallowed hard. He was aiming the M4 at it almost despite himself. He forced himself to look away from the strange spire.

'You getting this, Broadsword actual?' Chavez asked over the sat uplink. She had attached the DV camera to the mounting rails of her M4 carbine and linked it to the sat uplink so she could broadcast back to the CP. 'They want us to investigate,' Chavez told the rest of them. *I'll bet,* Barnes thought. 'Gonna tell us what that weird fucking thing is, Broadsword actual?' Chavez listened. 'That's a negatory on actual information,' she told the rest of the patrol.

'It looks like some kind of drill machinery,' T suggested.

'What are fucking coffee farmers doing with mining machinery?' Chavez demanded.

'Maybe FARC are using it?' T didn't even sound like he believed what he was saying.

'Mole people,' Earl said over the tac radio. Barnes was so surprised that he turned to glance at the sniper. Nobody seemed quite sure if the quiet Missourian was joking or not.

'Can you hear something?' Barnes asked. He'd become aware of a low noise coming from the direction of the spire, which according to Barnes' map was where the village was supposed to be.

'Chanting,' Earl said over the tac radio.

'What are they chanting?' T asked.

'I don't know. I can only swear in Spanish.'

***

'This what you were expecting?' Lockhart asked as he watched the grainy footage of the strange spire.

'This is so much more,' Asher said. There was a hunger, or a need, in his voice that made Lockhart very uncomfortable. The fat scientist turned to Lockhart and the commander grimaced as he caught a whiff of the off-milk smell that seemed to accompany the other man everywhere.

'It seems inert. We need to get in there, full biohazard protocol.'

'Let's see what they find first.'

***

The town was little more than a street lined with a few dilapidated houses. The biggest building, if you ignored the strange spire, appeared to be some kind of combined office, truck yard and police station. The trucks were for transporting the coffee beans, Barnes guessed.

The chanting was louder now. He'd asked Chavez what they had been saying and, after she had angrily pointed out that she'd grown up in New York, she'd tried to interpret.

'It sounds like gibberish, to be honest. The only words I can make out are "light" and "white flower".'

'They're talking in tongues,' Earl said.

'LT?' T said quietly over the tac radio. The SAW gunner was on the other side of the street between two houses, his weapon aimed up the road towards the spire. Barnes had been similarly concealed between two ice-encrusted houses but covering their back. 'See the weapons?' Barnes glanced up the street, where he saw there were a number of weapons, mostly old fashioned assault rifles, just lying in the middle of the road.

Maybe they've embraced peace, Barnes mused. The weapons looked like the sort of thing that some of the less well-equipped FARC units would be armed with.

'I like unarmed people,' Chavez muttered. Barnes had to agree with her.

They were close to the spire now but still could not see the base of it.

'Okay, lets move up and get eyes on,' Barnes told them over the tac radio. He reckoned they would see the base of the spire around the next corner.

'Jesus!' T had said it quietly but Barnes had still heard his exclamation. Barnes looked across the road. There was a figure in the doorway of one of the frozen houses. T had let his M249 drop on its sling and was holding his Mk 23 in one hand and pushing the figure back with the other.

'Earl cover our six, Chavez our twelve, keep shooting footage and eyes out all around,' Barnes said and, glancing up and down the street to make sure that there was no-one in sight, he quickly crossed the road.

'Ma'am, you need to go back into the house and lie down,' T was telling the woman who kept on advancing on him. Barnes' stomach churned as he caught a good look at her. She was clearly sick, very sick. She was repeating something in Spanish that he didn't understand but it sounded similar to what they had all heard being chanted.

The woman looked old, but Barnes knew that it could be difficult to judge age in parts of the world where life was hard. She wore a long skirt and a filthy t-shirt. There were seeping growths around her nose, her mouth and her eyes, which were milky and blank. She was obviously blind. The growths looked like externalised tumours to Barnes.

'Seriously, ma'am, you need to stay back,' T said. The woman wasn't listening. She kept on reaching for him as he pushed her back. Barnes saw that she had bleeding holes in her palms. They looked self-inflicted. He glanced down at her feet and saw that they were bloody as well. She was smearing her blood on T. The medic pushed her back hard and then brought his leg up and used that to gently kick her back even further into the house. Then he closed the door as far as he could with the ice covering it and held it there.

'Did you see her lymph glands?' T asked. Barnes shook his head. 'They were swollen. They'd gone hyperbubonic.'

'Disease?' Barnes asked, his heart sinking. *What the fuck have we been dropped into?* Barnes thought, trying to suppress his anger at command.

'Contagion,' T said. Barnes could see the medic was fighting to control his fear.

'Can you do anything for her?' Barnes asked. The woman tried to wrench the door open. T had to yank it closed again. For someone old and sick she seemed very strong.

'Give her something for the pain. Put her out of her misery.'

'She didn't look like she was miserable or in pain,' Barnes said as he drew the Mk 23 and began screwing the suppressor on it. T watched him. Both of them knew that the woman would give away their position, compromise the patrol.

'It is my medical opinion that there is nothing we could do for her and she attacked us,' T said, letting Barnes know he had his back.

'This is on me, understand?' Barnes told the medic. *Time to commit a war crime,* he thought. 'Open the door.'

T let go of the door handle and it was wrenched forward. The top of the diseased woman's head came off as Barnes fired. For a moment both men thought that she wasn't going to fall over. Finally she swayed and fell back. Barnes stepped into the house and put two rounds into her chest.

'Watch our six,' Barnes told T as he slung his M4. He wanted the suppressed pistol in case there were any more. T nodded, but Barnes knew the other man was worried about contact and infection.

'LT,' Chavez said over the tac radio. 'You're going

to need to see this.' Barnes glanced up and down the dirt track that passed for a street here. He saw a dog cross behind them but nothing else moved. Chavez was lying down by the bend in the road, using one of the ice-encased houses as cover. She was looking around the corner, the DV camera on her M4 shooting footage as she did so. Barnes made his way over to her and glanced around the corner.

'Shit,' Barnes said. The ground was broken and had then frozen over where the spire seemed to have pushed up out of the earth. It looked like it had partially destroyed some of the houses as it had risen from the ground. Around the base of the spire were people. Many of them looked like peasant farmers, but others had on the uniform of FARC guerrillas and others were better dressed, or didn't look Hispanic, suggesting cartel gunmen and mercenaries. All of them showed signs of the external tumorous growths and many of them were bleeding from what Barnes suspected were self-inflicted wounds. They were chanting gibberish and bits of Spanish as they swayed backwards and forwards towards the strange spire. Barnes was beginning to wonder if the spire, which seemed somehow inert to him, was some kind of delivery device for a biological weapon. Though whose, he couldn't even begin to imagine. Barnes ducked back behind the house.

'Estimate?' he asked Chavez.

'There's easily more that a thousand people there. They must have come from all over the local area. What's wrong with them, LT?'

Barnes didn't answer, instead he took the handset off the sat uplink on Chavez's back.

'Venom two-one to Broadsword actual, requesting an immediate medevac and quarantine, we have clear signs of a biological contagion here.' Chavez turned around to look up him. She looked scared and angry.

'Negative, Venom two-one. Make contact with the villagers. We need to know what's happening.' The voice giving the order was the same that had replaced Major Winterman's when they'd been re-tasked, except the background noise was different. It was clear that whoever was giving them orders was no longer in the CP. He was obviously transmitting from a helicopter in flight.

'I don't think you understand the situation here on the ground, Broadsword actual, I cannot risk further exposure of my people to whatever this is.'

'Venom two-one, one of the things about being a soldier is sometimes we have to risk death. One of the interesting things about orders, particularly ones like this, that come down from the Joint Chiefs like it had been written on stone by God almighty and handed to Charlton-fucking-Heston himself, is that they are non-fucking negotiable. You don't do what I am telling you to do and I will not only have you and your men court martialed for disobeying a direct order but for coward-ice as well and I will try very hard to make sure that the consequences are just as bad for you as if you'd caught the Black-fucking-Death itself. Do you under-stand me, soldier?'

Barnes tried to resist the urge to crush the handset.

'Fucking asshole,' Chavez muttered, having heard most of the conversation. 'I think he's going to have an accident if we get out of here.'

'I don't want to hear that, Chavez,' Barnes told her, though he was having similar thoughts himself.

***

'Fucking reluctant soldiers!' Lockhart spat as he threw the radio handset on the ground. Asher was struggling into his NBC suit in the cramped confines of the Sikorsky S-92, a civilian derivate of the military's Black Hawk helicopters. There were only two of the CELL military contractors with Lockhart in this chopper, not counting the door gunner. The rest of the personnel in the chopper were Asher's scientists. The other two S-92s, however, were both carrying full squads of CELL soldiers.

'How contagious is the virus?' Lockhart asked Asher. The scientist was sweating heavily, which made it very unpleasant to be in an enclosed space like a helicopter with him. Lockhart was looking forward to Asher being fully encased by the protective NBC suit.

'Unless they are caught in the initial sporeing they should be fine,' Asher told him.

'Then why the suits?'

'In case this time it's different. After all, we've only seen this once before and the resources to research the virus at the time were very rudimentary indeed.'

Lockhart gave this some thought and then continued putting on his NBC suit.

***

They had discussed it. Barnes had explained the order. If they just wanted to bug out he would understand and claim that he had given the order to hang back. It wasn't an unpopular suggestion, he could tell, but they were soldiers.

Barnes had told them that he was prepared to try and make contact with the infected on his own.

T had told them that if the virus was airborne then they were all already infected. If not and it was from contact then he was probably infected, so it would be best if he made contact with them. Also he had the best medical training out of the four of them. The cowardly part of Barnes had wanted to let T do it.

Chavez had said that she was filming it anyway and command seemed to want intel. She had sworn a lot more, but that had been the crux of what she had said.

Earl had said nothing, just waiting for the others to make their decision.

That was how Barnes had found himself, flanked by Chavez and T, walking down the middle of the street trying not to slip on the now wet ice. They were walking towards a very large group of very sick people who seemed to be worshipping the strange spire. Earl was nowhere to be seen. He was watching over them through the scope on his M14. Barnes felt envy for the sniper, but conceded that Earl was where he could do the most good.

Barnes and T had their weapons slung diagonally across their front. They had their hands on them but weren't pointing them at the sick people. Chavez's M4 was pointed at them but only, she told herself, because of the camera.

Barnes had no real idea what he was supposed to be doing. T was looking all around but all the people seemed to be at the spire. The sick people were ignoring them. The closer they got the more they could see the horrible, seeping, tumorous growths. They were concentrated around orifices but some of the people were obviously more heavily infected and the growths covered a lot more of their visible skin. Many of the people present were also suffering from self-inflicted wounds. Often the wounds were on palms, feet or in the victim's side. Barnes guessed they were supposed to represent stigmata.

'What've we got, Earl?' Barnes asked over the tac radio.

'If there's anyone else out here, I can't see them,' the sniper told him. It wasn't the most reassuring way to phrase it, Barnes decided.

They were less than a hundred feet away from the mass of people. They had beatific expressions on their face. They were staring at the spire with unbridled religious adoration and awe. They couldn't fail to notice the three soldiers stood out in the open, but were ignoring them.

'Erm, excuse me?' Barnes tried quietly. Chavez turned to look at him. It had been weak and he knew it. 'Can I have your attention please? We are United States soldiers, we are here to help you! Is anyone in charge? Is there a doctor amongst you?'

A few of them turned around but then went back to worshipping the tower, though to Barnes their worship looked a little like gibbering and drooling.

'Okay, now that we've tried to make contact can we leave?' Chavez asked.

Good idea, Barnes thought.

'Not until we get some intel,' Barnes said. *What fucking intel?* he wondered angrily, *these people are sick and mad.* Chavez looked like she wanted to object but kept quiet. After all, she had agreed to come with them.

'Are you the prophet?' the question was asked in good, if slurred and heavily accented, English. The man wore hard-wearing jeans and work boots but the dog collar gave him away as a priest. The man's throat looked swollen and there were growths all around his mouth, which explained the slurring, and the drooling. He had cuts all around his head. Barnes guessed it was supposed to suggest a crown of thorns.

'What?' Barnes was taken aback by the question. 'No sir, I'm a United States soldier. We're here to find out what's happening and then report back so your government – with our help – can better respond to the situation here.' Barnes cursed himself for mentioning their government. This area was controlled by FARC and there were FARC guerrillas amongst the congregation here.

'I think you are the prophet,' the priest said.

Well, this never happened in Iraq, Barnes thought.

'Have they converted to Islam?' Chavez asked.

'Yes, that's a Muslim mining drill they're worshipping,' T answered. The tension was apparently turning him sarcastic.

The priest started moving towards them. Other members of the strange congregation were starting to notice the three soldiers.

'Father, what's happening here?' Barnes asked. 'What is that thing?'

'It is a herald,' the priest told them. He was still advancing. Barnes found himself taking a step back and he noticed Chavez and T did the same thing. T slipped a little on the wet ice.

'A herald of what?' Barnes asked.

'The god who brings the white flower. The winged serpent, *Quetzalcoatl,*' the father told them. Barnes glanced at Chavez. She just shrugged.

'I think it was one of the words they were chanting,' she told him.

More of the strange congregation were getting up now and moving to join the priest.

'Maybe the cartel is testing drugs on them?' T suggested as his mind desperately grabbed for rational explanations. The priest, and now more of the congregation, were advancing on the three of them.

'Okay Father, I need you and the rest of your people

to stay back. You could be contagious,' Barnes told them.

'Just say the word,' Earl all but whispered over the tac radio.

'What we got, Earl?' Barnes asked.

'Clear behind, all X-rays are in front of you.'

'I think you are the prophet. There is light in your flesh. We must follow the light.' The priest was becoming more intense. Some of the people advancing on them were starting to gibber in tongues. Others were just repeating the word *profeta* over and over again.

'Sir, I'm going to have to ask you and the others to stay back!' Barnes repeated, putting every ounce of authority that had been drilled into him by military service into his voice. They kept coming.

'Just say the word,' Earl repeated.

'Yes, you are the prophet and the light and the flesh is the way to *Quetzalcoatl.*'

'Okay, get back now!' Barnes lifted the M4 and pointed it at the priest. T brought his weapon to bear as well. 'If you do not stop moving then we will fire!'

'I have a clear shot on the priest,' Earl told him. Barnes felt beads of sweat appear and then freeze on his forehead.

'The flesh and the light of the prophet is a sacrament and must be consumed it is the way to ...'

'Now,' Barnes whispered over the tac radio. Barnes actually felt the bullet go past. The priest's face collapsed in on itself and turned red. The priest remained standing for a moment and then toppled to the ground. 'Weapons free,' Barnes told the others.

The diseased congregation charged. Barnes had a moment to register a moving wall of people running at him. He opened fire, long bursts, the muzzle flash flickering at the end of the M4's barrel. They started going down, but not nearly enough of them. Those hit were carried along in the press of the charge or fell to the floor, tripping over others coming from behind them, but always another person took their place.

T was firing long bursts as well, playing them across the press of the diseased people who were charging the three soldiers. The M249 SAW was designed for suppressing crowds, but that didn't work when the people you were trying to suppress had no sense of self-preservation, when all they wanted to do was turn you into one of them.

Earl was killing with every shot from his concealed position, but there were still too many of them.

Chavez emptied the clip from her M4 then turned and ran to the next fall-back point.

'Reloading,' she cried over the tac radio as she ejected the empty clip, rammed another one home, racked the slide, charged the weapon and then grabbed a grenade from her webbing.

Barnes's M4 ran dry.

'Danger close!' He reached forward and squeezed the trigger on the underslung M203 grenade launcher, aiming it straight into the charging crowd that was nearly on him. He fired the grenade launcher but didn't stop to see the effects of the grenade. Barnes turned and sprinted towards the fall-back point. Earl was trying to say something over the tac radio as the fragmentation grenade exploded in the crowd. Bodies and limbs flew about the street. More of the diseased people went down as fragments flew through limbs and bodies at velocity. Barnes staggered as something sharp tore into his upper arm. Something wet hit his head, tearing his fleece hat off.

'Say again!' Barnes shouted as he sprinted, reloading the M4 and sliding another forty-millimetre grenade, a beehive round, into the grenade launcher.

'Grenade!' Chavez shouted as she threw a fragmentation grenade into the right flank of the charging diseased people, away from T on the left.

'They're flanking you, running behind the houses parallel with the street on both sides,' Earl shouted over the tac radio.

Chavez's grenade exploded amongst them, sending more flying, sending limbs spinning and cutting more of them down. Those that had been hit but not killed by fragments and bullets kept coming, limping, crawling or just pulling themselves along with their remaining fingers as others trampled them.

Barnes skidded to a halt by Chavez, turned and started firing. He saw T as he turned to run but they were on him, grabbing and tearing at him. He tried to break free but there were too many of them. Then those closest to T started dying. The top of the head of one came off. Another spun round as he got hit in the chest. Another went down, and then another, as Earl shot them from cover.

More of them were still running at Barnes and Chavez.

T broke free.

'Reloading,' Earl said over the tac radio. It sounded like a death sentence to Barnes. He reached forwards again and fired the M203. The beehive round filled the air with buckshot as if he'd just fired an enormous shotgun. A line of people directly in front of Barnes went down in a spray of red. He was trying to buy time for T.

They brought T down. The M249 was still firing and a few rounds impacted close to Barnes. Barnes shifted the M4 and started firing single shot at those around T. T was fighting like a demon. Barnes was horrified to see them trying to bite him, claw at him. He saw one of the diseased people, an old man covered in tumorous growths, tear T's cheek open with his teeth. The medic was trying to crawl out from under them. The last Barnes saw of him T was reaching towards them, then he was dragged back and disappeared amongst the diseased crazies.

One of the diseased people hit the ground, sliding across the ice, almost colliding with Barnes. He'd been shot by Earl. Barnes shifted aim and started firing as he backed away – they were almost on him again. He heard Chavez screaming. Barnes glanced to his right. They'd come pouring out of an alley between two of the houses. They had her and were tearing at her face, her arms, her legs, anywhere that wasn't armoured. She was already turning red. Her cries were cut off as her throat was torn open.

Barnes shifted aim, trying to help Chavez, knowing it was too late. He fired. It was a tracer round, warning him that he only had two more rounds in the magazine. He fired those and ran. He had no choice. She was dead already. He would just keep telling himself that.

Barnes pulled a fragmentation grenade off his webbing, pulled the pin, let the spoon flip off and then threw it over his shoulder in a way that he really hadn't been trained to do. He ejected the empty clip and tried to reload whilst sprinting but dropped the magazine.

Ahead of him he saw Earl move out onto the street, firing his M14 rifle quickly. Barnes was aware of bullets passing him. He heard people fall and others collide with them and go down, but there were always more.

He saw Earl's head jerk to the left. One of them came sprinting out of a gap between two houses. The diseased woman was practically on top of the sniper.

The grenade exploded behind Barnes and the pressure wave hit him, almost knocking him down. He felt fragments impact his Kevlar but he managed to keep running.

He watched as Earl grabbed his knife and moved to the side, ramming it into the diseased woman's throat. She ran past him a few steps and then sprawled out on the ice, turning it red. Earl drew his Mk 23 and began firing rapidly into the alley between the houses.

Diseased people were collapsing to the ground as they tried to reach the sniper. Earl kept backing away, firing the pistol.

Barnes felt someone grab the back of his webbing. Then another hand grabbed him, and another. He was yanked back. He slipped on the ice and was taken to the ground.

They were all around him, hands reaching for him. They threw themselves onto the ground next to him, on top of him. His vision was filled with beatific faces, tumorous growths and teeth. As they clawed at him he heard disturbing ecstatic moans.

'Run! Run!' he screamed at Earl.

He kicked, punched, tried pushing himself away from them. Somehow he had his knife in his hand. There was blood. He felt teeth and ragged nails against his skin and there was more blood.

He heard a sound like a buzzsaw. Diseased people started going down close to him. Hydrostatic shock blew limbs off sick bodies and sent them spinning into the air as a frightening amount of bullets rained down on the street.

Barnes renewed his fighting. There was no room for the advanced hand-to-hand combat techniques he'd been taught at Fort Bragg. He was kicking out with his feet, punching out with his left fist and every time he felt someone break skin he tried to stab them, a lot.

There was now the constant buzzsaw noise of mini-gun fire. Someone was cutting down the diseased like a scythe through wheat. Barnes kicked one of the diseased people in the face, a little girl. A man got Barnes' knife in the face. Barnes found that he had enough room to draw his pistol. He started firing the Mk 23 rapidly, trying to clear himself room. Firing one-handed he pushed himself to his feet. Someone grabbed at him. Their face caved in as Barnes shot him at point-blank range. The muzzle flash set the man's beard on fire. Barnes practically hurdled him as he broke free of the diseased people and ran.

He felt them grab at him again but he was free and ahead of the mass, but then there were more of them ahead of him. He fired at them on the run. One fell, but now his pistol was empty. As he ran he reloaded the Mk 23, trying not to drop the magazine again.

A civilian Blackhawk hove into view over him. It was flying sideways. Barnes had a moment to register that the door gunner was wearing a protective NBC suit. The door gunner's rotary minigun started firing. The muzzle flash was a constant as the buzzsaw noise started again and the diseased people chasing him started falling.

With it clear behind him, Barnes stopped running and started firing at the four ahead of him. He couldn't see Earl anywhere. He took the four sick people ahead of him down and then swung around. One of the diseased people had managed to avoid the minigun's onslaught. Barnes shot him twice in the head. The slide on the pistol came back, the magazine empty. Barnes ejected it and replaced it rapidly. His M4 had been torn away in the fight.

He was gasping for breath. There were three of the helos. He could see that now. All of them were pouring fire down into the village. One of them was firing into the rainforest. Bullets from the minigun cut swathes through the frozen trees, shattering them like crystal.

He looked around for more of the sick people. All he saw was a sea of corpses.

***

They circled the village looking for more of the infected to kill. Lockhart looked down at the patrol leader stood in the middle of the street, holding a smoking pistol, looking for more targets, his people gone. Lockhart felt sorry for the man.

'It's very exciting this,' Asher said. Lockhart wished that his orders had allowed him to ride in a different helo. 'Is it safe for us to go down?' Lockhart just gave the scientist a look of contempt.

The commander listened as he received a message through the headset he was wearing.

'Well?' Asher demanded. Lockhart took a deep breath.

'The Joint Chiefs have agreed with the boards' recommendation. The Firestorm protocol is enabled. The bird's already in the air.'

Asher nodded. 'Typical tiny military minds. We'll have to act quickly, then.'

'What about Lieutenant Barnes?'

'What about him?'

***

Barnes watched as armed men fast-roped out of two of the choppers, whilst the third chopper covered them. They were wearing NBC suits with body armour over the top.

Four of them advanced on him, covering him with their carbines.

'Lieutenant Barnes. I'm afraid I'm going to have to ask you to relinquish your weapon.'

'Are you fucking kidding me?! We're on the same side!' For one moment he thought that maybe they worked for the cartel, or FARC, except they had called him by his name. He handed over his Mk 23 and then sat down hard.

It was then he started to realise how badly hurt he was. He was covered in cuts, abrasions and bite marks. Some of them were deep and bleeding quite badly. He'd taken a through-and-through in his right upper arm, probably fragmentation from one of his own grenades. He had another graze on his forehead, either from another fragment or a bullet. Judging from how hard he was finding it to breathe he reckoned he had at least one broken rib, probably due to a stray round, at a guess from the minigun. It had only grazed his body armour. Frankly, he was lucky to be alive. He noticed that none of the people in the NBC suits were rushing to offer him medical aid. They *had* supplied him with a number of armed guards, however.

Then he started to think about T, and Chavez, and wonder where the fuck Earl was.

Then he remembered them all around him, reaching for him, teeth in his flesh. He started to shake uncontrollably.

***

The folding table had a number of scientific instruments on it. Asher was pouring over an instrument that Lockhart took to be some kind of microscope. Lockhart glimpsed the stopwatch on the table, checked the countdown, and then turned to look at the strange tower. Three members of Asher's team were using a plasma cutter in an attempt to remove part of it. Their attempt was working but it looked to be taking a lot longer than he would expect for a plasma torch to cut through anything.

'What happened here?' Lockhart asked the scientist. Asher sighed so theatrically that Lockhart was able to make it out through the heavy NBC suit.

'At a guess it was an incursion that didn't fully initialise. Probably due to a lack of energy.'

'And the virus?'

This time Lockhart heard the theatrical sigh over the radio link. The commander started grinding his teeth.

'Commander, I'm working in the most appalling conditions, under ridiculous time restraints and trying to do science through these preposterous suits, which is a bit like trying to play tennis whilst zipped into a body bag ...'

'Just answer the fucking question,' Lockhart snapped.

Asher stared at the commander. The effect was wasted due to neither of them being able to see very much as a result of the suits' masks.

'The answer to the fucking question, commander, is yes, according to my preliminary, and I emphasise the word preliminary, findings, this is very similar to the Tunguska strain.'

'Is it contagious?'

'In your terms that,' Asher pointed at the spire, 'is basically a big landmine crossed with a fungus.'

'An area denial weapon?'

'Whenever it breaches the surface it spores and, as far as we know, only those infected with the spores come down with the virus. The spores themselves become inert after an amount of time we have yet to determine.'

'So he's going to be fine?' Lockhart asked, nodding towards where four of his men were guarding Barnes. 'Even with the amount of contact he's had?'

'As far as I'm aware he'll be perfectly fine. Fit as a badly-beaten fiddle, right up to the moment that this area is sanitised.'

'And you have enough samples?' Lockhart asked. Asher didn't answer immediately. Instead he just looked around at the carpet of corpses on the ground.

'I think so,' the scientist finally said, sarcastically.

'Good. Get that sample of the spire and get your

people back on the helo.' Lockhart turned and started walking towards Barnes.

'Commander, I do hope you're not forgetting your instructions,' Asher said. Lockhart swung around to face the piggy little scientist.

'They're called orders, and I don't need a stinking little pig of a man to remind me of my duty, do you understand me?' Without waiting for an answer he turned back and strode towards the battered Delta Force officer.

***

Major Winterman strode across the playing field the US and UK forces were using as an airfield for their helicopters. He was heading towards the British quarter.

'No ma'am, in my opinion it is untenable to attempt to run special operations under these circumstances.' He was talking over a secure sat phone to General Pamela Follet, the commanding officer of United States Special Operations Command at MacDill air force base in Tampa, Florida. 'It puts every last one of my operators at risk and frankly, I feel it's an usurpation of military resources for corporate agendas. I have not taken this decision lightly, but I am tendering the resignation of my commission, effective immediately. I will of course serve out the remainder of Operation Scarface unless you see fit to replace me, which I would understand.' Winterman listened to the General's response. He had spotted the individual he begrudgingly wanted to speak to. He stopped walking. 'Frankly, General, the Joint Chiefs can kiss my ass and yes do please put that on record. If any of them have a problem with my conduct then they are more than welcome to come down here and discuss it with me personally. I should also make you aware that the moment, and I mean the very second, I am relieved of command I am going to find that so-called-commander-marine-washout-Dominic Lockhart and beat his bitch-ass to death. Yes ma'am, you have a good day as well.'

Having finished murdering his career, the major continued heading towards the UK part of the base as one of their Chinooks came into land. The man he wanted to speak to had noticed his approach and stood up.

'Major!'

Winterman turned around. He saw three members of D-squadron's recce/sniper troop running towards him. He recognised Sergeants Hawker and Cortez and second lieutenant Dunn. It had been Dunn who shouted.

'I suspect it's just mister now,' Winterman told them. The three of them looked like they had just come off a job. Dunn looked momentarily confused but just launched ahead anyway.

'Major, with all due respect, what the fuck is going on? Where is T's patrol? We get to the CP and they said you'd been relieved of command.' Winterman looked at the six foot tall operator. Dunn looked like he'd been carved out of stone. He knew that all three of them went way back with Thomas and Earl. They liked Chavez as well.

'You ready to get into some trouble?' Winterman asked. Cortez shrugged, Hawker grinned and nodded.

'Sure,' Dunn told him.

'Follow me.' Winterman turned on his heel and continued towards the obnoxious SAS "liaison" he'd been saddled with earlier in the operation. 'Sergeant!' Winterman shouted.

The squat, shaven-headed SAS trooper looked at Winterman and the three fully armed and still camoed-up operators he had with him.

'Is this a beating?' the SAS sergeant asked, wondering if he'd pushed the yank major too hard. 'Because the boys are right behind me in the tent and I'm not afraid to scream like a little girl if things turn nasty.'

'Who the fuck's this?' Cortez asked.

'No sergeant, it's not a beating,' Winterman told him.

'In which case, either call me Sykes or Psycho, guv. You go shouting words like sergeant around and people are likely to think I'm some kind of soldier or something.'

'I'm sure nobody would make that mistake,' Dunn told the Brit, smiling.

'What can I do you septics for?' Sykes asked.

'Septics?' Hawker asked.

'Septic tanks, yanks, it's rhyming ... never mind. This to do with the spot of bother you had this morning?' he asked Winterman. The Major nodded. 'What do you need?'

'I'm forced to go outside my chain of command. How much pull do you have with 7 Squadron?' the Major asked.

'I can 'ave a word if you like.'

***

Barnes watched the NBC-suited figure approach him. The man carried himself like he was used to command. He had seen most of the other personnel, except the fat one, defer to him. The NBC-suited figures were packing up the two choppers on the ground and getting ready to leave whilst the other chopper circled them. Barnes had been using his med kit to see to his own wounds as best he could whilst four of the gunmen guarded him.

The commander reached him and stopped, standing over the lieutenant.

'You're not going to take me with you, are you?' Barnes said, with a degree of resignation.

'I'm sorry, son.'

Barnes looked up at the man but all he saw was the mask of the protective suit.

'At least take my people's bodies with you.' The commander shook his head. 'Who are you people?'

'Do you want some advice, son?' The commander asked. Barnes didn't answer. 'Run, as far and as fast as you can. Head south, but start now.'

'Have I got it? The virus or whatever the fuck that nasty shit was.'

The commander shook his head.

'Am I a carrier? Will I be contagious?'

'No.'

Barnes looked up at the commander's mask.

'I'm going to find out what happened here, you understand me?'

'You need to get going, son, now.'

Tiredly Barnes stood up, got his bearings and, with every muscle in his battered and wounded body protesting, he started to run.

Lockhart watched him go and then turned and climbed onto the last chopper as it took off.

***

A Spirit B2 belonging to the 509th Bomb Wing out of Whiteman Air Force Base, Missouri, dropped the smart bomb from over ten miles away at a height of forty thousand feet. The bomb tracked the transponder left by Commander Lockhart at the base of the spire in the village unerringly. As it approached the spire a conventional explosive within the bomb was detonated, scattering the nanofuel over the surrounding area. That fuel then auto-ignited.

***

Barnes heard the explosion first. Then he was aware of a rushing noise as a powerful wind seemed to suck the oxygen out of the air. He had taken as many of the painkillers as he had dared from the med kit, but sprinting through a frozen jungle was still agony and he spent a lot of time slipping over and sliding into trees. Then the blast wave hit. The frozen trees exploded. Ice fragments filled the air. Barnes was torn off his feet and flung across a narrow gulley. He had just about enough time to realise that he was in real trouble.

***

The RAF 7 Squadron pilot had brought the HC3 Chinook to a hover. Major Winterman, Dunn and Psycho were all crowded into the helicopter's cockpit hatchway. They, along with the pilot and co-pilot, were staring at what looked like a solid wall of fire hundreds of feet high. It bathed the inside of the chopper in a hellish red light.

Lockhart leant out of the lead helicopter, looking behind him. They had just got clear of the fuel-air bomb's extended blast wave. It looked like the air itself had caught fire.

***

Below them was devastation. More than two square miles of rainforest had just ceased to exist. It was steaming, blackened ground now. Beyond that, many of the trees had been knocked over by the pressure wave and parts of the forest were burning.

'Psycho, what have you got us into?' the Chinook pilot demanded as he circled the area.

'Jimmy … I'd no idea,' Psycho said apologetically. 'Cool though, aye?' Dunn and Winterman turned to stare at the SAS trooper, appalled. 'I'm just saying,' Psycho said defensively.

'I've got smoke on our five,' Cortez said from the helicopter's main cargo area. Winterman and Dunn headed back to look.

'No shit, the jungle's on fire,' Psycho said as the pilot swung the Chinook around.

'I see it,' the co-pilot said, pointing at a thin plume of yellow smoke.

***

Barnes dropped the smoke canister he'd set off when he'd heard the chopper and collapsed to the ground and mercifully passed out.

He came to moments later to see the twin rotors of a Chinook overhead. Time skipped a beat. He came to again to see a squat, powerfully built, shaven-headed soldier holding a General Purpose Machine Gun standing over him.

'You're all fucked up, mate,' the soldier said in a broad London accent.

2 Days Later

'Yes sir, one of the Delta Force operators survived and

another is missing.' Lockhart said into the secure sat phone. 'Yes, sir, I am aware of Dr Asher's recommendation but it is my belief that a sanction will just draw more attention to the situation and frankly Asher is a horse's ass. That soldier fought hard and deserved to live.' Lockhart listened intently to what was being said on the other end of the line. 'I still have reservations about the whole program, but frankly I think Lieutenant Barnes would be an excellent choice if you're still intent on going ahead with it.' Lockhart listened again. 'Thank you, Mr Hargreave.'

Lockhart folded the sat phone away and took another sip of his Bourbon as he glanced out the window of the corporate jet heading north. On the table in front of him was a folder labelled Raptor Team.

Schism

'They call me Prophet. Remember me.'

The barrel of the M12 automatic felt cool against his head. He hadn't had cause to fire it at CELL or Ceph recently. Pressure on the trigger. Heat. Almost too hot for there to be pain. There was the weirdest sensation of something moving behind his eyes, inside his head, but just for a moment. He remembered sinking to his knees. He was dead then, but his brain was still receiving information. Nobody ever talked about this because nobody ever came back. The ground tipped towards him but everything went black before he face-planted.

He remembered speaking to Hargreave. He remembered being interrogated some time later. No, that wasn't him. He was dead. He remembered putting the bullet through his head. It was either that or he would have slowly turned into a Ceph, his body eaten by tumours and alien DNA, becoming an alien killing machine.

If he was dead then why was he running across the wasteland, a darkened New York behind him, the damaged skyline reaching up like so many broken fingers? His hands had been bloody before. He'd been little more than a boy, a junior officer, the first time he'd killed. It'd happened in Iraq. It'd happened very quickly and he'd done it over a distance of seventy feet. The first time up close and personal, the first time he'd felt warm blood on his hands, had been in Columbia. Now he had blood on his hands again, and this time he couldn't feel the warmth through the nanosuit. The blood steamed a bit in the cold air. Information on its chemical makeup scrolled down his vision from the suit's Heads-Up Display. He knew everything there was to know about this blood except whose it was and how they'd died. Though Prophet knew they must have died at his hands.

Bright light stabbed down onto the broken concrete and scrubby plants. One helicopter gunship and then another hove into view. Information on the model of the gunships, their capabilities and armaments, played down the HUD. He could hear the pilots' conversations with their control. They were CELL military contractors playing at being soldiers and getting paid more than real troops for their troubles. They were searching for an escaped nanosuit. Someone called Alcatraz. *Who the fuck is Alcatraz?* he wondered. Then he remembered the kid he'd pulled from the river. The wreckage of the USS Nautilus. The cold feel of the metal of the M12 against his head.

'Shit. I'm dead,' Laurence Barnes, who they called Prophet, said to himself, but he didn't stop running. He activated the stealth mode and the lensing field bent light around him. To all intents and purposes he disappeared as the harsh blue light of one of the gunship's searchlights swept across where he'd been.

He became a ghost.

***

'Okay, I'm gone now.'

'I think we both know that's not going to happen.'

'I have a life ... a family.'

The CSIRA Black Body Council interrogator glanced at the file.

'Not much of one, not from what you were saying.'

'You think you know me now, Roger?'

Prophet froze the footage that the suit was showing him. He could see how it was going to play out. He was lying down in a sewer trying to mask his heat signature from the thermographics that the pilots in the CELL gunships overhead would be using.

He now knew who he'd killed. Roger, the interrogator. The guy that CSIRA or CELL or whoever had sent to debrief him in the wake of the clusterfuck that had been his recent operation in New York.

He remembered the disease, the quarantine. He remembered CELL being called in as a military contractor to enforce martial law in the city. He remembered how they had hunted him. And he remembered the Ceph. The same aliens he'd first encountered in the Pacific on Lingshan. Cephalopod-like aliens clothed in hi-tech war machines far in advance of humanity's best military efforts. He remembered the suit melding with their technology. It hadn't been the last time.

He had been in control for some of it, or some mix of him and Alcatraz had been, but now the memories were fragmented. The events played like two pieces of film of the same events running just slightly out of synch with each other, one superimposed over the top of the other.

It was worse than that. It didn't stop the further back he went. He remembered Lingshan, but somehow he was also doing SERE training at Brunswick in Maine. He remembered Columbia, but he was ditching school and hanging with his friends. He remembered Iraq and at the same time reading comics, riding his bike, breaking into some kind of Sea World-style attraction. He remembered basic training and he remembered his Mom instilling the fear of god into him. The problem was that the mother he remembered, now superimposed on the hell of basic training, was white. Mrs Barnes had most decidedly not been.

There had been other signs as well. The fear as he'd lain down in the black water of the sewer – where had that come from? And Prophet's skull felt fit to burst. The pain was a burning white light behind his eyes. He was sure there was blood trickling out of his ears under the suit, but then corpses don't bleed. *Maybe it's the suit growing into my head to fix the problem,* he thought. The suit should have been able to tell him what was going on, what was causing the pain, but the medical outputs seemed conflicted.

Prophet knew that none of this mattered. The only thing that mattered now was the mission. The only thing that mattered was what he knew. What he'd been shown on Lingshan, in the ice. He knew it was far from over. When he'd put the gun against his head that had been because of the disease, he told himself, he'd had no choice. He tried to ignore how much the cool metal of the gun barrel had seemed like a chance to rest.

The pain made him scream. Blackness claimed him.

***

Olfactory sensor overload. Information scrolled down Prophet's vision, describing the chemical process of rot. It was biotelemetry telling him that he was sat in a stinking alley full of garbage.

There was someone else in the alley with him. Even as disorientated as he was, Prophet was shocked that he'd somehow managed to go from a nanosuited god-of-war to being blindsided in an alley. The man was well built, hair shaved at the sides, flat on top, green eyes but otherwise surprisingly non-descript. He looked to be in his early twenties. The jeans and t-shirt, despite the chill in the air, did nothing to disguise the man's military bearing. Prophet could make out the bottom of the winged skull tattoo. The skull had a diving regulator in its mouth and the words *Swift, Silent, Deadly* underneath it.

'Fucking jarhead ...' Prophet managed.

'Screw you, you army puke,' the other man said, without a trace of feeling.

The empty bottle he had thrown exploded against the wall of the alley. Prophet found himself alone. He pushed himself to his feet with difficulty. He staggered a bit but he could feel himself recovering. Presumably this was the suit working out how to deal with his bizarre situation.

Prophet became more alert with every step he took. He looked out of the alleyway. The alleyway led onto a rain-soaked boardwalk. Beyond the boardwalk was a beach, and then a dark rough sea.

The suit's nav-systems had been trying to tell him for a while but it took the boardwalk, all the neon and garish casino fronts, to drive it home: Atlantic City. *As if things weren't bad enough*, Prophet thought, *I'm in Jersey.*

It must have been late because there were very few people on the boardwalk. Still feeling a little disoriented, he decided that he wanted to see the ocean. He engaged the stealth mode, the lensing field ghosting him, and he crossed the street.

Glancing behind him, footage from a Macronet feed in the window of a bar caught his eye. He linked to the net with a thought, searched for the footage and had it downloaded to the HUD. He saw CELL military contractors brutalising and executing victims of the Manhattan virus. It cut to footage of Hargreave-Rasch board members being escorted through crowds of reporters. The headline read: *Hargreave-Rasch's board members to face congressional hearing over Manhattan Crisis.*

Prophet figured that mismanagement was what they called war crimes these days. He believed that the board members should be punished for what they had done, but he didn't hold out much hope. The system was too corrupt, and Hargreave-Rasch's PR were already spinning the New York events.

He reached the beach without drawing too much attention to his hulking form. *Mission, have to get back on the mission.* For the first time in a long time the mission was his. He wasn't doing what other people were telling him. And for the first time in a long time, he knew the mission was right. It was a simple matter of survival.

He was almost thinking straight now. The pain in his head had been a constant since New York, but the nausea and the acid burn in his stomach was gone. He'd always enjoyed looking at the ocean but tonight it disquieted him. He didn't like water anymore.

***

'You're back again, huh, mister?'

Prophet turned to find himself looking down at a young girl, maybe ten- to twelve-years-old, smiling at him. She was dirty, her clothes were ragged, and she had dark hair and green eyes.

What was going on? Where'd she come from?! Then Prophet realised that he was somewhere new.

He checked the GPS. Somewhere in Ventnor City.

The information came scrolling down the HUD for the asking. A working class neighbourhood that gangs and drugs were slowly claiming, thanks to the Double Dip Recession. He couldn't remember ever having been here before but the girl definitely seemed to recognise him.

He was stood in some trees out the back of a series of panel board houses that might have been nice places to live, once. The wooded area was scattered with old bottles, tins, needles and other drug paraphernalia. There was the remains of fire in a dip in the ground.

'I've been reading my bible.' The girl was talking again. 'Momma was always said it was a good thing to do. A righteous thing. Before they took her away.' The girl swallowed hard. She looked like she was about to start crying.

Prophet hadn't had much interaction with kids. He'd been good with them when he had to be, when his friends started pairing off and starting families, maybe a little too strict but that was the military in him. They'd liked him, though, he knew cool stuff and could do cool things. But he had no idea how to handle this.

He remembered her. Alice, his little sister. His parents had had children way too late. He remembered being surprised that his dad hadn't been shooting blanks at that age. He remembered how young Alice had been when Mom had been diagnosed with early on-set Alzheimer's. He'd wondered if she'd been suffering, undiagnosed, when she'd gotten pregnant in her forties. Maybe even earlier, when they'd had him.

The religious stuff had always been there. As an adult he'd become convinced that half of it was fear and half of it was his mother's need to look down on and judge others. When the Alzheimer's kicked in, well, then the real fun and games had started. He'd known it was the disease, but that didn't matter much when you were just a kid, getting beaten on and screamed at about how you were going to hell. In comparison the Marines had seemed like a pleasant alternative.

No! That never happened! My name is Laurence Barnes, I grew up in San Diego. They call me Prophet! Prophet knew these to be false memories. They were someone else's. Red warning signs were appearing on the HUD as the suit tried to understand what was going on in his head. He'd been in fire fights in over a dozen countries and here, in Jersey, confronted by a ten-year-old girl, who at some level he knew was his little sister even though he didn't have one, he was having a panic attack.

'Momma said that the bible had the answers. That's armour you're wearing, isn't it, mister?'

Prophet forced himself to calm down. The pain in the dead flesh of his skull was nearly overwhelming. He could see white lights and wanted to scream.

'You're an angel, aren't you, mister?' He almost laughed and thought he felt like throwing up, if only he still could. The things he'd done made that question seem like an obscenity. 'You've lost your wings. Is god angry at you?'

No, it just feels that way sometimes.

'Alice!' the harsh voice cut through the humid night

air. 'Where are you, you little bitch?! Get over here now or you'll feel the back of my hand.'

Prophet didn't like the sound of the voice. He stepped back and engaged the stealth mode. It was only then he saw how frightened Alice was.

Alcatraz had always tried to be hard where his mother was concerned. He'd had no problems about cutting her off after she'd been institutionalised. He'd always told himself that there'd been no guilt about never going to see her. Despite how she'd terrorised him growing up, Prophet knew this to be a lie.

When she'd ended up in the psych ward his, *no, Alcatraz's*, dad had basically wasted away. He'd gone out with a whimper, not a bang. Alice had ended up in a foster home. There had been tear-filled conversations, with her older brother promising her that as soon as he was back home she could come and live with him.

'Then I just went and died in New York. Sucks, huh?' Prophet whipped around, looking for the source of the voice and seeing nothing. The weasel-faced man in the wifebeater, pyjama bottoms and, oddly, spats, must have heard something because he looked around to where Prophet was hidden. Deciding it was nothing he turned back to Alice. His bloodshot eyes full of anger. The girl was shaking with fear.

'What'd I tell you?' he demanded.

'Which time?' she asked, confused and terrified.

'Are you trying to get fresh with me?' He lifted his hand up as if to backhand her. She shrank away from it in a way that told Prophet she'd been hit plenty of times before.

'Hey,' Prophet said softly. The man froze. 'Turn around.' The man managed to control his fear long enough to do as he was told. He couldn't see anything. He looked around and, still finding nothing, his fear was replaced with anger as he started to turn back towards Alice. Prophet made sure that the man saw him appear out of nowhere. The man let out a high-pitched scream. The scream was choked off as Prophet grabbed him by his chin and lifted him off the ground. The man soiled himself.

This I understand, this situation I can handle, the proper and correct application of fear and violence.

He could feel the man's jaw crack and then splinter under his power-assisted fingers. The man was somehow still making whimpering and squealing noises as he drooled blood.

'I could be anywhere and you'd never know,' he whispered to the man. 'You're going to look after Alice and all the other children in your care to the best of your abilities. You will never raise a hand to them, or even an angry word. You will treat them with as much kindness as your resources will allow and you will stop drinking or doing whatever it is that turns you into a foul smelling, evil, little worm, because I will be checking. I will be checking frequently, and if I don't like what I see I will remove limbs and solder the wounds shut. Do you understand me?' The man didn't answer. 'I said, do you understand me?'

'I don't think he can talk,' Alice managed through the terror. At the sound of her voice Prophet felt the guilt wash over him. He'd forgotten she was there. This was just another bit of violence for her to witness. He dropped the man, who curled up into a ball and made whimpering noises.

'Get out of here,' Prophet said quietly. The man didn't move, he just whimpered. Prophet took a step towards him and the man made a run for it, scrambling away on all fours.

Prophet looked down on Alice.

'I'm sorry,' he said.

'God will forgive him for his sins, and you.'

He felt like crying. He knew that this frightened young girl was concocting an elaborate fantasy around this strange figure she'd been confronted with. That he was an angel fallen from grace and that to earn his redemption he would watch over her and keep her safe. The awful knowledge that under the carboplatinum-reinforced coltan-titanium exoskeleton was the animated corpse of her older brother somehow made it all the more horrifying.

'Did you mean what you said? Will you be watching over me?'

Prophet thought long and hard about lying. He desperately wanted to. He just wanted to tell her what she wanted to hear, but he couldn't. She was far too nice, forgiving and naïve to survive in the situation she had found herself in.

'No,' he told her. 'What I said was to frighten him

into looking after you. It might work but probably only for a little while. You've got to be smart, keep your head down, keep out of his way and look for a safe way out as soon as you're old enough, and I mean school not the streets, and Alice, you've got to learn to look after yourself, stand up to people. You don't want to get in a fight if you can help it, but if they hit you, hit them back, harder. You understand me? God will understand.' *Or fuck him, quite frankly.*

She nodded, tears in her eyes. It wasn't enough. It wasn't nearly enough.

'I guess you've got other kids you've got to help, right?' she asked through the tears, wiping her nose on her sleeve.

No. There's the mission and only *the mission, if your brother will let me.*

He nodded, mumbled platitudes at her and then turned away. He made himself walk away by promising that he would come back and check up on her. There would have been tears in his eyes as he lied to himself, if he hadn't been a walking corpse.

He all but staggered past the Green-Eyed Man from the alleyway, trying to ignore him. The man watched him pass. The expression in his eyes was unreadable.

***

'Prophet?'

More voices in my head?

'Prophet. I know you can hear me,' The voice was

familiar and it sounded like it had been trying to speak to him for some time. Prophet looked around at his surroundings and sighed. He'd lost time again. He was sat on a detritus-strewn beach. He wondered why the other guy never took him anywhere nice when he was in control as he watched a flock of scavenging seagulls take to the air. On the other hand, in the nanosuit, he guessed he was a little conspicuous.

'Prophet, this silence helps neither of us. I think you're in trouble and I think we can help.'

He recognised the voice now. Karl Rasch. The CEO of Hargreave-Rasch Biomedical. The company that had developed the living weapon that animated the distinctly *un*living body he had stolen.

Hargreave-Rasch were also the parent company of CryNet Systems and CryNet Enforcement and Local Logistics, the so-called "military contractors" who had spent a lot of time shooting at him in New York. He'd killed a lot of them, as well as a lot of Ceph.

'I will find a way to break this comms link permanently,' Prophet muttered. As he said it the HUD was already showing him options for the nanosuit's comms as the suit's heuristic systems went to work.

The Green-Eyed Man was back, looking intently at Prophet and listening to one side of the conversation. He was sat on a pile of driftwood, the seagulls ignoring him.

'Is that a good idea?' Rasch's voice was cultured, educated, with a thick German accent. 'You don't sound well. We have the facilities to help you.'

'It's not over. I know what the Ceph are planning. We have no future ...' Prophet cursed himself. The Green-Eyed Man continued staring at him.

'We can help you, we want the same things.'

'Bullshit, you want to skin me. Use me, like your company always has.' He remembered the argument he'd had with Psycho on Lingshan. The Brit had been convinced they were little more than test beds for Hargreave-Rasch's experiments.

Rasch did not answer immediately.

'You're a soldier, Prophet. There has to be risks involved in that. There has to be somebody giving orders, and there have to be sacrifices. You − more than anyone − know what's at stake,' the old man said finally.

'Yes, I do. I just don't think that you're the ones to deal with the problem.'

'We want to deal with the Ceph as much as you do. And I need your help for that. There's no future for any of us if the aliens take over.'

'I want this planet to survive. You and your company just want to profit. Besides, are you sure there will be anything left of you after the Congressional Inquiry?'

There was a dry chuckle over the comms link. 'I think we both know that's not how things like that work.'

No, consequences are for poorer people, Prophet thought.

'I'm not coming in. I don't trust you, and I have a job to do. I know the Ceph are still active out there, and I know you're looking for them as well.'

It was hollow machismo and Prophet knew it. The comms link went quiet again.

'The way you integrated with the Ceph tech in New York may make you our greatest hope. I think you're having problems. We're not sure what happened. We're not sure how your personality survived but we do think that it's affecting you. A conflict with the remnants of callsign Alcatraz's personality.'

You mean the mind that this body belongs to? Prophet looked over at the Green-Eyed Man. He was smiling at Prophet. The smile had little humour in it.

'Being Hargreave's puppet got people under my command killed. It got me killed. It got this poor bastard whose mind I'm riding around in killed, and as much as I enjoy your Victor Frankenstein impression, I'm not coming in. You know what I'm going after. If you say that we're after the same thing, if you truly want the Ceph defeated, keep your people out of my way.'

'You know that's not going to be possible. I don't have control over all of CELL's people. Working with us will be the best way to accomplish your mission. I know there are some ... wrong-headed elements in this company, but you can trust me. You need to come in. The Monster lived a lonely existence and came to a cruel end ...'

The suit showed him the way to sever the comms link. He did so and then audited the suit's internal systems, looking for any other ways that Hargreave-Rasch or CELL could contact, or worse, track him against his will, but he found none.

'What am I to you?' the Green-Eyed Man asked him. 'The zombie that carries you around? A drone, a weapons platform that you're the operating system for? What?'

Prophet put his head down and tried to ignore him. He heard the Green-Eyed Man laugh.

'You think I'm going to go away?' Suddenly the Green-Eyed Man was kneeling down next to him. 'Know what I think? The suit becomes your skin. We're superhuman, yeah, but the sensors still feed back everything directly to our nervous system once the suit fuses with flesh. We still feel every hit, every shot or knife wound, each fall or burn. Feels like we've died a thousand times, doesn't it? That's what I think I am to you. I'm armour. I'm here to soak that shit up. All the pain.'

Prophet finally looked up.

'I think you're here because you're trying to hold on.'

He was just talking to the sky. The Green-Eyed Man was gone.

***

'I know you're in here.' The voice had the surety of a fanatic. Prophet had heard its like before, in the Middle East, in Columbia.

He was in a small institutional room. It was bare except for a bed with restraints. The window was small and made of thick, reinforced safety glass. It was some kind of psych ward. He'd visited men and women who'd once been under his command in places like this before.

The woman strapped to the bed was gaunt to the point of cadaverous. Although washed-out, her features lacked the slackness of the long-term institutionalised. Instead she looked alert, intent, but there was more than a little madness in her eyes. She must have been in her late forties or early fifties, far too young for Alzheimer's this severe.

He'd come to as if waking, alert, from a deep but dreamless sleep. He was in the corner of the room. The nanosuit's stealth mode was engaged. The lensing field bent light around him. In theory it make him invisible.

'Show yourself,' the woman hissed. Apparently he wasn't invisible enough to hide from Alcatraz's mother. 'And there met him out of the tombs a man with an unclean spirit. Who had his dwelling among the tombs; and no man could bind him, no, not with chains. Because he had been often bound with fetters and chains, and the chains had been plucked asunder by him, and the fetters broken in pieces. Neither could any man tame him. And always, night and day, he was in the mountains, and in the tombs, crying, and cutting himself with stones.'

There was just something about quoting the Bible, Prophet thought, which meant you could always find relevance somewhere to your current situation.

He had no idea what to do. If he showed himself to the woman then he would just be torturing her, further feeding into the religious aspects of her dementia. On the other hand, she already knew he was here. Alcatraz must have given himself away.

Now you decide to visit your mother? He was more than a little pissed off. Maybe torturing her had been the point. Maybe this was payback.

C'mon Alcatraz, you're better than this, Prophet thought. He wasn't sure if the distant answering howls of rage were his imagination or not.

'Son?' she asked.

Shit.

'Mom?' Prophet found himself whispering.

Where the fuck had that come from?

The madness was gone from her eyes. He saw only what you were supposed to see in a mother's eyes – unconditional love.

The lensing field collapsed as it ran out of energy. *How long was I stood there for? How long was she raving at the invisible ghost in her room?* He glanced down at her wrists and ankles, which had been rubbed raw and bloody by the restraints. This must be more than Alzheimer's, he decided. There was an aspect of religious mania to whatever was wrong with her.

She looked up at near-enough six and a half feet of armoured-carbon nanomyfibrils with recognition and love in her eyes.

Then, with a sinking sensation, he watched her face harden.

'You're not my son,' she said, her voice laced with venom and suspicion. Was he supposed to say something,

Prophet wondered? 'Who are you!? Where's my son?'

I'm the ghost possessing your son's corpse. He died fighting aliens.

'He was a good boy.' She wasn't looking at him now. 'Oh, he did wild things. Some days I thought there was the devil in him, but I knew, deep down, he was a good boy. He serves his God and his country, you know?' she said with pride, and then looked up at him, eyes narrowing with suspicion.

'Ma'am.' *What are you doing, Prophet?* he demanded of himself. 'I'm afraid I have some bad news.' Her eyes were shining with tears now. It was the start of the conversation that all family members of soldiers dreaded, and she knew it. Some part of her, the lucid part, would have been expecting it ever since her son had joined the Marine Corps. 'Your son was killed in action. In New York.' *New York*, Prophet thought, *we weren't supposed to die in New York. We were supposed to die in places like Iraq, Columbia, Afghanistan, Sri Lanka, Lingshan. Foreign places, exotic places, not the Big Apple.* 'He fought hard, he died bravely. He was a credit to his fellow marines, the Corps itself and his country,' he finished meekly. He could hear the hollowness of the platitudes in his own words.

'It was the violence, wasn't it? And the drugs they gave you. And fallen women. They follow soldiers like flies to excrement. And the drink, all your friends would want you to drink with them. You were always such a popular boy. Is that how it got in?'

Now he was her son again, it seemed. Prophet told

himself that he just needed to leave. This was accomplishing nothing. Suddenly she looked up at him again. The madness was back in her eyes again, stronger than ever. Righteous hatred was written across her severe features.

'Was that how the demons entered your flesh? They try and put them in my body, with the needles and the pills, but my faith is strong. God and his angels watch over the righteous. They protect their own. I saw the devils on the net in the common room. They were walking the streets of Sodom-on-the-Hudson! Bold as brass! Hell has boiled up like a blister and burst in the streets of New York!' She was thrashing around in the bed like a woman possessed. Her arms and her ankles were bleeding. Spittle flecked her mouth and chin. 'I know what you are, demon! Get out of my son's body!'

She was praying. Screaming her exhortations to God, trying to cast the possessing demon out of her son's body, when the orderlies arrived to sedate her. Prophet bent light around himself. It wasn't difficult to sneak out of the room.

The daughter had seen an angel. The mother had seen a demon. Prophet guessed that the daughter had more hope. He was worried that the mother was closer to the truth.

What do you want from me? Prophet demanded. But the Green-Eyed Man was nowhere to be seen.

***

The pain in his skull was so extreme that he was staggering. He had only just managed to get out of the hospital without being detected. He sank to his knees. This couldn't go on. He had no idea where he was or what he was doing half the time. Sooner or later he was going to get seen and caught. By the local authorities if he was lucky, by CELL if he wasn't.

He was beginning to think that Rasch was right, that they were the only ones who could help him. He just didn't think they would. The mission was nowhere. If this continued then all he was doing was trying to avoid the inevitable when he was lucid and in control and rushing toward it when he wasn't.

White light. Agony. The pavement was rushing up to meet him but he blacked out before it reached him.

***

Somehow he knew he was moving. He was being just stealthy enough to avoid being seen by civilians and police. It wasn't like he was trying to hide from military contractors or hostile aliens. If he was to remain fused to this suit, which was now synonymous with remaining alive, then this was just a stroll for him. This level of sneaking about would become his life until he got careless, got caught and got dead.

Except Prophet knew he was just a passenger now.

***

'I think we need to talk.'

Prophet opened his eyes. The Green-Eyed Man was sat opposite him. They were both sat at a simple table in an otherwise empty room with bare walls. The day outside the window looked grey and bleak. The landscape beyond the glass was featureless.

'Is this real?' Prophet asked.

The Green-Eyed Man pointed at him. 'I want my body back.'

'You're dead.'

'Which makes us equal. I watched you put a bullet in your own head, except the dead flesh you're possessing came with my mind when I was born. Not yours.'

Prophet wanted to smile. The kid was cocky but he thought he wouldn't have minded having him under his command. The smile went away as he remembered just how many people had died under his command. That was a whole different set of ghosts.

'What is this? Where are we?'

The Green-Eyed Man frowned. 'I think you're changing the subject.'

Prophet noticed that he wasn't wearing the armour anymore. He was in dress fatigues that he hadn't worn in years.

'Just because you outrank me doesn't give you the right to take my body.'

'There is no right here. There's just what happened, and there's dealing with it.'

'You could let go, old man.'

'So could you.'

'It's my fucking body!' The Green-Eyed Man lunged across the table and grabbed Prophet by the lapels of his dress uniform. Prophet didn't move. Instead he took the time to stare deep into the other man's eyes. Taking stock of him, measuring and, if he was honest, judging him.

'I don't know where we are, but do you think this will help?' Prophet asked quietly. Alcatraz slumped back into his seat, calmer. He looked fatigued. *I guess haunting someone really takes it out of you,* Prophet thought. The Green-Eyed Man looked up at him.

'I'm not haunting you. I'm haunting my body.'

'Is that what you are? A ghost?'

'Maybe. Or a partially erased program, or information given form by the suit's systems. Or maybe I'm just you having a breakdown. Ever consider that? What about you? What do you think you are?'

'I'm Proph ...' he started.

'You used to be Laurence Barnes, didn't you?'

'I still ...'

'He's dead. Maybe you died when you put the suit on, maybe when you put the gun to your head, but you're dead now. You're a ghoul inhabiting a stolen corpse, a demon possessing a body, a Frankenstein's monster of animated dead flesh and alien technology.'

'You sound like your mother.' Prophet had meant it as a provocation.

He watched Alcatraz's face harden.

'Fuck that bitch.'

94

Yeah? Who are you trying to fool, kid? Prophet was pretty sure that wasn't even how Alcatraz spoke. That was language learnt for the barracks. A front. Prophet shrugged.

'So?' he asked. 'What do you want from me?'

'For you to let go. To get out.'

'What are you going to do with your life?'

'What are you, my dad?'

He'd have needed beating into shape first if he had been under my command, Prophet decided. The conversation was starting to sound like the arguments he'd overheard between his sister and her teenaged kids.

'It's a serious question.'

'What life?'

'Semantics? Really?' Prophet was becoming more exasperated.

'No, that's the thing, see? I'm not being semantic. I'm going to lay myself to rest. We're both dead. We need to let go. We're just a grotesque joke now.'

There's more of your mother in you than you'd like to admit, isn't there, son? Prophet thought but decided to keep it to himself.

'Sorry. I need your body for something more important.'

'Like what? We're a corpse in a fucking suit.'

'Did you just forget about New York? The fact that we're being invaded by alien squid?'

'That's fucking over, man. I ... we dealt with that shit.'

'It's not over.' The Green-Eyed Man swallowed.

Prophet looked at him hard. It was the sort of stare he'd given subordinates back when he'd been conventional army, 82nd Airborne, before Delta. Prophet tapped the side of his head. 'Yeah, you've seen it, haven't you, son?' Alcatraz didn't answer. 'You fought hard. You did well. You were a good soldier ... and I'm sorry – I really am – but your war's over.' The Green-Eyed Man opened his mouth to retort, but Prophet cut him off. 'What do you think you've been doing? Visiting your sister? Your mother? Where are we now ...?'

'We're here. You need to ...'

'Where are we in the real world? You're saying goodbye, son. I'm sorry you died. I think you've more than earned your rest, but I need your flesh and you're just going to have to take my word for it that it's important. If you know what I know, if you've seen what I've seen, then you won't even have to take my word for it.'

'It's my body,' Alcatraz said quietly.

'Do you want to fight this war?' Prophet asked. More and more he himself was starting to realise that he didn't want to fight the coming war either. He just didn't see any other way.

'It's over,' Prophet told him. 'It was over before it began, and I think you know that. You're right, this is your body, and I think that if you'd really wanted it you would have taken it by now.'

Prophet watched the knowledge settle in, the resignation. Tension leaked out of the other man. Prophet stood up. He smoothed down his uniform and then held out his hand. Alcatraz stared at the offered grip. Prophet couldn't quite read the expression on the Recon Marine's face. Finally Alcatraz stood up.

'Alice?' he asked.

The mission, Prophet thought.

'I'll look in on her when I can.' He almost believed the lie himself.

Alcatraz nodded.

'What's your name, son?'

Alcatraz told him.

***

He was stood alone in a graveyard under a slate grey sky. He looked down at the gravestone.

A heuristic system: experience-based problem solving. In other words, learning. *Just how smart is the suit?* Prophet wondered. Then he corrected himself. How smart was the alien tech in the suit? The Ceph were a reactive species, they responded to external stimuli. Once something had happened to them they would change their approach the next time round, and the next, until they either succeeded or were destroyed. The suit had known there was something wrong with Prophet. Or rather, it had known there was something wrong with its CPU. Had it found a way to fix it, he wondered? Or had it made a choice between Prophet and Alcatraz? Prophet found that he didn't want to think too hard about that possibility ...

It was only then that he realised just how envious he

was of Alcatraz's peace, even if that peace was merely oblivion.

He thought back to something a senior NCO had told him during training: In a fire-fight, you find cover or you find religion. It didn't seem that Alcatraz had had much of a choice.

He looked down at Alcatraz's father's grave. Then he turned and walked away, with the marine's last words ringing in his ears.

'They call me Alcatraz. Remember me.'

Archaeology

St. Petersburg, 2024

Amanda looked down into the darkness. It was total. The complete absence of light. Intellectually she knew there was light down there, somewhere, but it felt like she would descend into blackness forever. It was still, cold, and there was little air movement. The lights attached to the steel frame of the elevator illuminated the smooth rock wall of the shaft. The rock looked natural, but according to her briefing the shaft had been cut by the Ceph aeons ago.

Hundreds of feet above her was the Hermitage and the freezing temperature and thick snow of a St. Petersburg winter. The opulent decadence of an imperial culture was on display for all to see. It was a strange contrast with the darkness, the minimalist rock and what they had found here so deep below the Earth's surface. She was starting to see a faint glow below her now.

***

The elevator carried her into the main site. The

roughly hemispherical cavern was lit with portable lights. Amanda could hear the steady diesel throb of the generators. It was freezing down here, despite the freestanding heaters. Amanda wrapped her long coat around herself. The rock floor of the cave was a series of gentle rolling rises and indents that looked like they had been caused by water, and a number of small streams ran through the cavern.

The main cavern – or Site A – was a hive of activity. All across the rock floor men and women, clothed in layers and layers of threadbare clothing, chipped away at the rock with a variety of hand and power tools. As the elevator got closer to the cavern floor she could see seams of metal running through the rock. The seams didn't look natural. They looked like they formed particular defined shapes. The best way that Amanda could think of describing it was that it looked like someone had fused circuitry with the rock. That, however, did not do the alienness of the tech in the ground justice. It was technology that had been there a long time before there had even been a humanity. Having lived through the crisis in New York, Amanda had a healthy respect and fear for the Ceph and their tech. Amanda could understand the need for Hargreave-Rasch to research the Ceph technology caches they were finding, but after her experiences in New York the alien technology made her very uncomfortable indeed.

The entire site was being watched over by CELL gunmen. There were two waiting for her as the elevator came to a halt and she stepped out into the cave.

'Alan, Mikey, how's it going?' Amanda asked, her strong New York accent unmistakeable. She was genuinely pleased to see the two contractors she'd worked with for three years, up until she had been demoted and left out in the cold by her employer.

'Good to see you, Cross,' Alan said, smiling. The well-built American with the brown eyes and the short, cropped dark hair and the flat face went all the way back to SRT with her. She had talked him into joining CELL when he'd left the military police. She regretted that now.

'Boss,' Mikey said and hugged her. It wouldn't have been so long ago that she would never have tolerated such a thing. Now, frankly, she couldn't give a shit. Things had not been going terribly well career-wise since she'd left the army.

They exchanged news but it was the casual stuff, nothing about the current situation. Amanda knew them well enough to know that they were hiding something.

'So what's the boss like, this Walters?' she asked. Mikey and Alan exchanged a look.

'Asher wants to see you.' Mikey told her. The Afro-Caribbean Brit wouldn't meet her eyes. Security was supposed to be run by John Walters. He had a reputation as a competent, if unimaginative and overly rigid, commander. He'd inherited Amanda's team after she'd been demoted. She had spent the last eighteen months as little more than a mall cop.

It was bad news, however, if Dr Asher, the dig's overseer, was trying to control security as well. Security was supposed to create a physically safe work environment, but under an independent command, as security matters had to sometimes override the day-to-day running of the operation they were protecting.

Also, Amanda knew Asher's reputation. He'd been a high flyer before the New York crisis but something had happened with a subordinate of his, a Nathan Gould, which had meant Asher had fallen from favour. Amanda had also heard mutterings that before he had fallen from grace his security detail had had to cover up some of his more unsavoury activities more than once.

'I'd rather meet Walters first, if I'm going to be his two IC,' Amanda told them. Again there was the exchange of looks. 'What the fuck's going on?' Amanda demanded. Since New York she hadn't really cared about her career. This was the first break she'd had since her demotion. She was looking forward to working with her old team again, because she felt that she'd taken the time to train them up into something better than the rest of the grunts and toy soldiers that CELL employed. Largely, however, she just wanted to coast until she could cobble together some kind of retirement plan. Though with the constant changes to the terms and conditions of what could laughingly be called her contract, retirement seemed to be getting further and further away.

'Seriously Amanda, Asher makes things difficult for people who don't do as he says, could you just talk to him first?' Alan said. Amanda didn't like the tone of his voice. He sounded beaten.

'Is everyone alright?' Amanda asked as she shouldered both her kit bags. Another look was exchanged. 'Okay, tell me right now.'

'It's Sam,' Mikey said. Mikey was a tough guy. He had been a military police officer in the British army, a close protection specialist, but he sounded upset. Sam had been the youngest member of her team. She had been forever playing catch-up. Unlike most of them she had come straight from civvie street. What she had lacked in competence she had more than made up for with being likeable, and she had been improving. At the time that Amanda had been removed from command of the team Sam had been showing a great deal of promise and had acquitted herself well, or as well as any of them had, in New York. Amanda felt her stomach drop. She wasn't going to cry – she had learned long ago to never show weakness in front of others. When she got the chance she'd kill a bottle of vodka on her own and cry then. It was easier that way.

'What happened?' she asked controlling her emotions. Mikey and Alan said nothing. The other two contractors would not meet her eyes. 'Was it down here?'

'You need to speak to Asher.' Alan said. 'He's ... er ... well, he's dealing with this morning's situation.' Amanda looked between the two of them. She felt her blood run cold.

'Are there active Ceph down here?' she demanded. There was no answer. She slumped against the metal cage of the elevator. The nightmare visions of New York that she had tried to ignore returned stronger than ever. Contractors from other teams blowing away those affected by the Rapture, the Manhattan Virus. Seeing her brother, infected. Half her team dead, torn apart by armoured aliens, and somehow this had all happened in her home town.

She wanted to tell them to get everyone out. Fill the caves with CELL spec ops teams or, better yet, flush the tunnels with fire. She knew from bitter experience that Hargreave-Rasch Biomedical, the parent company of Crynet Enforcement and Local Logistics, invested an awful lot more in its interest in the Ceph technology than it did in its personnel.

***

Dr Herman Asher found himself appalled at the appearance of the new head of security for the dig. The wiry-looking African-American woman's hair had been shaved into some kind of Mohawk that had then been braided. Both ears were extensively pierced and she had a plug in the left. Her nose had a stud in it. She had on combat boots and bloused fatigue trousers and her CELL issue body armour, but the body armour was hanging open and he could see a white t-shirt. The t-shirt had the words London Calling and the Clash written on it, along with a picture of a man smashing a guitar on the ground. She had a tatty old long coat over the top of her body armour.

'Miss Cross, what is the meaning of your appearance?' Asher demanded.

'Punk rock,' Amanda told the bespectacled, grossly fat, piggy-looking dig supervisor. She had been thirteen years old when she had snuck into CBGBs on the Bowery in the Lower East Side for the club's final ever gig. After New York, once she had realised that her career was over and she didn't much care, she'd decided to go back to her old style. It reminded her that she had a personality outside of CELL. Right now, however, Amanda was more concerned with the twisted body of Lieutenant Commander John Walters that was lying on the floor of Site D.

Walters' head had been twisted around a full hundred and eighty degrees. His chest cavity was a ruin. It looked like something had punched him in the rib cage, very hard. She reached into one of her holdalls and found a pair of surgical gloves and a pen. She inspected Walters' chest wound and confirmed what she had expected.

'He would have died from the blow to the chest but he was killed when his head was twisted around. Mikey, check the Grendel.'

Mikey pulled off his standard-issue gloves, which could leave fibrous trace on the assault rifle lying close to Walters, and pulled on the surgical gloves that Amanda handed him. He checked the magazine.

'We've got six rounds missing,' Mikey told her. It tallied with the spent casings on the ground. Amanda had a look around the small cave. There were at least three tunnels coming into it. Much of the cave floor had been chipped away and they were standing in trenches embedded with the alien technology.

Amanda looked at how the body had fallen and then around the cave. She pointed towards one of the tunnel entrances.

'Alan, check around there, see if you can find the impacts.' Alan switched on the flashlight attached to the mounting rail on the side of his Grendel assault rifle and went over to check the area Amanda had indicated.

'I expect you to conform to basic CELL grooming standards at the very least,' Dr Asher told her.

'So?' Amanda asked distractedly.

'I beg your pardon?' Dr Asher asked, feeling himself getting angry. Amanda sighed and looked up at the scientist. She didn't think she was going to like the man. She had always wondered about people like him. Why would they try and make life difficult for people who were more than capable of beating the shit out of them? The piggy little scientist was flanked by two more of the security detail. One of them was Safiya, who'd worked with Amanda before. Safiya was third generation French/Algerian. She had been a police officer in Marseilles. The other guard was a weedy-looking buck toothed guy she didn't recognise.

'I'm going to assume for a moment that you're not a complete idiot,' Amanda told Asher. 'That the body of your head of security lying right here hasn't escaped your notice. And that this is the second corpse on your watch …'

'On Sub-commander Walters' watch …' Asher began. *Pass that buck,* Amanda thought.

'You don't give a fuck about how I'm dressed. It's a power play. It's about establishing control. Let's just skip it. You do your job, I do mine and we both try to piss each other off as little as possible.'

Asher stared at the woman. Once again he was at a loss trying to work out why these semi-literate grunts would even bother speaking, when all that was required of them was to do as their intellectual superiors told them to.

'Oh dear,' Dr Asher said, with mock sadness. 'There seems to be some confusion. I will try and explain the situation in as simple terms as I can manage. You do what I tell you to do when I tell you to do it, and you do it without question.'

Amanda looked up at him. There was no anger in her expression, just weariness.

'No,' she told him simply. Asher started turning a funny red colour. Amanda guessed that he wasn't used to being told *no* by his subordinates. 'Look, I tried the career thing in this fucked-up job, it didn't work out for me. You've got nothing to threaten me with. You don't like me? Send me packing, or even better have me fired, you pathetic little pig of a man.' The bucktoothed member of Asher's security detail endeared himself to Amanda by trying to suppress a grin. Asher was turning puce now, but he managed to get control of himself.

'You have family in New York, don't you, Miss Cross?' Asher said, smiling.

'I did until CELL had them evicted for whatever it is they're doing there. Imagine how popular that will make me at Thanksgiving.' Amanda didn't like how this was going. She could not for the life of her understand why Congress had handed control of the ruined city over to CELL after the mess they had made during the quarantine.

'I believe that they are in a refugee camp just outside of Sleepy Hollow. I can make life very difficult for them, as well as for the members of your team.'

Amanda stared at him. She felt the same cold rage that she always felt when someone threatened people that she cared about. Don't blow, she told herself, bide your time.

'Boss,' Alan said returning. Amanda was grateful for the interruption. She'd been worried that she was going to say or do something really dumb and possibly quite violent. 'I've got three bullets imbedded in the wall. They were tightly grouped. The other two rounds I can't account for. I reckon they got shot down the tunnel deeper into the cave complex. I can go look for them.' Amanda was already shaking her head.

'No way. We go out, we go mob-handed.' Alan looked relieved. 'You said two.' Alan held something up. 'Seriously, what did I tell you about handling the evidence?' Amanda asked, pained. Mikey was grinning. Alan looked embarrassed. Amanda took the object off him and examined it.

'Impacted six-point-eight millimetre full metal jacket from the Grendel. Standard issue because CELL doesn't know enough to issue low-impact rounds to the half-trained fuckwits they employ as grunts. It hit the cave wall,' but even as she said it she knew something wasn't right.

'Thing is, boss, I found it right in the middle of the tunnel entrance,' Alan told her.

'Walters the kind of guy to panic?' Amanda asked.

'No, he was solid,' Safiya said in English. Her accent was a mix of French and Algerian. 'He wasn't in New York but he'd helped clear out a few Ceph nests and he'd been on the sharp end in Sri Lanka with your 10th Infantry.'

'Which ties with the tight grouping. So why didn't he hit what he was aiming at?' She pointed at the tunnel entrance. 'So something comes at him. He gets off two three-round bursts. He hits it but no blood?' she looked at Alan. Alan shook his head. 'It closes in the face of automatic weapon fire and not only overpowers a trained ex-soldier but twists his head round.'

'So Ceph, right?' the bucktoothed guy said.

Amanda glanced at Asher.

'Anything you want to share, doctor?' Amanda asked. Asher had a good poker face.

'You thinking Stalker?' Mikey asked.

'No plasma burns, no shard wounds. Stalker would be my guess.' She stood up. 'Alan, how many of the detail down here?'

'Now? Ten, including you.'

'And from the old team, other than the three of you here?'

'Daniels, Schmidt and Okobe. O'Donnel got crippled in a bar fight in northern Finland ...'

'Yeah, I heard about that, shame, good people when she could control her temper.'

'Marceau got fired after that shit in Manchester. Couldn't get work, couldn't get welfare, he ate his own gun ...'

'Shit. I didn't know about that. And Harrison bought it in Nigeria?' Alan nodded. 'Then three new guys?'

'Including this bucktoothed motherfucker here,' Alan said nodding at the fourth member of the security detail present.

'Hello, bucktoothed motherfucker,' Amanda said to him warmly. New Guy smiled and nodded. 'I like him, particularly the way he just won't shut up.'

'Everyone calls me Hank, ma'am,' the bucktoothed contractor told her.

'Alabama?' Amanda asked.

'Hell no! Southern Georgia.'

'You got problems with us coloured folks?' Amanda asked.

'Ignoring your racial profiling of me as poor whisky tango, only in front of friends and family back home.'

Amanda had to smile at this.

'You in off the street or did you serve?' Amanda asked, standing up and brushing herself down.

'1st Marine. Caught the tail end of Sri Lanka. We

were in New York trying to evacuate civilians. Under Colonel Barclay.'

'He's good people,' Mikey assured her.

'Miss Cross,' Asher began irritably. 'My time is very valuable and you have work to do.'

'Okay, I'm through playing detective. Standard operating procedure is you pull everyone out of here and you call in spec ops. They hunt and kill this thing and then you can go back to work.'

'No, I don't think so,' Dr Asher said.

'It's the SOP,' Amanda said, feeling her heart drop. Asher wouldn't want to shut down the operation and call in spec ops because it would mean a loss of productivity and a loss of control. In short, it wouldn't help him crawl back up to the corporate trough.

'There's ten of you and one of these things . . .'

'And we have to keep the dig secure and hunt this thing and possibly sleep as well. There are hundreds of miles of tunnel down here, not to mention that this could be the tip of the iceberg. My experience is that if there's one, there's probably more.'

'I've read your record. Military police Special Response Team and then you transferred to the Defence Criminal Investigation Service. You have the skills to deal with this situation. In fact, you were a very promising young CELL officer until you disgraced yourself by disobeying direct orders and abandoning your post in New York.'

Amanda clenched her jaw but did not rise to the provocation.

'Fine. Shut down sites B through E ...'

'No. In fact, as soon as we're finished here have the body cleared away, because I'm bringing another team in. The fact that it killed here suggests that this site may be more important than we initially thought. Just find this thing and kill it.'

'We can't protect everyone at all five sites. People are going to die.' Amanda said through gritted teeth.

'And with the death of Walters and your presence here, we have proof that dead people can be replaced. Are there any other simple concepts that you would like explained to you before you get on with your job?' Asher asked.

Asher turned to leave. Safiya and Hank stayed put. Asher turned back to them, clearly furious.

'You two with me, now!' he snapped.

'You're going to keep two of my detail with you?!' Amanda said, incredulously. Asher just looked at her as if she was a moron. 'Doctor, I need at least one of them with me.'

'Already your incompetence is annoying me. It only takes a phone call ...' He left the rest of the threat about her cousin and their family in the upstate New York refugee camp unsaid.

'You need to be careful that you don't push so hard that the other person feels that they've got nothing left to lose,' Amanda told him. Asher started going red again, furious.

'You, inbreed,' he finally said to Hank. 'Stay with her.'

'Yes sir,' Hank said mildly.

Amanda would have preferred Safiya, and she didn't like the way that Asher was looking at the attractive French/Algerian contractor. She did, however, have perfect confidence in Safiya's ability to look after herself.

Asher left.

'So, he seems nice,' Amanda muttered. Mikey laughed, Alan and Hank smiled.

***

She had gathered them all in site A. They were sat just behind one of the light rigs, in a circle. Okobe, Daniels and Schmidt had all greeted her warmly. Genuinely pleased that she was with them again.

'You're supposed to be like plod, aye?' Kearney asked. He was a wiry, thuggish-looking kid from somewhere called Wolverhampton in Britain. Apparently he'd ended up in CELL due to the UK's Penal Conscription Act. Amanda found this a little strange. She had thought that conscripts under the act were supposed to end up in Britain's actual military, not as corporate military contractors.

Amanda narrowed her eyes at Kearney and just shook her head in bewilderment. His accent was almost impossible to understand.

She'd secured her body armour and was wearing a holstered Hammer II automatic pistol on her hip. She was in the process of reassembling and checking her Alpha Jackal combat shotgun. She had just attached the fore grip to the mounting rails under the barrel and was in the process of attaching a flashlight to the mounting rails on the side of the weapon.

'He wants to know if you're police,' Daniels translated for her. He was another Brit, who'd served with the Royal Engineers. He was a middle-aged man going to seed. If CELL had any sense he would have been working for them servicing vehicles and weapons, but in a very military show of logic he'd ended up carrying a Grendel in a security detail.

'I used to be an MP,' Amanda told Kearney.

'So you gonna' investigate this?'

'It's not an investigation, it's a hunt. It doesn't matter who or what did this or why, we just need to find it and kill it. And I've got some bad news for you, kid.' Kearney narrowed his eyes. 'Go and relieve Safiya and send her back here.'

The young British kid opened his mouth to protest but Daniels looked over at him and just shook his head. The kid remained quiet and headed over to where the doctor was looking over some findings.

'We going into the caves?' Coyle asked, sounding worried. Coyle was another of the new guys. An American who had served in a tank regiment. He had the look of a soldier who'd stopped caring about himself, or anything else for that matter.

'We'd just get lost unless we've got solid intel as to its whereabouts.'

'Do you know what this place is?' Alan asked Amanda. Amanda laughed.

'I got put on a transport flight from Lagos. I wasn't even told I was going to St. Petersburg.' There was some laughter from around the circle.

'Asher talks openly in front of us. He thinks anyone carrying a gun is a mental sub-normal who wouldn't understand what he's talking about.'

'Yeah, he's a charmer alright,' Amanda said. 'So?'

'He thinks this is part of a birthing chamber. Somewhere below here are Ceph, or things that will become Ceph, or at the very least some of their tech, just like New York.'

'Nice. So if one of them is awake ...' Amanda asked as she slid the extended magazine into the Jackal.

'Then they're probably trying to find a way to wake the others.'

'And we end up with another New York right here in St. Petersburg.'

'Which won't matter to us,' Daniels said. 'Because we'll be overwhelmed immediately.' He had been with them in New York. He'd seen what the Ceph could do.

'I just want some payback for Sam,' Okobe muttered. There were nods from Mikey and Schmidt as well. Okobe was ex-Nigerian army. He was tall, rake thin but somehow still powerful looking. Normally quiet but he had been close to Sam and it looked like her death had hit him hard. Amanda reached out and grabbed the Nigerian's arm. She had liked Sam as well.

A harried-looking Safiya joined them.

'I've only got a little while, he's less than pleased

at the swap,' she told them. There were some angry mutterings.

'Okay, ideas?' Amanda said.

'Claymores?' Daniels suggested.

'Do you have any?' Amanda asked. Daniels shook his head. 'Probably for the best. We can't have some junior xeno-archaeologist spread themselves all over the local area.'

'It might catch Asher,' Schmidt suggested. There was more laughter. Schmidt had been a tank gunner in the German army. The German looked after himself. His flattop blonde hair and blue eyes made him look like the Aryan ideal. His appearance was at odds with his apparently generous and friendly nature.

'We've got five caverns to cover, not to mention intervening tunnels, and Asher wants all the sites up and running. Even one person per cavern, we're going to struggle if we want to sleep and someone's going to have to stay with Asher and hold his hand,' Mikey pointed out. Amanda was already shaking her head.

'We rotate whomever's on that fat fuck so Safiya's skin doesn't crawl off on its own.' There were a few more chuckles. Safiya's laughter seemed forced. 'Six on, three off, staggered sixteen hour shifts,' Now there were groans. 'The three off sleep here in the main cavern. The other six work in two patrols of three, working round all five sites. None of us go anywhere unless we have two others with us, clear?' There were nods from the others.

'That's still pretty thin,' Alan pointed out.

'Give me an option. I'm guessing that Sam and Walters were both on their own?' There were nods from around the circle. 'What are comms like?'

'They've got transceivers attached to the walls of the tunnels. Basically you've got good coverage at the five sites and the tunnels directly between, but get off the beaten track and it's for shit,' Hank told her.

'You thinking cameras?' Daniels asked. Amanda nodded.

'And I want the cameras streaming to phones carried by each patrol. Can you do that?'

Daniels was nodding.

'I should be able to sort something, though I can't promise total coverage.'

Amanda knew it was busy work. She was just giving them something to do. They were glad that someone was here making decisions, and that that person could do a good impression of competence.

The cameras might help but she was of the opinion that it would be the Stalker, or whatever Ceph monstrosity that was down there with them, that would set the tempo of their hunt. Unless they could divine a purpose and work out its whereabouts, or when it was going to strike, they were just going to be reacting.

Amanda was of the opinion that she might be able to do something if Asher would pull everyone back into Site A in the main cavern. With them spread out like this, people were going to die.

The light started to shake. Everyone looked up. Amanda realised that it was the ground shaking. The lights toppled over and smashed. Around the cavern similar things were happening as the dig personnel staggered around. Some of them were grabbing lights and other pieces of equipment trying to steady them.

There were explosions of rock all around the cavern. There were cries of pain as sharp fragments of flying rock hit people. It looked like the seams of metal in the stone had come to life. The organic, almost bone-like metal was pushing through the stone like the tips of claws. It was glowing with some kind of internal light.

This is it, Amanda thought, *they're waking up. We're dead.* She felt the same terror she'd felt in New York grab her. Then, as quickly as it had started, the shaking stopped. Amanda could hear the moaning and whimpering of frightened and, in some cases, wounded people in the main cave.

They were all looking to her now. She was desperately trying to hide her fear.

'Mikey, Schmidt, stay here with Coyle. You do not help these people, even the wounded, you stick together and work the perimeter. Alan, you take Okobe and Safiya, check sites B and C. Daniels, you and Hank are with me.'

She ignored cries for help. She ignored Asher shouting at her as she headed for the tunnel, the Jackal held tight into her shoulder. As Amanda scanned left and right she noticed that the internal light from the metal was going out. It was as if it had become inert.

'Where's Kearney?' she asked. Nobody had an answer.

Amanda swallowed hard. This wasn't what she had expected. The lights had gone out in site E. Like site D it was a much smaller, irregularly shaped cavern worked smooth by water over its millennia of existence. The floor of the cavern was a series of rough, narrow trenches chipped out of the stone. As in the main cavern, it looked as though the segmented, bone-like Ceph tech had momentarily come to life and fused together, breaking through the rock. Also like the main cavern, the process seemed to have been interrupted. Unlike the main cavern there looked like there was something wrong with the visible protrusions of the Ceph tech. It looked sick somehow, or perhaps even dead.

Kearney's corpse lay on the floor but she didn't have time to check it yet. First they had to secure the site as best they could.

The beam from the flashlight attached to the barrel of her combat shotgun shook as she searched for the alien killer in the pitch darkness of the cavern, over a mile beneath the surface of the Earth.

***

They had found nothing. After the chaos and the panic things had calmed down enough for them to get light back on in Site E. After significant reassurances that

119

it was as safe as it was going to get, a very angry Dr Asher had joined them. He assured Amanda that she would be held responsible for her incompetence in allowing the site to get damaged. He didn't say anything about the corpse lying on the floor. Amanda had to stop Daniels from tearing into Asher.

'So what do you think happened here, doctor?' Amanda asked once Asher had finished admonishing her.

'Isn't it obvious? A Ceph bioform, probably a Stalker, came in and killed your man.'

'Weird damn way to kill him,' Hank said.

'You do know what the word alien means, don't you?' Asher asked scathingly.

'He was killed with what looks like a bladed weapon through the base of the skull and up into the brain ...'

'A Stalker bone spur ...'

'Maybe, but with a full investigative team here I might be able to find out more ...'

'What more do you need to know? You have a Stalker ...'

'Stalkers don't kill like that,' Daniels told him from his position, where he was watching one of the dark tunnels. Asher looked like he'd been slapped.

'Keep your men under control!' he spat, genuinely offended.

One day we need to examine the basis for your apparent superiority, Amanda thought.

'He's right, they slash, like with a sword,' she told him.

'You need to stop thinking so narrowly. This species isn't like us, they adapt reactively between generations. Given time, and they don't need that much, they develop the tools they need.'

'So we could be dealing with something new here?' Amanda asked.

'Perhaps.'

'Does it have anything to do with the Ceph-tech initiating?' Hank asked. Asher looked angry that the bucktoothed southerner had dared speak to him.

'Perhaps, or perhaps it was just reacting to the presence of a Ceph-bioform. Now as much fun as trying to teach monkeys algebra is, I have work to do.' Asher turned to leave, motioning Safiya to join him.

'What's wrong with the Ceph tech in here, Asher?' Amanda asked. She watched him swallow hard.

'I don't know what you're talking about,' he finally said.

And that's a fucking lie, Amanda thought, *but that's all I'm going to get out of you, isn't it?*

'Okay doc, thank you, we'll call if we think you can help any more,' Amanda told the piggy-looking scientist. Asher opened his mouth to protest being dismissed by a subordinate, but Amanda had already moved on. 'Mikey, get your people's heads down, try and get as much sleep as you can because you're on again at 1600 zulu,' she said over the tac radio, pausing for an affirmative. 'Alan, I want your people doing sweeps, leave the main cavern, it's going to hit us where we're lightest. Concentrate on sites B through D, I think it's

121

finished with E.' Amanda glanced up at Asher, looking for a reaction. He looked angry at his dismissal but he turned and left Site E. Safiya followed him.

'Poor kid,' Daniels said looking down at Kearney. 'He was a little shit but you could see something worthwhile in him trying to get out.'

I didn't even get a chance to know him, Amanda thought. She couldn't muster up much feeling. She'd seen young lives wasted before. It was clear that Daniels had liked the kid, however.

'What do you think?' Daniels asked looking away from Kearney's body.

'I don't think it's a Stalker,' Amanda said. The British engineer was nodding in agreement.

'You even think it's Ceph?' he asked.

'Has to be,' she said sounding not entirely sure. 'The tech's initiating for a reason.' She pointed at the trenches full of inert Ceph tech fused with the rock. 'No reason to do that unless it's Ceph. If it isn't because of this killer then we've got bigger problems.'

'What, then?' Hank asked.

'I think it's something higher up the squiddies' evolutionary chain and that makes me nervous,' she told the Georgian. He nodded and then looked troubled. 'Spit it out.'

'I don't mean to offend you none ...'

'Something that's almost always said before someone offends me.'

'I've come to terms with how CELL left us in the shit in New York. That wasn't you people's call but I heard stories about you. Abandoning your post, deserting your people.'

Amanda glanced over at Daniels. He shrugged.

'We told him to talk to you about it,' the Brit told her.

'Look, you seem cool and everything, but I just want to know who I'm working with.'

'Fair enough. That's exactly what I did in New York,' she told him evenly. Hank just watched her, saying nothing. 'I had family in New York. The whole place was crawling with Ceph, there was the virus and there were CELL units brutalising and executing refugees and people suffering from the virus. I left my people to go and try and get my family out. Same thing was to happen, I'd do it all over again.'

Hank nodded.

'We would have gone with her,' Daniels told him. 'We were all going to desert but Amanda knew it'd sink our careers, such as they are. She slipped away when we weren't paying attention.'

Hank was nodding.

'If it's kin I guess I can understand.'

'If I'd still been in the army it might have been difficult but frankly, fuck CELL. All they are to me is a rapidly shrinking monthly pay packet. In fact if you were in New York under Barclay I'm surprised you joined up with CELL.'

Hank shrugged.

'Times is tough. I got kin as well.'

Daniels and Amanda nodded in agreement.

'Let's get these cameras up and running,' Amanda said. She glanced down at the corpse. It would be sent up in the elevator like Walters had been, to be disposed of in the most cost-effective way possible. Until that happened it would be stored in one of the caves, one that wasn't imbedded with Ceph tech, close to the main cavern. His next of kin would be notified via text over the Macronet, maybe. 'Poor kid,' Amanda echoed Daniels.

***

C site was a long thin cavern. The floor was crisscrossed with trenches, like all the other sites. One of the light rigs had been broken when the ground had shook and as result the end of the cavern opposite the exit was in darkness. The eight workers in here were staying close to the light and the exit that led to the tunnel, which in turn led to the main cavern.

Amanda didn't know much about archaeology or recovering ancient alien tech that fused with rock, but the workers chipping away here didn't look like they were doing a particularly good job. Several of them either were or had been crying. A number of them were still shaking badly and all of them kept looking into the darkness at the end of the cave.

The workers looked like poor locals who had been given minimal training and less pay. They slept down here on floor mats and in sleeping bags, huddled around the heaters in the main cavern. They looked at

Amanda, Daniels and Hank like they were their prison guards.

We're not the enemy, kids, Amanda thought as she and Daniels moved past, weapons at the ready, the flashlights attached to the barrels of the weapons stabbing into the thick, inky, seemingly total darkness. Hank covered them from further back.

'Clear,' Amanda said as they finished checking the cavern. The word felt like a lie. There were so many caves and so much darkness down here that whatever was killing people didn't have to be very far away from them for it to be impossible to find.

Asher didn't seem to understand that the dig workers were not going to be very productive just because he had told them to be and because it was their poorly paid job to be so. He didn't understand why people couldn't or wouldn't just do what he told them to. He couldn't understand that the fear, exacerbated by the dead bodies that they had all seen dumped just outside the main cavern, was going to impact on productivity. Asher couldn't understand that in the long run he was more likely to achieve what he wanted by rolling up the operation, having the threat dealt with and then coming back. In other words, it didn't matter how much of a martinet Asher was, they were always going to be more scared of the alien creature killing them silently than they were of him.

One of the workers had, in broken English, accused Amanda of using them as bait. If she'd had her way she would have evacuated everyone, and as *de facto* security chief it was her call under CELL operating guidelines, but the reality of the situation had prevented that. So she had to work with what she had. If she was honest, the worker hadn't been wrong. Her best chance of finding the thing was when it was in the act of either killing people or trying to initiate the Ceph tech.

As she exited site C she glanced down at one of the workers. She was gaunt, haggard and probably not even out of her teens. The look the worker gave her back was resentful to the point of hatred.

It's not me, she wanted to tell them, but she knew she was part of the problem now.

'Boss?' Daniels said, out in the tunnel leading back to the main cavern. Amanda didn't like the frightened tone in the Brit's voice. She looked around to see what was bothering him. The tunnel wall was glowing with shifting symbols made of neon light. It looked like the walls were alive with some sort of circuitry, clearly Ceph tech.

'Another activation?' Hank asked. He was covering one way up the tunnel. The tunnel lights, the ones put there by humans, started flickering. The three of them switched on their flashlights, though there was a lot of light coming from the alien-tech in the tunnel walls.

'Mikey, where are your people, over?' she said into the tac radio. Alan, Okobe and Safiya were getting some rest. Amanda was exhausted, she had managed to get some sleep on the flight from Lagos but she was nearing the end of sixteen hours on. Between a long shift and the nervous tension, she knew she was too fatigued to be thinking clearly. Amanda didn't want to start on the amphetamines as she would never get to sleep when her shift ended and she didn't want to go there again, at least not unless she had to.

'Cross, what the hell is going on?!' Asher demanded over the radio.

'Doctor, get the fuck off this frequency! Mikey, report, over.'

'We're coming into … contact!'

Gunfire echoed through the tunnels. Two short bursts, then a longer less disciplined one. Then the gunfire stopped. Daniels was up and starting to move.

'Wait!' Amanda ordered. Daniels did as he was told. The beam on his flashlight was shaking badly as he covered the tunnel. Hank was covering behind them. Amanda let the Jackal drop on its sling as she grabbed the phone from her coat and switched it on. They had set the cameras to stream to the phone, but the cameras on B site were down. 'B site. Now.'

*****

The light illuminated the smoke from the cordite swirling in the air. There were spent shell casings on the ground and a lot of blood. The lights had been smashed as well. The beams from their flashlights and the glowing alien symbols in the rock were the only illumination. Amanda stared in horror. She wanted to be sick.

She had seen death before. She had seen a lot of it in New York, the horrors of the Manhattan Virus and the violence of the Ceph and in some cases her CELL colleagues. She had lost people before, but this assault had just seemed so easy for the Ceph bioform. Despite the weapons, the armour, the training and the experience, something had just snuffed out Mikey, Schmidt and Coyle like it was standing on bugs. Perhaps, to the Ceph, that was exactly what it was doing.

'It's gotta still be in here,' Daniels said. The fat, middle-aged British ex-soldier was breathing hard, staring at Mikey. Daniels had always pretended not to like Mikey as the other Brit had been an ex-military police officer, like Amanda, and there was little love lost between enlisted men and MPs, but in truth the two had been close. The front of Mikey's neck was a gaping red mess. The Ceph killer had nearly sawn his head off.

Amanda swallowed hard and tried to control the shaking, she just needed to cope long enough to give orders that wouldn't get any more people killed. Her flashlight played across Schmidt's body. He was laying half in and half out of one of the shallow trenches glowing with alien technology. His back had been broken. The angle that he was lying at looked horribly unnatural, to the point of obscene. Amanda could still make out the look of surprise on the German's face.

'H... help ...' The voice was weak. Amanda and Daniel's flashlights played all across the floor of the cave. Only Hank remained calm, using his flashlight to search the back of the site. Daniels found him. It was Coyle. He was frothing up blood.

'Daniels ...' Amanda started to warn the other contractor, but it was too late. Daniels had moved to Coyle and knelt down in the trench next to him.

Amanda shifted into the position where Daniels had been standing, trying to control herself. She had the feeling that there was something else in there with them. She felt a mounting terror that there was something just out of view, avoiding the light.

'S'okay mate, we're going to get you out of here. You'll be fine.'

'There's nothing there ...' Coyle managed, his voice sounding wet, like he was trying to talk through a mouthful of liquid. Coyle started to shake uncontrollably. Daniels tried to hold him. The American contractor was vomiting up frothy blood, then he lay still.

'Cross, report!' Asher demanded over the tac radio. 'Get the rest of your men back to the main cave right now!'

'Doctor, shut the fuck up!' Amanda demanded. She could hear boots running through the tunnel towards them.

Daniels was staring down at Coyle. The blood on his hands looked black in the light of the flashlights. Coyle's abdomen was little more than a red ruin.

'Boss,' Hank said quietly. He was just about able to keep the tremor out of his voice. 'I think there's something in here with us.'

Amanda felt her blood run cold. It felt like she followed the beam of Hank's flashlight in slow motion. It was aimed just past Daniels, who was shaking like a leaf. Amanda saw nothing for a moment. Just the rock and the glowing neon figures of the alien symbols imbedded in it. The symbols didn't look right. It was as if they were refracting off or through something. Amanda froze.

Daniels was frantically trying to get something he was holding in his hand to work. The emergency flare sputtered into life. It almost blinded Amanda and Hank with its phosphorescent, flickering glare. There was something wrong with the light from the flare. Just behind where Daniels was knelt over Coyle the flickering light was not behaving as it should. The misbehaving light moved. Daniels started screaming. He was lifted up into the air. There was more movement in the light and Daniel started spraying blood all over the cave.

'Don't you do it!' Amanda was screaming. Amanda threw herself to the side as Daniels was flung at her.

Hank started firing. The staccato hammering of the Mk 60 medium machine gun in the enclosed space was deafening. The muzzle flash from the MMG created a strobing effect in the near darkness.

Amanda started firing as well, the recoil of the automatic shotgun hammering into her shoulder. In the confusion of flares, glowing alien symbols and muzzle flashes she had no idea what she was shooting at but she wanted a wall of fire between her and that thing.

Alan was suddenly next to her, his Grendel assault rifle at the ready. He was searching through the tech scope for a target but finding nothing. There was a popping noise as Okobe fired the underslung grenade launcher attached to his Grendel. The flare grenade exploded deep in the other tunnel that exited B site.

Amanda's shotgun ran dry. Hank had already stopped firing. The air was thick with choking cordite smoke now. Their ears were ringing. Both the flares bathed them in flickering light. Okobe was reloading his grenade launcher. At the back of her mind some old training instinct was telling her that she should reload the shotgun. She ejected the magazine, stowed it and slid another home. She was just numbly going through the motions.

'Boss?' Alan asked. Amanda ignored him. She felt a hand on her shoulder. 'Amanda?' Her head shot round to look at him.

'It's got a cloak,' she said. Alan looked confused for a moment. 'A cloaking device. We can't fucking see it.'

***

They had returned to the main site. Amanda was still shaking. She was almost spilling the coffee over herself. She didn't want to watch the footage but she was forcing herself to. The shitty holo-projector was building the three-dimensional image from 2D footage, the final result was grainy and incomplete, but it showed them what they needed to see.

The dig workers had fled the moment the Ceph-tech had come to life. There was about fifty seconds of footage of the empty cave and then Coyle, Schmidt and Mikey had entered the cave cautiously, weapons at the ready. The beams of the flashlights on their weapons had caused the camera to flare. Despite his caution Mikey hadn't even been aware of what had happened to him. It looked like some old horror film about demonic possession. Mikey's head was yanked back. Then his throat had seemed to open of its own accord. Amanda paused the image and looked closely enough to see grainy imprints on Mikey's face where the killer's invisible fingers had gripped the head.

The camera flared again from the muzzle flashes from the Grendels, then an apparently invisible force picked up Schmidt and flung him into the camera.

That was the end of the footage. There was silence.

'Did it know about the cameras?' Alan finally asked.

'I think we have to assume so,' Amanda said.

'How?' Okobe asked.

'What if it's got our comms?' Amanda asked.

There was silence. People looked around the diminished circle. Safiya had joined the surviving members of the security detail now. Asher was, after all, in sight of the entire team.

'Would it even understand us?' Alan asked.

'They're clearly intelligent,' Amanda pointed out.

The few remaining workers in the sites outside the main cavern had refused to continue work. Amanda couldn't blame them, either. The remaining security detail had escorted them back to the main cavern. Asher had spent some time screaming at them to get the workers back to work and how much they had failed. Nobody had shot him.

'I've seen a cloak before,' Hank told them. Eight eyes turned to look at him. 'In New York we'd been trying to get the refugees out. We were working with elements of 4ᵗʰ Marine Recon. One of their guys, a fella by the name of Alcatraz, apparently got hisself some kind of experimental armour. It had a cloak but he was on our side. That marine was hell on wheels in a fight. Best weapon we had against those things.' Alan and Amanda shared knowing glances. 'What?' Hank asked.

'Tinman,' Alan said. Okobe looked up at him. It got Safiya's attention as well.

'What's Tinman?' Hank asked.

'Someone in some kind of experimental armour killed a fuck load of CELL contractors and Spec Ops guys. You heard of Dominic Lockhart?'

'The guy who used to run the military side of CELL? The guy who fucked up the New York operation?' Hank asked.

'The guy who got blamed for fucking up the New York operation,' Alan said. Amanda held her peace. She had her own opinion on Dominic Lockhart. 'Well, this Tinman was supposed to be the one who killed him during an attack on a CELL complex. We're right in the middle of an alien invasion and this Tinman turns on the very people who're trying to do something about it.'

'Look, Alan, I don't want to get up in your face about this or anything, but CELL did things in New York …'

'That the liberal media …' Alan began.

'Enough,' Amanda said. 'Hank, what's your point?'

'Whatever this Alcatraz or Tinman was about, he was about fighting Ceph. Asher said they're reactive. They evolve from generation to generation in response to their environment. If they'd seen this cloak in action in New York then maybe their next generation will all pack a cloak.'

'Some of the Ceph had cloaks in New York,' Amanda said quietly. The others looked at her in horror.

'There's something else,' Safiya said. 'I overheard Asher speaking with one of the technicians. We were in site E. Asher had some kind of weird device that he hooked up to the Ceph tech fused into the rock itself. It was weird. The thing looked like their technology.' Amanda thought back to how she had realised the Ceph tech imbedded in the rock had looked strange after the murders. 'Asher said that it was all dead. That it had been infected by some variant of the Tunguska strain.'

'So this thing is harming the Ceph tech?' Okobe asked. His deep rumbling voice often made people think he was slow. Amanda knew that the quiet Nigerian just preferred to think long and hard about things. He was not infected with the westerners' love of hearing their own voices.

'So it could be the Tinman, then?' Alan said.

'How?' Hank asked. 'This Alcatraz was a Jarine, another throwback with a gun, just like me. He was hell on wheels in a fight when he was in the armour and he could kill swift, silent and deadly with the best of them, but he sure as hell wasn't no Apex-Predator, invisible serial killer.'

'Tell that to Dominic Lockhart and his men. He murdered fucking hundreds of CELL contractors. People just like you and me ...' Alan said angrily.

'Look buddy, I'm no fan of New York but what those CELL guys were doing ...'

'Enough,' Amanda told them. 'Forget about New York.' She wished she could. 'The fact is, it's murdering our people. I don't care whose side it thinks it's on or what it may or may not have done in the past. It's no friend to us. In the unlikely event we see it, we light it up.'

'What do you want to do, boss?' Safiya asked. Amanda could hear the fear in the other woman's voice.

'We bug out,' Amanda said. 'This is way above our pay grade. Even if we had K-Volts and Mikes, I wouldn't want to fuck with this thing.'

'Asher?' Alan asked.

'His career's in the pan. He doesn't want it to look like he's fucking up this dig and he wants the glory if we catch or kill whatever this thing is. Hopefully he's realised that this is beyond our collective capabilities, if not ...'

'I'll handle the creepy fat fuck,' Safiya said. The look of disgust overcame her obvious fear. 'Anyone else noticed he smells of sour milk?'

'If it comes down to a bullet I do it, you understand me? Nobody else, just me.' There were grumblings around the circle. Nobody would meet her eyes. 'I said just me. Understand?' There were muttered assents. 'Okay, let's go and speak to him.' Amanda made as if to get up. 'No comms, understand me?' she asked. They nodded and stood up. Amanda switched the magazine on her Jackal combat shotgun. Replacing the clip with the volt rounds she had been issued in New York. Each cartridge contained electrostatically-charged ball-bearings. She hadn't used them. She was grateful for that now.

***

They were moving past the cave where they had stored the bodies when they heard the noise.

Alan had point, followed by Okobe, Amanda and Safiya, and Hank had the tail. They kept the flashlights off and moved as quietly as they could. They were relying on the light bleed from the main cavern for illumination. Amanda would have killed for even one pair of night vision goggles about now. The cave was wide and low. There were natural columns where stalactites and stalagmites had joined together.

Backlit by the lights of the main cave, they threw long shadows across the floor. Amanda cursed and switched on the flashlight attached to the side of her shotgun. The beam sliced through the darkness. The others were taking their cue from her and doing the same.

They moved to the side of the entrance, forming a line against the rock wall. Using the flashlight beams to check all around them.

Amanda played her flashlight over Daniels' body. There was muttered cursing from the others.

'Quiet,' Amanda hissed. She noticed the beam of her flashlight was shaking again. She played the light over Coyle. Schmidt. Mikey. He had been her oldest friend on the team after Alan.

The crunching noise had probably been quite quiet. To Amanda it sounded deafening. She watched Mikey's body jerk as if it had been nudged by someone trying to get past. *It knows we're here and it doesn't give a shit,* she thought.

It was almost an automatic response. Her finger curled around the shotgun's trigger. She squeezed. Four rounds. The hammer hitting the cartridge. The charge in the cartridge exploding. The powder propelling electrostatically-charged ball-bearing down the barrel. A long tongue of flame from the barrel of the shotgun lit up the cave. The spent cartridge was expended from the weapon. The same thing happened three more times.

The electrostatically-charged ball-bearings filled the air over Mikey's corpse. Amanda was tangentially aware of the ball-bearings blowing bits out of the body.

Lightning arced around a massive, powerfully built but human-shaped figure, standing over Mikey's body. The illusion cloaking him flickered and then failed in sparks of electricity.

The figure was wearing a suit that, to Amanda, looked like it had been made from muscle-like metallic cables in an armoured exoskeleton. Its face was covered by mask and visor. The figure was looking between them, taking its time. Unhurried. Unworried.

'Light it up!' Alan shouted and started firing burst after burst from his Grendel assault rifle. Safiya and Okobe started firing as well. The multiple bullet impacts wreathed the armoured figure in sparks. Hank hesitated but opened fire with the Mk 60. He was firing the MMG from his shoulder. Tracers and armour piercing rounds impacted into the figure. Staggering it. The tracers were bouncing off the armour and arcing into the darkness of the cavern.

Darkness started to envelope the figure once more as it stood up. Amanda realised that it was trying to use the cloak again. She fired the three remaining volt rounds, dressing the figure in lightning and dropping the cloak.

There was a load popping noise as Okobe fired his grenade launcher. The grenade hit the figure, staggering it, and then exploded. The overpressure rammed them all into the wall. Amanda's head was ringing as she staggered to her feet. She shouted that she was reloading, but couldn't hear herself. She tried to pull herself together enough to eject the mag from the shotgun. The shotgun's empty magazine fell to the ground while she clutched at her webbing for another one.

It came stalking out of the darkness, all pretence at stealth gone. Smoke pouring off it. The armour had changed. Flattened, somehow, into overlapping plates. It strode straight past her, ignoring her. Only Okobe had the presence of mind to fire. Amanda cried out as a ricochet from one of the Nigerian's rounds caught her in the shoulder, spinning her around.

Amanda spun back just in time to see the armoured figure push a knife through Okobe's body armour and then lift the tall Nigerian off the floor. The screaming stopped. Okobe went limp as he slid down the knife until the figure had his lower arm inside Okobe's torso.

Her hearing returned. It took a moment for her to realise that the screaming in her ears was Asher demanding to know what was going on. Shaking fingers finally managed to ram a fresh magazine into the combat shotgun.

An enraged Alan jumped on the armoured figure's back. The figure cast Okobe's body aside casually, grabbed Alan easily from his back and threw him into the cave wall. Even through the ringing in her ears and Asher's incessant babble, Amanda could hear the cracking noise and Alan's scream.

Hank fired a long burst at nearly point-blank range. Sparks and ricocheting tracers lit up the cave. Safiya went down as one of the ricochets caught her.

'Wait! Cease fire! Cease fire, goddamnit! Stop fucking shooting!' Amanda screamed.

Hank ceased firing but rapidly backed away from the figure, which had turned to face him. Safiya, on the floor, scrambled away from the armoured figure as well. The French/Algerian woman grabbed her Grendel as she did so. Alan was groaning. That was good, Amanda thought, it meant he was alive.

'Please! I know you can hear me,' she shouted into

the tac radio. 'We'll leave you the fuck alone, just please stop killing my people,' she begged.

It turned to look at her. She found herself facing an expressionless armoured mask.

'Is it here?' the figure demanded. It had a low bass voice. There was something emotionless and cold in it.

'I don't know what "it' is, but this is a really fucking unimportant facility.' The figure just stared at her. 'Look, you just tell me what it's going to take for you to stop killing my people and we'll do it, okay?'

'Alcatraz, man?' Hank tried. She could hear the terror in the ex-marine's voice. The figure turned around to look at Hank.

'I know that name. I am not him,' he/it said.

'What do you want?' Amanda asked.

'Access,' the figure said.

'We're just going to leave, okay?'

The armoured figure said nothing but it didn't make a move to kill them all, which Amanda put in the win column.

'What the fuck are you doing?!' Asher's voice went very high pitched when he screamed, Amanda noticed. Amanda suddenly realised that the voice wasn't just in her ear now, but in the cave as well. Both she and the armoured figure turned around to look at the piggy scientist. Amanda was surprised that the fat scientist was brave enough to get this close to the thing-in-armour. 'What are you fucking talking to it for, you stupid bitch? Shoot it!'

'Fuck that!' Amanda said emphatically. 'We are oscar mike.'

She turned and headed over to Alan, hoping that he was well enough to move. Hank was helping Safiya to her feet.

'Shoot him! Shoot him!' Asher was screaming. The armoured figure was just staring at the two of them.

Amanda didn't think that Alan's back was broken. Not that it mattered, she didn't think that she had any choice but to try and move him.

'I'll see you dead for this! I'll have your family fucking murdered!' Asher screamed at Amanda. A shot rang out. Asher collapsed to the ground, holding his stomach. He started crying and letting out little squeals of pain. Amanda looked at the smoking Hammer II heavy automatic in her hand.

'What did I tell you, Asher? You've got to leave people with something to lose.' She threw the Hammer to the thing-in-armour. 'Looks like you disarmed me and shot Dr Asher here,' she told him/it. The figure nodded. 'Use him for whatever you want, we're taking our dead.' The figure considered this and nodded again.

Amanda and Hank helped Alan up. He was moaning, fading in and out of consciousness. They headed back to the main cave. She glanced over her shoulder. Her last view of the Tinman was him advancing on the squealing gut-shot Dr Asher.

Her face hardened into a mask of hatred.

You killed my people, she thought, *this isn't over, motherfucker.*

Daimyo (a fragment)

Quantico Marine Base, Virginia, 2024

He'd read all of the warrior philosophers. Sun Tzu, Musashi, Clausewitz. The practical stuff, whilst much of it was often common sense, was a useful grounding in strategies. *The rest of it's navel-gazing bullshit to try and rationalise away killing a lot of people, in this marine's opinion* General Sherman Barclay thought as he looked at the half-full crystal glass of single malt whiskey. *There's no decency in war. Sometimes, if you're lucky, you're defending your country, the rest of time you're proving to some intransigent that you're a bigger bastard than they are.* In short, if you were a soldier, you did what you were told. He was a four-star general and commandant of the, until recently, United States Marine Corps. He'd got the job as a result of the cluster-fuck in New York. It was a rank he'd never wanted, but now that he had it he found that he also didn't want to do what he was told.

The screen on the wall of his study was showing a newsfeed from the Macronet. His story hadn't been at the top of the program, but he knew it was coming. The lead story was still CELL related. He watched a tall, old man, with features that reminded him of a hunting bird of prey, walk out of a huge skyscraper in Frankfurt into an explosion of camera flashes. His security were pushing reporters and paparazzi out of the way as he made his way to the waiting eight-wheeled armoured Mercedes limousine.

'The boardroom coup ousting of Karl Ernst Rasch, CEO of Hargreave-Rasch BioChemical, comes as no surprise to business analysts in the wake of his comments criticising their subsidiary company, the CELL Corporation. Hargreave-Rasch has had some turbulent years, culminating in a name change to distance themselves from alleged unethical medical experiments. Rasch publicly spoke out against the energy giant's alleged use of Ceph-derived technology in its New York facility ...'

'And fuck you, too,' Barclay said and muted the sound. He was sat at his desk, still in his dress blues, his service M1911 on the blotter paper in front of him. He had disassembled it and cleaned it. The drilled-in repetition of the process helped him clear his mind. The whiskey had helped him fuzz it up some. He rapidly reassembled the .45.

During Operation Iraqi Freedom, as a young Captain, he had talked to a special forces operator who had told him that if anyone ever pulled a pistol on him, he should just turn and run. The operator had been of the opinion that pistols were so inaccurate that if you added the stress of combat, people had next to no chance of hitting anything. After that conversation

Barclay had made it his business to be the best damn combat pistol shooter in the Marine Corps. A skill he'd had to put to good use on more than one occasion.

He slid a magazine into the pistol and worked the slide to chamber a round. An empty gun was nobody's friend. He left the pistol hot, the safety off. It was against Corps regulations. It was a special forces trick, they wanted to draw and fire rapidly and smoothly. After all, it wasn't like he had to worry about kids or grandkids in the house. He didn't even have to worry about a wife anymore. Susan had told him when she had left that the marines were his mistress and she had never been able to compete.

He held the M1911 up and let the side of it rest against the grey hair on his temple. The black metal was cool against his head. He put it down on the gun-oil stained blotting paper. Next to his pride and joy.

Barclay had grown up in New York in a hard, working-class, Irish-American neighbourhood in the Bronx. His dad had loved westerns and from his dad he had inherited a love of America's frontier history. As a child his father had taken him to Woodlawn Cemetery in the Bronx, to see the grave of William Barclay Masterton, better known as Bat Masterton. Masterton had been a buffalo hunter, army scout, Indian fighter, a gunman and a lawman. He had been a contemporary of Wyatt Earp's. A young Sherman Barclay had been struck by the coincidence of sharing the same name with Masterton, even if it was only the gunman's middle name.

He had been a newly promoted first lieutenant when the gun had come up for auction. A .45 Colt Peacemaker owned by Bat Masterton his own damned self, complete with notches on the grip. What had tickled Barclay about the pistol most of all was that it hadn't been the one used in Dodge City or in Colorado during the railroad wars. It was one of two pistols that Masterton had bought from pawnshops in New York when he was working there as a newspaper man and writer in the latter part of his life. He'd cut notches in them and sold them to people, telling them they were the pistols from his gun-fighting days.

It had taken every last penny of his savings and a loan that he'd lied to the bank about. Susan and he had only just got married and it was one of the worst arguments they had ever had, but he had bought the gun. Over a period of years he'd lovingly restored it, and then, because he hated useless things, he'd learnt to shoot with it. That hadn't been easy. He suspected that throwing live canaries at a dartboard would prove to be more accurate than the damn Peacemaker.

He had just finished cleaning the Peacemaker when he appeared on the news feed. His dress blues hadn't been in disarray this morning, when he had betrayed every instinct he had, not to mention a number of regulations and outright laws. When he'd held his impromptu press conference at Arlington Cemetery.

The caption under the footage read: General Sherman Barclay blows the whistle on CELL's control over Marines.

He hadn't intended on being a soldier. Even as late as college he wasn't sure what he had wanted to be. Football had secured him a partial scholarship, damned hard work on the part of his mother, father and older brother had made him the first person in his family to go to college. His father and brother were heating contractors. They had worked in downtown Manhattan a lot. His father had seen the lifestyle of the people who worked downtown, and he had wanted that for his son. Sherman had been less sure. Both his father and his brother had been in 7 World Trade Centre on the ninth of September 2001. He had joined the marines after he graduated the following year.

Then, like Susan had said, he had fallen in love. The United States Marine Corps was older than the country it served. It had fought in every significant conflict America had been involved in. From fighting for the country's independence in the American Revolutionary War to going toe-to-toe with alien invaders in the streets of his hometown. He didn't mind admitting that they'd had their arses kicked in New York, but he was proud of every last one of his men and women who had conducted a fighting retreat from alien war machines long enough to evacuate civilians from the ruined city.

The marines had made mistakes, no doubt about it. He'd witnessed atrocities, seen the shelling of civilian population centres. There were monsters and cowards in its ranks, though he had rooted those he could find out with ruthless efficiency when he had taken command. But he was more proud of the men and women who had served the Corps than anything else in a long, bloody, exciting, hard life.

Then the companies had come. He had watched the privatisation of war with disgust throughout his military career. In his opinion, the moment the focus went from duty and loyalty to the man next to you to a pay cheque, the coherence wrought by military discipline was gone. At best you got badly equipped individuals in way over their heads. At worst you got atrocity.

He wasn't some peace-loving, anti-capitalist hippy protestor. He remembered when they had occupied Wall Street. Unlike many amongst his peers, he had had respect for them. Rightly or wrongly, they had taken a stand for what they believed in. He'd been furious when they'd started getting beaten and moved on, silenced. Their right to voice their opinions was one of the things he had thought he'd been fighting for. Nowadays they would just be branded as terrorists and mown down by corporate goons, like the so-called *Resistor* group that had been protesting outside a CELL facility in Tokyo. Barclay had read the intelligence briefings on them. They hadn't been terrorists, that was spin bullshit. They'd just been kids.

He'd studied business in college. He had no problem with capitalism. His dad had made him believe that if you worked hard you should get rewarded for it. The double dip had proved that capitalism and corporations needed restraints. That compassion and responsibility had to be more important than the rapacious profiteering of a tiny minority. Some things just couldn't be left to an institute whose primary concern was the generation of wealth, the wellbeing of the people of your country being one of them. Instead the world had gone the other way.

And now the same company who had come for his beloved hometown had come for his beloved Corps. He didn't care that it had all been agreed in Washington, set up by bribe-welcoming politicians in shady backroom deals. CELL had control of the Corps now, and could use them for whatever they wanted.

'Not on my watch,' he muttered, only slurring a little bit.

He didn't even flinch as the lockbuster shotgun rounds blew off the hinges of the door to his house. *Little dramatic,* he thought. He picked up the Peacemaker and stuffed it into the waistband of his dress trousers.

They sauntered into his office. They had checked first and seen a broken-down old man slumped in a leather chair with a whiskey in his hand. There were five of them. He could hear others moving around his house. Things were being loudly broken in other rooms. They wore sharp suits, carried piece-of-shit Feline SMGs and were dumb enough to wear sunglasses inside. Barclay didn't think he would have liked them even if they hadn't just damaged the door on a house more than a hundred years old.

'Sherman Barclay,' one of them started. He was stood in front of Barclay's desk. He had the false confidence of someone with a gun facing a broken man. Though he did glance down at the M1911 lying on the blotting paper on Barclay's mahogany desk.

'General Barclay,' he corrected the man.

'Not any m ...'

'Are you wearing perfume, son?' Barclay demanded.

'Erm ... What?' the man was taken aback by the tone of command in the General's voice. 'It's aftershave.'

'Perfume. My marines don't wear perfume, and neither would you if you had any goddamned self-respect. What the fuck are you and your little pantywaists doing in my house other than using up perfectly good oxygen?'

'We're here ...'

'You address me as sir, or General, or you can get out of my house, understand me, boy?'

The boy with a gun in front of him was starting to lose confidence in his ability to deal with this mean old man. He glanced down at the M1911 again. Barclay followed his gaze and then looked the gunman in the eyes. He just saw himself reflected in mirror shades, but he knew the other man looked away first.

'Sir, we're here to take you into custody ...'

'Under whose authority?'

'The board of CELL ...'

'Who are a private company. This makes about as much sense as being arrested by Ronald McDonald. I don't recognise their authority. What am I supposed to be charged with?'

'Treason against ...'

Barclay was on his feet. Five SMGs were suddenly pointed at him by very nervous corporate gunmen. He was pointing at the man in front of him. Whiskey or no whiskey, his hand was steady.

'You listen to me, you failed abortion, my loyalty, my duty, my honour ...' one of the gunmen laughed, a sneer on his face. '... has been proven in fire and blood. You stand where thousands of men and women far better than you have stood and you have the gall to accuse me of treason. Your very presence here is a goddamned insult to every marine who died in some godforsaken shithole, from Tripoli to Okinawa, for your fucked up sense of entitlement and your disrespect. Get the fuck off my base now, before I beat you off it!'

'... Against CELL,' the gunman finished. Barclay just stared at him. Then he started laughing.

'What does that even mean, boy?'

'It means you have to come with me.'

'Or what?'

'We're authorised to use force in your apprehension.' Barclay nodded.

'You sure about that, son?' he asked.

'General, sir ...'

If they had sent marines, even MPs, instead of these suited, pencil-neck, executive gunmen. If they had saluted him, shown respect to the rank, the Corps that he had been commandant of until this morning, a rank he had earned the hard way, he would have gone quietly, maybe.

He grabbed the M1911 from the desk. The first shot was one-handed and it was point blank range. He put the big hollow-point round between the gunman who'd been doing all the talking's eyes. The back of his head came off as the hollow point mushroomed.

He shifted, moving to one side. Bringing his hand holding the M1911 into a two-handed standing position. The one who had laughed was next. Nothing petty, but that one wanted to shoot, Barclay had recognised the type. Two rounds. He went down.

He moved, crossing behind his chair. *Don't stand still in a gunfight, bullets will come looking for you.* Two more rounds. He was sure he had just winged the gunman closest to the door but he went down and didn't start firing.

The last two had started firing now. Inexperienced as they were, they had at least managed to react. Bullets blew splinters out of a desk more than two hundred years old. His crystal decanter exploded, spraying him in whiskey. He was still moving to the side. He fired twice more and a gunwoman went down. The final gunman was firing the Feline, spraying wildly as he made for the door. Barclay registered the look of panic on the gunman's face. A round caught Barclay in his left shoulder, knocking him back. He took aim. The gunman saw his death coming and he couldn't understand why the gun bucking away in his hand wasn't going to save him. The round caught the gunman in the head. He walked another step, still firing and then collapsed to the ground.

Cordite smoke filled the room. Then the pitiful whining of the wounded started. It was just like any other battle. It was the one closest to the door who was still alive. He had just winged him. The slide on his M1911 was back, the gun empty. *No,* he thought, *not a battle, a gunfight.* One of the things that Barclay had always liked most about the stories of Bat Masterton was that the gunfighter had apparently been a genuinely good shot. Not a spray and pray merchant.

He heard them first. They came charging through the double doors. Barclay let go of the empty M1911. He fast-drew the Peacemaker from his waist band. *Oh, how long I practiced that.* They started firing. He fanned the hammer on the single-action revolver rapidly, firing from the hip. The M1911 hit the desk. The hammer on the Peacemaker clicked down on an empty chamber.

Somehow he'd hit all three of the entering gunmen. With six rounds, fanning, firing from the hip, admittedly at close range, he'd hit all three, as it mattered in a gunfight.

'Can you see me now, Bat?' he said to himself and smiled, and then he staggered back and sat down hard in his chair. The one in the gut hurt the most but he was sure it was the round in the chest that would kill him. Breathing was difficult, like there was some kind of obstruction to it.

All the warrior philosophy was bullshit. Eight dead young men scattered around his house, sent by cowards, proved that. If he had managed, somehow, amongst all that bloodshed, to be a decent man then that was something his father had taught him. It hadn't come from a book. But he had taken two things away from all that bullshit. Sometimes questioning and disobedience were the most patriotic things that you could do. The Founding Fathers had taught him that.

He could hear vehicles skidding to a halt outside. Footsteps, running. There was shouting outside.

The second thing: when a *samurai* disagreed with his *daimyo*, his lord, the ultimate protest he could make was to take his own life. This ritual form of suicide by disembowelment was called *seppuku*.

That was bullshit as well, Barclay thought as shaking fingers managed to put one more round into the Peacemaker. *I just want to make the decision on how I go out.* He had never felt that anybody owed him anything, not the country, not the people, not the marines, not the government – well, maybe the government sometimes – but as a reward for more than thirty years of service: *frankly, this sucks ass.*

As he put the barrel of the gun to his head and cocked the hammer he thought about Susan. He thought about his father.

They burst into his office brandishing weapons and shouting. There had always been shouting in his life, ever since he'd joined the Corps anyway.

'Semper Fidelis,' he told them. He squeezed the trigger.

None of them noticed his final act of "treason". The camera in the plant pot in the corner, broadcasting to the Macronet.

*

'There are those who argue that everything breaks even in this old dump of a world of ours. I suppose these ginks who argue that way hold that because the rich man gets ice in the summer and the poor man gets it in the winter things are breaking even for both. Maybe so, but I'll swear I can't see it that way.'

William Barclay "Bat" Masterton, New York City, 1921

Refuse/Resist

HMS *Robin Hood*, Shakedown Run, Atlantic Ocean, off the Eastern Seaboard, 2034

Captain Cyrus Harper stared at the hardcopy of the order. He glanced over at the holographic image of the target. He could see the thermal imagery of the forces gathering amongst the ruins of Yonkers. He also noticed that part of the image had been redacted. The part of the image that would have shown exactly what was going on NY. The image had been shot from orbit. He guessed it had been shot by one of the CELL satellites linked to the Archangel orbital weapons platform. *Why didn't they just use that?* the cowardly part of him wondered.

'Sir,' his executive officer Commander Stevens demanded. 'We have our orders.' Harper looked up at his XO. The man was tall, very thin and had a predatory aspect to his features. This had earned him the nickname "the ghoul" amongst the men. He was one of the breed of men that Harper had come to think of as "corporate" officers.

Next to his XO was Lieutenant Zinah Talpur, the

commander of the small complement of Royal Marines on the *Robin Hood*. She looked less than pleased to be involved in this. Not so long ago, it seemed, an XO would have never dared to question – let along try and strong-arm – his captain like this, but things had changed. The navy had been privatised. The CELL Corporation, the monopolistic economic superpower in its own right, had bought the military from an increasingly close-to-bankrupt country.

Many of the officers in the navy had attempted to resign their commission only to find that their "contract terms" had changed. Harper hadn't been one of them, but then the maiden voyage of the HMS *Robin Hood* was going to be his last voyage. He had joined at the turn of the century. Now in his mid-fifties, they would either try and give him a desk job or assign him to a training post. The latter appealed more than the former but neither appealed enough for him to stay. He had not renewed his term of service before the buyout. He was still able to leave. The Navy was, if nothing else, an enormous bureaucracy. Once something was done it was very difficult to undo it.

'Sir!' His XO was even more insistent now. Harper's eyes flickered up to see him. He had not liked Stevens from the moment he had met him. He didn't like his attitude, his style of command or the way he treated the men. He could see the hunger in the XO's eyes. CELL ownership meant opportunities for the right kind of people. Stevens wanted Harper to refuse the order from their new owners, the order to fire on another sovereign nation to secure corporate interests, so he could take command. For him, career advancement was more important than anything else, even honour.

Harper, however, had misgivings. He didn't care if the American government had okayed it. He didn't care that it would be part of what passed for a combined-arms operation under the auspices of CELL. A company with this amount of power didn't sit right with him. He had always assumed that anti-capitalist sentiments were for hippies and dropouts who couldn't or wouldn't play the game. Now he was less sure. CELL seemed like capitalism taken to such extremes it had started to resemble feudalism. That said, he had never disobeyed an order in his life and he wasn't keen to start now.

'Mr Stevens. I don't know who you have served under before, but I am not in the habit of having my XO bark at me,' Harper began.

'Sir, it is my ...'

'Or indeed interrupt me. I have received the orders. We are still more than seventeen hours away from the point at which they will need to be acted on. I fail to see why you are here acting this way. In fact, I could do with an extremely good reason why I shouldn't have you removed from duty and confined to quarters. Lieutenant Talpur, frankly I expected better of you.' The young Pakistani woman at least had the decency to look guilty. Harper was less than pleased when he noticed that Stevens had his sidearm at his hip.

'Sir, you do not have the authority to remove me

from command,' Stevens said, a little too smugly for Harper's taste.

Captain Harper's anger moved like a thundercloud across his face.

'Why? Has God come on board in the last five minutes?'

'Sir, these are decisions being made at board level by CELL command. They feel that you may not be prepared to properly execute their orders.'

'And I wonder where they got that opinion from?' Harper demanded. His reply was one of Steven's thin, evil little smiles. That was it. He turned to Talpur.

'Lieutenant, do you still recognise me as Captain of this ship or are you in mutiny as well?'

'Now just a minute!' Stevens objected.

'You, sir, will remain quiet!' Harper shouted. He rarely raised his voice.

'Yes, Captain, but ...'

'Mr Stevens, you are relieved of command. Lieutenant, escort Mr Stevens to his quarters and confine him there.'

'Mr Stevens,' Lieutenant Talpur said, gesturing towards the door. He turned to look down at the much smaller woman.

'Are you out of your mind?!' he demanded.

'Don't make this any more difficult than it has to be please, sir.'

Stevens swung round to face Harper again.

'You're going to pay for this!' he spat.

'Another word and you're confined in the brig.

Lieutenant, relieve Mr Stevens of his sidearm, please. Leave it on my desk and escort him out of here.'

The lieutenant removed Steven's M12 Nova from his holster and laid it on the Captain's desk. She all but had to drag the protesting XO out of Harper's stateroom.

Harper sagged in his chair as soon as the door closed. He had lost his temper and he knew it. He had let the evil little shit get under his skin and he had done something rash.

He glanced over at the half-full bottle of good whiskey next to the model of the 55-gun ship-of-the-line HMS *Prince Royal*. He desperately wanted a drink but knew he wouldn't succumb to the desire. Not this time.

Any kind of ruckus of this nature on a Royal Navy ship meant a serious black mark on everyone involved's record. The problem was he didn't appear to be in the Royal Navy anymore. It seemed that they were even going to change the name of the ships. They would no longer be *His Majesty's Ships*.

He glanced in the mirror over the sink in his cramped stateroom. He was tall, craggy, and had a hooked nose, which along with his eyebrows gave him a bird-of-prey-like appearance. Despite having waged constant war against middle-aged spread he normally thought that he was doing well for his age. Today he just looked tired, tired and old. He cursed this so-called "anti-CELL" resistance movement. If only they had left it another month before starting, he would have been out of the navy.

He could understand why CELL wanted some

assurances that he would follow orders when the time came. If he balked at the last moment it could really mess up their plans. CELL had a lot of influence with the US government and although they had managed to buy the US Marines, which effectively had its own navy and air force, it had not bought the US Navy. The HMS *Robin Hood* was their best hope for a naval bombardment in the area. Though why they hadn't chosen to use what had been, until recently, the US marines was beyond him.

Most of the conflicts that Harper had served in during his thirty years had been so-called low intensity conflicts: Iraq, the London Emergency, Sri Lanka, Columbia, even dealing with Ceph nests. Too many of them had involved him firing guns or missiles into civilian centres. Next to none of them had been standup fights. Once again his targets were 'terrorists'. He knew that Yonkers had mostly been evacuated when CELL had effectively annexed New York in the wake of the Ceph invasion. On a conceptual level, Harper still had problems with an alien invasion of New York.

The problem was, he knew the people he was being asked to bombard. Not personally, though it wouldn't surprise him if there were a few familiar faces amongst them. But these were the same people he had known all his life. They were military people. He had served with their like. He understood why they were fighting. They were angry about the stranglehold that CELL's energy monopoly had on the world and their privatisation of the militaries of a number of different nations.

He knew his orders were wrong, but he'd known orders had been wrong in the past. He had been aboard HMS *Anguish* when her Captain had been ordered to fire on south London in the face of widescale social disorder. That had been wrong. He'd spent the next four years as a functional alcoholic as a result of watching the south London skyline burn.

More than once he had questioned orders to fire on civilian population bases in Sri Lanka. By questioned he meant internally, of course, not out loud. He couldn't afford to not play the game, not in His Majesty's Navy. Not if he wanted a career.

At least he knew that he would be firing at soldiers who were under arms and intent on violence. He just wasn't sure he disagreed with them. Just like he didn't want to be taking orders from a rapacious multinational company.

Just one more month. Rachel and he had intended on using what was left of their savings, the little they had managed to protect in this apparently never-ending recession, and their paltry pensions to buy a place in Dorset. She would continue to teach, he was hoping to get work as a consultant for companies with ship building contracts with the navy.

He slumped in the chair and looked at the whiskey again. He knew what the easy option was. He knew what he owed Rachel, particularly after she had stood by him after the London emergency. After all, it wasn't as if he hadn't bombarded cities from the sea before.

What he needed was intelligence. The problem was

that he was the only one he trusted with gathering the information. He didn't want to leave the ship – in fact, it could be seen as treason – but he was running out of options. *Actually, you old fool, you still have two, you just don't like them*, he thought. He didn't trust his new employers. The Royal Navy wasn't meant to be the enforcement arm of a multinational corporation. He needed to know more about the armed insurrection. The resistance wouldn't risk their comms discipline to speak to him. That left speaking to them face-to-face, and the only person he fully trusted to do that was himself. He told himself that it was because he wanted to make an informed decision. He stood up and left his cramped cabin.

***

Harper reflected that he had a love-hate relationship with the HMS *Robin Hood* as he made his way towards the bridge through the ship's narrow corridors. It was a superb vessel. It had a trimaran hull that incorporated SWATH – Small Waterplane Area Triple Hull – technology to minimise the ship's volume at the surface area of the sea, where it would encounter resistance from wave energy. This meant reduced acoustic and wake signatures, which added to the vessel's stealth capabilities. It also made the guided-missile stealth destroyer very fast. During test runs they had managed to get the ship up to speeds of just under sixty knots.

It packed a punch as well, even though its stealth properties precluded it from having the main gun that many other ships of its class were armed with. It had been designed as a near-invisible missile platform, a surface ship with comparable stealth capabilities to a submarine. Although without a main gun, it was armed with two fully automated 30mm Bushmaster auto-cannons and two rotary, radar guided, 20mm Phalanx close-in weapon systems designed to shoot down incoming missiles. As well as air defence missiles and ship-to-ship torpedoes it also carried 24 CVS401 Perseus multi-role cruise missiles.

Its inward sloping, or tumblehome, hull design, its lack of vertical surfaces or right angles and its construction out of hardened, molecular-bonded carbon fibre all added to a reduced radar cross section as well as reducing its heat and sonar signature.

However, the most impressive aspect was the cloak. An array close to the stern of the ship was capable of projecting a lensing field that bent light around the ship. This effectively made the *Robin Hood* invisible when it was stationary or travelling at speeds below twenty knots, and significantly obscured views of the ship at speeds in excess of twenty knots.

Harper had had to see it before he believed it. He was still less than convinced that the cloak wasn't going to give the entire crew cancer. Allegedly developed from technology derived from the US government's Project Rainbow, a smaller version of the cloak was rumoured to have been utilised by US special forces operators in the Pacific during the Lingshan incident and again in New York during the Ceph incursion.

The cloak was the reason that Harper had a love-hate relationship with the *Robin Hood*. Not because there was something sneaky, or indeed un-gentlemanly about an invisible ship, though the old fashioned, traditional, hidebound part of him felt there was. The hate he felt for this amazing ship stemmed from the cost.

A company that had been bought out by CELL had built the ship. The cloak had doubled the price of the vessel and the ship had come in significantly over budget. The *Robin Hood* and its two sister ships had significantly contributed to the financial strain that had forced Britain to sell its navy, which, despite its size, was arguably the best in the world. CELL had squeezed and squeezed the Admiralty, and then the Treasury and then the government. That was why Harper found himself hating the ship, despite how hard its capabilities tried to woo him.

***

The bridge was in the centre of the ship. It contained a series of dark carbon-fibre workstations illuminated by the holographic projections from the various departments: helm, weapons, engineering, communications, navigation etc.

Lieutenant Commander Samantha Swanson didn't seem surprised to see the Captain, despite it being her watch.

'Captain on the bridge,' she announced, saluting. Harper returned the salute. She relinquished his raised leather swivel seat, which allowed a commanding view of the bridge, and stood with her arms behind her back by the navigation area. She was too professional to question or even show any reaction to his presence, though Harper guessed that Stevens almost certainly would have spoken to her and she would be aware of the *Robin Hood*'s orders.

Harper had worked with Swanson before, and had found the tall, sandy-blonde-haired woman to be a capable officer. He had recommended her for XO of the *Robin Hood*, which might have resulted in her eventual captaincy of the vessel but politics, and it was starting to look like corporate rather than Admiralty politics, had resulted in Stevens being foisted on him.

'Navigation, plot a course to the west end of Long Island Sound, please. Engineering, enable the cloak. Helm, I want you to remain steady at twenty knots. Let's see if this cloak can do everything they say it can. We are going to be giving our new employers a demonstration of their stealth technology.'

'Sir, should we make Liberty Station aware of our new heading?' Midshipman Walters, the head of comms, asked. Liberty Station was the CELL installation at New York that was ostensibly in command of the *Robin Hood* at the moment.

'The purpose of this exercise is to test the *Robin Hood*'s stealth capabilities. We are going to see how close we can get to New York without being detected. Comms discipline will be maintained.'

'Aye sir.'

Swanson glanced at the Captain but said nothing. She knew he was disobeying orders, and those that knew the purpose of the *Robin Hood*'s mission out here also knew that they could bombard the rebel positions in Yonkers from over a hundred and fifty miles away if they so wanted. A few people swapped glances but nobody raised any objections.

He felt rather than heard the background hum of the cloak as it initialised. The ship changed course. Even on the choppy sea the ship's ride was so smooth it felt like they were sailing silently across silk.

***

They passed the lights of New London, New Haven, Bridgeport, Norwalk and they were heading towards Stamford on the northern, Connecticut shore of Long Island Sound. To the south, Long Island itself was dark. After the Ceph incursion and CELL's aggressive land grab, real estate prices had plummeted horribly. Now the wealthy neighbourhoods like Port Jefferson and Whitestone had been abandoned. Empty mansions were homes for the displaced poor from the city, rats and wild dog packs.

Despite the tension that he could feel in the bridge, Captain Harper was appalled at how easy this was. Particularly as by now CELL must know that the *Robin Hood* was missing.

'Mr Hamilton, will the East River provide you with any significant problems?' Harper asked.

'Er ... no, sir,' Lieutenant Hamilton said, not sounding entirely sure of himself. Harper had never worked with the plump moustachioed man before, but he had reviewed the navigation officer's record and it had seemed more than adequate. You had to be something of a high flyer to have been posted to the *Robin Hood*.

Closer to the city, more and more of the surrounding habitation had been abandoned. There was mile after mile of dark empty buildings that used to be some of the most desirable real estate in the world. Now they were ghosts of suburbs and, as they got closer to the city, the neighbourhoods of New York. The only light or movement was from the occasional CELL patrol vehicle or helicopter, their searchlights lancing through the darkness.

What had once been a very busy waterway was now all but empty. The patrol vessels they did see in the distance, mainly CELL but some were US Navy, they gave a wide berth to. Nobody challenged them. Nobody even noticed them. The stealth field was working perfectly.

'This is obscene,' one of the ratings in the comms section muttered before being shushed. Harper wasn't sure that he disagreed.

As they entered the East River, New York was a faint glow to the southwest.

Inside the bridge the silence was only broken by the occasional quietly spoken instruction. The tensest moment came when they passed within two hundred feet of a patrol vessel. The craft's searchlights were being played across the dark riverbanks on either side of the river. They were presumably looking for resistance fighters. Lieutenant Chalmers, who ran the weapons section, glanced up at Harper but the Captain said nothing. He wasn't even sure what he was going to do if they were discovered. Would he fight or surrender? If he fought would the crew follow his orders? The searchlight must have shone straight through the *Robin Hood* but the patrol craft did not notice them.

How can they not be aware of something this size so close to them? Harper wondered. *Can't they feel us?*

'Helm, bring us to within five hundred feet of the northern shoreline,' Harper ordered. To the south of them was Rikers Island, the infamous prison now abandoned following the attack on New York. Information was exchanged rapidly, verbally and electronically, between navigation and the helm. Harper felt the ship change direction. 'Hold position here. Lieutenant Commander Swanson, the planning room, if you will.'

The captain stood up and headed to the room adjoining the bridge. Swanson followed him. The room contained a conference table with a holo-projector in the centre and workstations around the side. Other than a picture of HMS *Hood* the room was bare.

'Sir?' the lieutenant commander asked, barely suppressed curiosity written all over her face.

'I'll be blunt, are you prepared to follow my orders?' he asked.

'Are these in contravention of our orders from CELL?' she asked, equally bluntly.

'I will say no, they are not,' he lied, and he lied obviously. *Understand what I can't come out and say,* he willed her. *Take the word of your Captain when he lies to you.* This would be the only protection she would get. It probably wasn't enough. He saw the understanding on her face.

'You can trust me, sir,' she told him. He nodded, believing her.

'I am going to be leaving the ship,' he told her.

'Sir ...? Why?' Her surprise was visible.

'To gather intelligence.'

'Sir, we have people ...'

'I ... we need to make an informed decision. It needs to be me, I'm afraid.'

Now the young Lieutenant Commander looked less sure.

'Does that change your decision?'

Swanson gave it some thought.

'No, sir, I don't believe it does,' she told him, resolved.

'You know, with me gone there will be a lot of pressure ...' She just nodded. 'Very well. My standing orders are to remain here and remain hidden until I return.'

'And if you don't, sir?'

They now had eight hours before they were due to fire on Yonkers.

'Then I am afraid the decision will be down to you,' he told her. He left out that it would come down to her conscience. He left out that regardless of her decision it would haunt her for years. He knew Swanson to be twenty-eight years old, young for her rank. *Too young for a decision like this,* he thought.

She swallowed but nodded.

'Rules of Engagement, sir?'

'You will only fire if the lives of the members of this crew rely on it. The emphasis is on being sneaky.'

'The ghoul? I mean Commander Stevens?'

'He remains confined to quarters. If he gives you any trouble then put him in the brig.' She nodded. 'Anything else?'

'No sir.' She went to leave but hesitated. She turned back and offered her hand. 'Sir, it's been an honour.'

Harper looked down at the hand.

'I am intending on coming back,' he told her, smiling. She nodded and went back to the bridge.

***

Lieutenant Talpur's cabin-come-office was next to the bunk area for her marines and it was tiny. This wasn't too much of a problem for the Lieutenant as she was quite small. It was unpleasantly cramped for the Captain.

The Lieutenant handed the Captain a mug of tea.

'I'll be blunt. Can I trust you?' the Captain asked. Talpur's presence during Stevens' insubordination earlier had soured his view of the marine officer. She sighed.

'That it has come to this,' she muttered.

'Lieutenant, we don't have a lot of time.'

'It never occurred to me that I would ever disobey an order from the Captain of a ship that I was stationed on. The problem is, our chain of command has changed.'

'An officer still has the right to refuse to follow orders for reasons of conscience.'

'Until the terms and conditions of our contract are changed, and then their career will be over.'

'Do you want a career in this service?'

The Lieutenant looked at the Captain, holding his eyes for a long time, measuring him, trying to decide what to say. She rubbed her face tiredly. 'No.' The Captain started to say something. 'But I want to put food on the table for my family. I'm not sure that I have the luxury of your principles, sir.'

Neither do I, Harper thought as his heart sank. Although small in number, the marines would be crucial in maintaining control of the ship.

'So I can't rely on you, Lieutenant?'

'No, sir, I'm sorry.'

She slid a piece of paper across the table. Harper picked it up and read the list of six names on it. Lieutenant Talpur's was at the top.

'Lieutenant?'

'You need to relieve me of command and confine these men to quarters, as they all have dependents and quite frankly too much to lose. Sergeant Martin is unmarried with no children that he is aware of. He is also an outspoken critic of CELL. You can rely on Sergeant Martin, sir.'

'The men won't like that.'

'And women. It's been discussed, sir.'

Harper looked at the list and then back to the Lieutenant.

'Thank you, Lieutenant.' Talpur just nodded. 'There is one other thing, Lieutenant. Do any of your men ... people ... have criminal records?'

Talpur looked pained.

'Sir, a number of my people are in due to the Offenders Conscription Act. What do you need?'

'A car thief, ideally.'

'A Liverpudlian, then? I have just the man.'

***

It had been incredible, Harper thought. The inflatable raiding craft had been lowered between two of the tri-maran hulls. Looking up and around him he could see the composite carbon-fibre of the ship's structure. As the coxswain had taken the boat out from under the *Robin Hood*'s superstructure Harper had felt a moment of ionisation as they had gone through the lensing field. He glanced behind him and the *Robin Hood* was nowhere to be seen.

The other three people didn't seem to be enjoying his moment of wonder as they made their way slowly and quietly towards the dark Bronx shoreline. The coxswain was intent on piloting the boat. Private Fry, more frequently known as Scouse, was manning the MMG at the prow of the small craft. Corporal Fenn, a tough young woman from rural north Yorkshire, had her SCAR assault rifle at the ready and was scanning the surface of the river as they headed towards the Bronx shoreline.

Harper knew that the Bronx borough of New York used to have a fearsome reputation for crime, particularly the South Bronx. Now all they would have to worry about was the occasional groups of homeless, even more occasional CELL patrols, and wandering dog packs. Though there were rumours of leftover Ceph bioforms. Despite having seen the whole thing on the news and acting as part of the rapid response force formed as a result of the alien incursion, Harper still had problems crediting the whole thing. Aliens on the streets of Manhattan still seemed too much like science fiction to him.

With a navigator's eye Harper had used landmarks on the surrounding riverbanks to triangulate the position of the *Robin Hood* for his return journey. He was carrying a GPS device and had memorised the co-ordinates of the ship but he would not input them until the last minute in case someone got hold of the device.

***

They had come in under a rotting pier. Harper had told the coxswain to wait there for eight hours or until they returned. They had found a ladder that didn't look too rotten and headed up into the eerily quiet borough.

A four-wheel drive vehicle would have been more useful, but the only thing that Private Fry had managed to find and get working was a compact. They had siphoned as much fuel as they could find whilst Corporal Fenn watched over them. In the distance they could hear the howls of a hunting dog pack. Further afield they could see lights in the sky. A CELL helicopter, heading towards Manhattan and whatever it was that CELL was doing there.

The sound of the compact's engine starting up seemed incredibly loud amongst the dark, empty streets.

With two big marines and their weapons, the interior of the compact was quite cramped. Both the marines, like Harper, were out of uniform, wearing what dark-coloured civilian clothing they had found. They were still wearing their webbing, however.

'I think it only fair to warn you that if we're caught in civvies we may be executed as spies. If either of you want to back out, I'd understand,' Harper told them. Fenn said nothing.

'I hope we see one of these Ceph,' Fry said in his strong Scouse accent as he flipped the night vision goggles down over his eyes. 'I've never seen an alien before.'

***

Fry had studied the map, and many of the old street signs were still present. The Scouse marine had adeptly navigated through the abandoned city. They'd had to detour around rubble, push burnt wrecks of cars out of the way and, with an eye on the deadline, their journey had seemed horribly slow.

Harper had visited New York on a number of

occasions. The place had always seemed teeming with life. This ghost husk of city he found impossibly eerie.

They had caught sight of Manhattan on several occasions. It was lit up, but lit up like a construction site. Much of the most famous skyline in the world was dark and broken-looking from damage received during the Ceph invasion. Harper could see new structures going up but struggled to make out what they were from this distance.

They saw nothing on their journey, not even wild dogs, the only movement the lights in the sky from the helicopters over Manhattan.

***

They crossed over the Bronx River and into Southeast Yonkers. The city was built on a number of hills rising from the Hudson River in the west. Like everywhere else, it seemed deserted. They were travelling along a wide road lined with empty apartment buildings and deserted businesses.

'Sir?' Fry asked.

Harper knew that the Resistance had spread out across the city in a bid to avoid making themselves one big target. Harper knew that this was one of the areas where CELL's Archangel orbital weapons platform had found heat readings.

'I would imagine they should find . . .'

Headlights dazzled them. The glare momentarily blinded Fry, and he cried out as he simultaneously tried to push the NVGs up and bring the car to a halt. Harper was thrown forwards but was aware of Fenn bringing her SCAR up to bear. Fry was reaching for his weapon.

'Wait! Stand down!' Harper shouted. Some kind of aging armoured vehicle had been pulled across the road in front of them. There were dark figures running towards the car. The car doors were yanked open and Harper found himself face down on the tarmac, his hands being cable tied behind his back.

***

Harper felt that his explanation, that he was the captain of a stealth missile destroyer well within firing range of them and that he needed to speak with their commanding officer, lost something of its import when delivered through a black hood.

They had been searched, searched again, searched one more time in a way that bordered on violation, and marched to a number of different places before finally being tied to chairs. Harper's hood was removed and he found himself sat on a chair in a basement that had several inches of water covering the floor. Fenn and Fry were on either side of him, still hooded.

There were three people in here, all male. The first was a stern looking Caucasian man in his early sixties wearing urban pattern combat fatigues that looked very worn but still serviceable. He was in excellent physical condition for his age. His arms were crossed and he looked less than pleased to see Harper and the marines.

The second man was Hispanic. His hair was closely cropped, and he looked to be in his early thirties. He wore sleeveless jungle pattern fatigues under body armour and had an enormous Majestic revolver holstered at his hip.

The third man was sat opposite Harper. He had no hair and was thin, verging on the gaunt. He looked to be in his eighties but in very good shape for it. His eyes seemed younger, somehow. They were very much alive. He looked familiar to Harper, like someone he had seen on television.

'Do you know who I am?' the man asked. He had a strong German accent. Harper finally placed the man.

'You're Karl Ernst Rasch, the ousted head of Hargreave-Rasch BioChemical,' Harper said warily. He glanced at Fenn and Fry.

'And CryNet Systems, who own CELL, who in turn now own the Royal Navy. Or should that be the CELL navy?'

'My name is ...' Harper started.

'We know who you are. We have had your identity confirmed.'

Harper didn't even ask how.

'And these gentlemen?' Harper asked.

'Don't particularly want their names known,' the stern-looking man said. He was clearly used to command. Something about him made Harper think special forces. He wore no insignia on his uniform, just a small stars and stripes patch on one shoulder.

'You are the Captain of the *Robin Hood*?' Rasch said. Harper nodded.

'They know where you are,' Harper told them.

'That was to be expected. Whilst I was CEO at Hargreave-Rasch I was aware of the contract to provide the *Robin Hood*. I am aware of its rather frightening capabilities. CELL have chosen not to deploy what used to be the US marines in New York due to fear of mutiny. Provably loyal CELL military contractors defend the city. In many ways, the *Robin Hood* is our biggest threat.' He paused as if considering something. 'Some would say it is an odd thing for its Captain to be riding around South East Yonkers at this time of night.'

'I need to know why,' Harper told Rasch. Corporal Fenn turned her head as if to look at him through the hood.

'Are we courting the HMS *Robin Hood*?'

'I need to know that this isn't some kind of corporate vendetta.'

'Think we'd be here if it was, *ese*?' the Hispanic soldier asked him.

'Please take the hoods off my men,' Harper said. 'And we're unarmed, you can remove our restraints, you have my word that we will take no actions against you.'

The Hispanic soldier laughed. Rasch looked to the stern-looking soldier, who nodded. The Hispanic soldier took the hoods off Fry and Fenn and then cut the cable ties off their hands with a knife that bordered on machete-sized. The marines rubbed their wrists and looked around but said nothing.

'I would imagine,' Rasch began. 'That like most rational people, you have significant doubts as regards the privatisation of previously national militaries.'

'A national military is accountable to its government and ultimately to its people. A company is accountable to its shareholders at best, but more likely its bottom line.'

'I left Hargreave-Rasch, a company I helped found ...' *That can't be right,* Harper thought. Somewhere at the back of his mind he was sure that the biomedical company had been founded in the early 20th century. 'Because I had become significantly concerned with its practices. The company as itself was out of control. There was no one person running it, no strong personality with a grasp of morality at the helm after the death of my partner Jacob Hargreave.'

'Yourself?'

'It was easy to get rid of me when I started objecting to policy. There was a board-wide vote of no confidence. The problem is that it is a company doing what a company will do, taking corporate capitalism to its *nth* degree because there is nothing to tell it to stop. With the energy monopoly, it now has endless resources. It has stopped being something that we would recognise as a business. Instead it behaves like a particularly rapacious virus. It will consume and consume until there is nothing left. It is the corporate meme out of control, and it will settle for nothing else than total global domination.'

'Is that not the nature of the system?' Harper asked.

'Do you mean, "has someone won capitalism"?' Rasch asked.

The stern-looking soldier snorted and shook his head.

'Tell that to the people it's enslaving, *holmes*,' the Hispanic soldier said grimly.

'This "live debt-free" scheme?' Harper asked.

'See, the energy they have is supposed to be generated free, right?' the Hispanic soldier continued. 'So they undercut the opposition and drive them out of business, then the costs start rising and rising. People get in debt if they want to be warm and cook and shit. So they look at this scheme, but once they're in that's it. They never quite seem to get out of debt. CELL owns them.'

'Modern day indentured service,' Rasch said. 'And it's not like they can really refuse to use CELL's products. Now I'm the first to admit that democracy is a flawed system. It certainly got in my way more than once when I was CEO, and we used well-paid lobbyists to hijack it when it suited us to do so. At its basest democracy is legitimatised mob rule but I suspect we'll miss it when it's gone.'

'And you feel a terrorist attack is the way to get your point across?' The two soldiers with Rasch bristled at the word "terrorist". Fry was trying to suppress a grin. Corporal Fenn remained impassive but kept on looking behind her into the darkness in the corner of the room.

'If I could vote against it, write to my congressman or otherwise do anything about it, I would. I was probably the singularly most well-placed person to stop this company running out of control and I couldn't. We're not trying to get our point across, or terrorise anyone. We have a very specific goal to accomplish.' The craggy-faced soldier cleared his throat. Rasch turned to look at him. 'We will get nowhere with half-truths and obfuscations, Major.' He turned back to Harper. 'We are going after the mechanism for the CELL global monopoly on energy. The Ceph are a threat, and we will deal with them later, but right now we need to prevent my old company becoming even more powerful.'

'It's here in New York?'

Rasch didn't answer. The stern-looking major looked less than pleased. Harper realised that he was dead if he didn't join them. It might not even be that simple. Even if he agreed he would have to convince them he meant it.

'They'll hit you with the Archangel,' Harper told them. Rasch was shaking his head. 'They have to. If the source of their control is in the city they'll have no choice.'

'They can't risk it. They may damage some of their valuable resources. Captain, it's no coincidence that CELL are using New York as their base. They are harvesting the aliens' technology and believe me, the last people in the world you want with that technology is a global super power that is accountable to no-one. Not if you ever want to live free again.'

'Hyperbole,' Harper said, finding himself angry. *No, not angry,* he thought, *frightened.*

'We look like peaceniks, pinkos and hippies to you?' the Major asked. 'You know military men and women. What do you think it would take for them to get to the point where they are prepared to take an action like this?'

Distractedly Harper noticed Fenn glancing behind again. He was tempted to look himself.

'I think you know this is true, Captain. I think that you have watched it slither slowly in over the past few years like a snake. I think you've known it was happening but desperately wanted someone else to handle it. Well, we've run out of people to handle it. There's just us, here, now and as you can imagine we have a lot to do so I'm afraid I'm going to have to press you for an answer.'

Harper swallowed hard.

'I'll help you,' Harper said. Somehow it still felt like betraying his country. Rasch nodded and then looked into the corner where Fenn had been looking.

'Dane. Is he telling the truth?'

Harper watched as darkness seemed to recede around a massive and very powerful looking figure. *It's a cloak,* Harper realised in amazement. The revealed figure was bizarre. It wore some sort of armoured exoskeleton made of thick, muscle-like cable. Half of the armour's torso and helmet were painted white to resemble a skull and bones. Beads, feathers, bones and the skulls of rodents and birds were affixed to the armour in various places. The armoured figure wore a number of dog tags on a chain around his neck. There was a large automatic at his hip and he had some kind of sniper rifle in a sheath across his back.

'His stress markers are all to shit,' a surprisingly spacy sounding voice said. 'But he's telling the truth.' The figure was looking away from the six people, as if staring at something none of them could see. Harper, Fenn and Fry were staring at the armoured man.

'Are you an alien?' Fry asked. The figure turned around to look at the scouse marine.

'No,' he said simply. The scouser looked crestfallen.

'Yes, I could see why you'd be disappointed,' Harper said to the marine.

Dane turned to Fenn. 'You're good.'

Fenn didn't reply. She just watched the figure suspiciously.

Rasch looked up at the major.

'Major Winterman?'

The Major was giving some thought to this.

'I don't like this,' Winterman finally said. 'There are too many ifs. Yes, the *Robin Hood* would be of a tremendous amount of use, possibly pivotal, but even allowing for the good captain's willingness he still has a sizeable crew that needs to do as he says.'

'The Major is right,' Harper said. 'Normally the discipline on a royal navy ship is excellent. CELL's takeover has changed things. There are elements on board that would oppose supporting you and others who would wish to distance themselves from being seen to be doing so.'

'I'll go with him,' the armoured figure said casually, though his focus still seemed to be elsewhere. 'It'll be fun.' Harper turned to look at the bizarre but obviously powerful individual.

'Dane, we'll need you in the final assault.' Major Winterman said.

'S'cool, man. You got a boat you can loan me?' Dane asked a surprised Harper.

'Er ... yes, an IRC.'

'I'll watch the rockets, it'll be like the Fourth of July, man. Really pretty. Then make the rendezvous with my man Chino.' He nodded towards the Hispanic soldier, who nodded back smiling at the armoured figure.

'It's your decision, Major,' Rasch said. The Major gave it more thought but then nodded to Chino. Chino took a laminated map out of one of his fatigue pockets and gave it to Harper. It was a map of New York with grid references and co-ordinates on the back.

'Our biggest problem, captain, is a series of automated and manned gun emplacements. They have near total coverage and can deny us movement on street level,' the Major told him.

'What about moving underground?' Harper asked as he studied the co-ordinates.

'Much of the city is still flooded, much of the underground may still be extensively damaged due to Ceph action, and we can't know what changes CELL have made beneath the streets. If the *Robin Hood* takes these gun emplacements out you will save a lot of my people.'

'The spirits of dead warriors will look on you and know you to be righteous,' Dane said. Fry was staring at the armoured figure and then started to laugh.

'Don't worry about my man Lazy Dane none,' Chino said. 'He's just been living in that suit a little too long. It's cooked his head.'

'My righteousness aside, how good's this intel?'

'Swift, silent, deadly, *ese*. Forward observation a speciality,' Chino said proudly.

'Yes, well I understood what some of that meant.'

'The intel's solid, captain,' Major Winterman assured him.

'When?'

'Zero five hundred eastern standard,' Winterman told him. It was the same time that Cell had ordered him to fire on Yonkers. He had four hours to get back to the *Robin Hood* and prepare.

'It's been a long time since a British ship has fired on an American city,' Harper said.

'1814. The War of Neutrality,' Major Winterman supplied.

'It's alright man, we're on your side this time,' Chino told him.

***

Captain Harper was sure that the battered Bulldog light transport vehicle was older than Private Fry and maybe Corporal Fenn as well. With a four-wheel drive and Lazy Dane, who could apparently see in the dark, at the wheel they made much better, if more frightening, time back.

The only thing that the large armoured warrior had said on the return drive was to ask if they could "see them all". It had both the marines searching the surrounding area with their weapons at the ready until they had realised that Lazy Dane was seeing things they weren't. None of them had any idea what the strange figure had meant and not even Fry had wanted to enquire further.

The coxswain had moved into good cover and didn't come out until he was sure that it was the Captain and the two marines returning. The boat pilot was nervous of the massive armoured warrior but said nothing.

Harper typed the co-ordinates that he had memorized into the GPS device as they made their way across the black waters of the East River. There was just the slightest glow on the eastern horizon now. Fry was manning the MMG again. Fenn was looking all around, her SCAR at the ready. Dane was sat in the centre of the boat, his legs crossed.

Harper looked up. There was a ripping noise. His brain registered lights coming towards him. Something hit him hard. He was in the water. Panic. He could see the water churning close to him, darts of phosphorescent light shooting through it. Someone grabbed him and dragged him to the surface. He gasped air into grateful lungs. There was more of the ripping noise. The boat was gone. It had ceased to exist, along with

Private Fry, Corporal Fenn and the coxswain, who Harper was pretty sure had been called Harman. The water was churning again as tracers hit it from the Phalanx 20mm rotary cannon.

He could see the muzzle flash. It looked like a constant flickering illuminating the darkness. The muzzle flash was refracting strangely with the *Robin Hood*'s cloak, distorting it. The ship had moved. Not far, just enough to have had them heading towards the wrong place.

'Hold your breath, man,' Dane was next to him in the water. The armoured soldier must have knocked him out of the boat. 'I'm going to have to drag you.'

Harper had enough time to take a mouthful of air before he was pulled under the cold, cold water. He mastered the panic of submersion, the helplessness as he was dragged along at a surprising speed. Then panic again as he realised that Lazy Dane was swimming towards the *Robin Hood*, not towards the riverbank. Then panic as his chest started to hurt and he desperately needed to breathe. *Can the suit breathe under water?* his frightened mind thought. He was sure that Dane was going to forget about his dependency on oxygen.

'Breathe, hyperventilate, saturate your system with oxygen and then a final deep breath,' Dane told him. It took a moment for Harper to understand that he was on the surface again and interpret Dane's instructions. Then they were under again.

Hyperventilating shouldn't be a problem was the most lucid thought he managed, but even that was tinged with more than a hint of hysteria.

He had no idea how long it took. It seemed like he was underwater for an age, the cold trying to rob his precious breath, and that he was only on the surface for moments. Everything was black under the water except the occasional flickering light above them. Harper's fatigued and frightened mind finally managed to work out that the light was the Phalanx firing again.

Somehow they were under the *Robin Hood*. He was at the surface. Gasping air into lungs that didn't feel like they were inflating properly. His heart felt funny in his chest. There were ratings in the boat bay. Harper knew their names but couldn't bring them to mind. They were armed. They were shouting something at him and pointing weapons. Harper was struggling to work out what was going on. One of them had a red beam of light coming out of his chest area. The red beam went away and two red holes appeared in the rating's chest and he tumbled into the water. The other rating was turning, raising his weapon, and pointing it at Harper.

At your captain! an outraged and barely rational part of Harper thought. The top of the rating's head came off and he fell into the water as well.

Harper turned and saw Dane, still in the water, the big automatic in his hand, a suppressor attached to its barrel.

He's killing my men, Harper thought. Dane seemed to surge out of the water and grab hold of the ladder leading up to the raised boat bay. There was flickering light from the boat bay and Harper could see bullet impacts against the hull of his ship. The armour that Dane was wearing changed somehow. It started to look more like overlapping plates. The armour was lit up with sparks as multiple impacts knocked Dane around, but he continued climbing the ladder. The hatch to the boat bay was closing.

You can't assault the ship on your own, Harper thought, *there's Royal Marines on board!*

Dane, still taking fire, leapt off the ladder and grabbed the edge of the boat bay hatch as it was sliding shut and pulled himself up. The hatch closed.

Harper realised that he was shaking badly and still struggling to keep his breath. He knew that he needed to get out of the water or he was going to die. He struck out towards the ladder below the boat bay hatch. It was only then he realised just how strong a current there was in the East River. Harper had always prided himself on keeping in good shape. He had never felt his age so singularly as he did during that long, long swim.

His hand grabbed the lowest rung of the ladder. He found that he did not have the strength to pull himself out of the water.

Is that it? he demanded of himself, *you get this far and you quit?* He remembered the pathetic mess he'd been in the wake of the London Emergency. The excuses and lies he'd told Rachel. *Is that who you are again? Are you just going to lapse into self-pity and letting people down again?*

It took everything he had to pull himself out of the water. Then again as he pulled himself up to the next rung. Then again, but it was getting easier. The hatch above him started to open. The shadow of a figure stood in the warm light of the boat bay. Harper just kept climbing.

'I've got you, Captain,' Dane said and all but picked Harper up and deposited him on the floor of the boat bay. Harper saw more dead sailors, at least six more, men and women. He scrambled backwards across the floor, away from the armoured figure. Harper frantically tried to drag something out of the pocket of his sodden coat. Eventually he managed to free the wet Browning Hi-Power automatic pistol and, shaking like a leaf, he pointed it a confused Dane.

'Stop killing my men, you bastard!' he screamed.

'Captain, they're trying to kill us,' Dane said, reasonably.

'I don't care! No more killing! Do you understand me?'

Dane shrugged.

'Sure, there's no need to shout.'

Harper climbed to his feet. It was only then that he realised how astonished he was to be alive.

'You need to get out of those clothes, Captain,' Dane told him. 'And I don't think that the Browning's going to fire now.'

Harper stared at his service weapon for a moment as he collected himself.

'Can you still cloak?' Dane nodded. 'Do so and watch the hatches.' It took moments for Harper to find a towel and some clean clothes in one of the lockers. He stripped, towelled himself dry and changed as quickly as he could. He was dressed as an able seaman now, and the only shoes he could find that came close to fitting him were a pair of garishly coloured trainers.

People came into the boat bay. He heard shouted orders, a brief burst of gunfire that made him jump and then duck for cover. This was followed by the sounds of physical violence and some unpleasant snapping noises.

Harper emerged from behind the lockers to see Dane standing over three battered and mostly unconscious ratings lying on the deck.

'It might have been useful to interrogate one of them,' Harper suggested.

'You're a very hard man to please,' Dane replied calmly.

Harper relieved one of them of their M12 Nova sidearm and some spare magazines. He pointed at the opposite hatch to the one the sailors had just come through.

'That way.'

Dane moved in front of the Captain. Harper watched as the lensing field bent light around the armoured figure and seemed to swallow him. There was a slight disturbance in Harper's vision if he looked hard enough, presumably due to the movement, but otherwise he could see straight through Dane's armoured form as if it wasn't there.

A rating came round the corner. He saw the captain and started bringing his SCAR to bear. The SCAR was yanked up as the sailor was beaten into the bulkhead by an invisible force. The gun disappeared, enveloped by the cloak's lensing field. Another sailor opened a hatch and peeked out, a pistol in his hand. He was yanked out of the hatch and flung into the opposite wall, before being slammed into the ground.

Oh well, at least they're not dead, Harper thought.

They turned the corner. Two sailors were waiting for them. When Harper saw the muzzle flash from the barrels of the SCARs he knew he was dead. He raised his arm up pointlessly to ward off the bullets. The automatic weapons fire was deafening in the confined corridor. He heard a grunt of pain and felt something stumble against him. Dane became visible again. The armour changed. Harper actually heard the sound of plates sliding across each other. Dane started striding forward. The front of his armour was wreathed in sparks as the sailors panic fired at the strange figure. He reached the two sailors and Harper watched as the armoured figure did something unspeakably violent to both of them. Harper was transfixed for a moment and then remembered what he was doing. As the last of the shots stopped ringing in his ears he realised he was hearing shouts.

He tried opening the door to Lieutenant Talpur's cabin and found it locked.

'Dane, if you would,' Harper said. The armoured figure stalked back down the corridor and tore the lock out of the door.

'Sir?' A slightly surprised looking Lieutenant Talpur said as she glanced at Dane's armoured figure.

'Report,' Harper ordered.

'Commander Stevens and a number of the junior officers have taken the ship,' the marine lieutenant told him.

'Lieutenant Commander Swanson?'

'Executed for mutiny along with Sergeant Martin. Most of the crew are too frightened to do anything. Those that wouldn't go along with him are confined to quarters under guard.'

'How'd he get the drop on you, Lieutenant?' Harper asked, trying to ignore the hammering and shouting from the marines' bunk area next to the Lieutenant's cabin as they broke through the locked door.

'Unbeknown to me, Stevens had a key to the armoury. He armed his supporters. Those of my men on duty found themselves confronted with a lot of armed matelots. Those off duty were caught unawares. Nobody wanted to start shooting in the ship.'

Not the Royal Marines' proudest moment, Harper thought. That said, there were a lot more sailors on-board than there were marines.

'Lieutenant, I need to know where you stand and I need to know right now.'

'Sir, did you not hear me correctly? He executed Sergeant Martin.'

Harper nodded. Dane handed her the SCAR as the marines kicked their way out of their bunk area. The remaining twenty men and women of the platoon started spilling out. The first two grabbed the guards' SCARs and spare magazines.

'Stevens' people have all the weapons,' Talpur told

him. Dane told some of the marines where they could find more SCARs, those that he had left littered around the ship. A few of them headed off to collect the weapons.

'This Stevens?' Dane asked.

'Him you *can* kill,' Harper said grimly, thinking about the promising young Lieutenant Commander and the marine sergeant who were now dead. 'I want no unnecessary firing, Lieutenant.'

'Describe necessary, sir?' one of the marines who was armed, a young woman, asked. Harper thought he heard Dane chuckle.

'Where possible I want to speak to them,' Harper said. The marines looked to Talpur.

'Sir, with all due respect I'm not going to needlessly endanger my people. If they are at risk, taking fire, then they're damn well going to shoot back.'

'I said where possible.'

'So *they're* allowed to kill the sailors?' Dane asked.

'Yes, they're not bloody Americans. Now lead the way and try and soak up some of the gunfire.'

***

Stevens had, of course, secured the bridge. Ratings loyal to him had barricaded the approaches and were using open hatches as cover. Harper had his back to one of the bulkheads. He, Lazy Dane and the marines were hiding round the corner from one of the three corridors that lead to the bridge.

'We need to assault the corridor, sir,' Talpur told him.

'I can clear it,' Dane told him.

'Wait, both of you,' he said. 'You men, listen to me. This is your Captain speaking. I don't know what Lieutenant Commander Stevens has told you, but he is a mutineer who has murdered two members of this crew. Anyone aiding him is also a mutineer. I will show leniency if you put down your weapons now and surrender immediately. If you do not then you will be dealt with by a platoon of very angry Royal Marines who are looking for revenge for the death of one of their own. You may get some of us, though I think it unlikely. You will all, very certainly, die.'

He waited. He could hear talking.

'We're coming out. Don't shoot.'

Harper nodded, relieved. The sailors were roughly manhandled, relieved of their weapons, cable tied and left lying face down.

'We need a plan to assault the bridge,' Lieutenant Talpur said. 'Shit!' Harper just strode up the corridor.

'Don't fire. I'm coming in!' the Captain shouted and stepped onto the bridge.

'I like him,' Dane said to the appalled-looking marine Lieutenant.

***

Harper walked onto the bridge, all eyes on him. There were a dozen sailors in here with SCARs pointed at him. The cadaverous form of Stevens was stood in front of the Captain's seat, pointing a pistol at the Captain.

'Drop the weapon, Harper,' Stevens said.

Harper looked down at the pistol. He had forgotten it was there.

'It's Captain Harper, Commander Stevens.' He glanced at his watch. 'We don't have much time. Put your weapons down now,' he told the armed ratings.

'They are under orders from their new Captain. You, on the other hand, are guilty of mutiny!'

'Guilty? What, no court martial? And you have replaced me as Captain on what authority?'

'Orders from our new ...'

'Owners! Son, the closest thing the Navy has to an owner is His Majesty the King. Did he tell you to mutiny?'

'Like it or not old man, things change. The government, our actual employers, have sold us ...'

'Then the government has failed! We are the Royal Navy, we serve, we defend the people of the United Kingdom of Great Britain. Our only consideration is the best interests of those people. Those interests will not be served as the maritime enforcement arm of a rapacious multinational company, responsible for a number of atrocities and reintroducing indentured servitude to the civilised world.'

'So what? We make up our own orders, become little more than pirates guided by Captain Harper's morals? The same morals you had, presumably, when as the ranking weapons officer on board the *Anguish* you fired on your own capital city?' Stevens demanded.

Harper closed his eyes for a moment. He remembered Battersea Power Station backlit by flames, but he pushed it down. He couldn't afford to dwell on that now, to falter.

'Stevens, we're British. We ruled the sea. We have a proud history of piracy.' There were a few chuckles from around the bridge. 'And the most important thing any officer possesses is a conscience. The world knows full well of the horrors of military men forgetting that. You know that this order is wrong. You know that working for CELL is wrong. You know that killing Lieutenant Commander Swanson and Sergeant Martin was wrong. And you know you're not doing this out of any sense of duty. You're doing this because you know that you will be rewarded for it.'

Harper had noticed that the majority of the sailors had lowered their weapons now. Stevens was still aiming his pistol at Harper, however.

'I'm not an officer anymore, sir,' he all but spat. 'I'm an executive.' He started to squeeze the trigger. Then the gun wasn't there anymore, and neither was his hand. There was only a bleeding stump. Stevens looked at his wrist in horror. Dane flickered into view holding a large and very sharp knife with a bloody blade.

'Get that corporate piece of shit off my ship,' Harper ordered. Dane thought about refusing – strictly speaking Harper wasn't in his chain of command – but he grabbed the now howling Stevens and started dragging him off the bridge.

Talpur and the rest of the marines poured into the

bridge and started removing weapons from the sailors.

'Lieutenant, can you please let the rest of the men out of their quarters?' Talpur nodded and took six of the marines with her, leaving the rest to secure the bridge and finish disarming the sailors who had been watching the other entrances.

'Any of you who do not wish to follow my orders, please leave the bridge now.' A number of ratings and officers left their stations, but not so many that the ship wouldn't be able to function. 'Navigation, set a course for the Atlantic by the most expeditious route possible that doesn't involve going past Manhattan. Engineering, keep the cloak up. Helm, as soon as we are in open water I want fifty knots out of her.' He was giving these orders as he walked across to weapons, glancing at his watch. They had little time left.

The commander of the weapons section was standing up as Harper arrived at his station.

'Lieutenant Chalmers?' Harper asked.

'I'm sorry, sir,' Chalmers said. He wouldn't meet his Captain's eye.

'Get off my bridge,' Harper ordered, disappointed. He turned to the second in command of the section. The petty officer had not moved. He handed the man the laminated map. 'You have ten minutes to plot firing solutions for those co-ordinates. Can you do that, Bridges?'

'Yes sir.'

***

'No, no, please god no!' Stevens begged as Dane dragged him through the corridors of the ship. Dane stopped and turned to the Commander.

'Seriously, you have to come to terms with this. This is no good for you. This is the fulfilment of your *dharma*, it's a shitty *dharma* for sure, but you need to deal. This,' he pointed at the sobbing man. 'This is no good, there's no dignity here for either of us.'

Stevens just gaped at him and then started crying and begging again. Dane sighed and resumed hauling the Commander through the ship.

***

Dane dragged Stevens up onto deck just as the hatches to the vertical launch systems were opened, revealing the warheads of the twenty-four Perseus cruise missiles.

'There's a beauty in the focused purpose of a weapon like that,' Dane said. He kept a tight grip on Stevens as he watched the Bronx riverside go by. He watched it until the sight of all the ghosts got to him and he had to look away.

'Please, please, I can tell you something?' Stevens begged.

Dane turned to look at him.

'Think of something good to say, man,' Dane said.

'They knew that Harper might be problematic and they were worried about him absconding with a ship that has the *Robin Hood*'s stealth capabilities. They knew I would be loyal ...'

'Harper's loyal. You can be bought.'

'They gave me a transponder,' Stevens told him.

The suit was picking up lots of strange atmospheric readings, as if the air was ionising. *They know where we are,* Dane thought. He looked up. The clouds. They looked funny. Then they caught fire. He jumped. Everything became light and heat.

Dane jumped through steam and hit the molten riverbed of the East River. Then the water came back. He realised he had been screaming. The armour on his back, made from nearly indestructible alloys, had blistered and then turned molten and then fused with his flesh. All the times he'd fallen, been shot, stabbed, beaten, battered, run over. All the times that it had felt like he had died, none of it compared to this. This was pain in its purest form. Pain so extreme that it was an abstract. He was only conscious because of the suit's advanced medical systems. No human had ever experienced this degree of pain before. Then, mercifully, he died.

***

The suit forced him back to life minutes later. The water all around him was boiling from the heat of the armour. He died again.

***

The suit had to block signals from a lot of his nerve endings before it could shock the soldier back to life with the built-in defibrillator. Dane came to again on the side of the river, amongst the ghosts. He did some more screaming but managed to get it under control. He lay in the mud, making it steam. He looked back upstream. The East River was moving quickly, trying to replace the gap where a significant part of the river had just been vaporised. Plumes of steam were still shooting high into the sky. The suit was repairing itself, separating away from Dane's flesh and doing its best to return to a functional state.

The thing was *they had missed*, he thought, when he could think like a human again. The *Robin Hood* was gone, certainly. *More ghosts.* But had it been a direct hit he would never have survived, armour or not.

In the distance, the suit's enhanced hearing brought him the sound of rapid large-calibre weapons fire. *New York*, he thought, *I have to get to New York.*

The Goat

Chinatown, New York, 2034

FUBAR. Clusterfuck. There were so many good ways to describe what had just happened to them, Chino thought. The Brits, the fucking Brits, had let them down. Left them badly blowing in the wind. It had been foolish to trust them.

CELL had played it smart. Let them come in to the city proper. Let them get in underneath the framework of the dome they were building over the city destroyed by the Ceph incursion. Then the CELL gun emplacements had started up. They'd torn into people on the street. The rounds had ripped through cover. The fire had been so intense it had brought buildings down on top of the resistance fighters inside.

The gun emplacements broke them, split them, sent them running. Then CELL moved in on the ground, supported by VTOLs and helicopter gunships in the air. Their spec ops teams had gone after the resistance's hard core and the leadership. The rest they had left to the rank and file. What they used to call contractors, now they were more like indentured gunmen. The resistance fighters, most of whom were experienced soldiers, many with special forces backgrounds, tore into the CELL gunmen, but there were just so many of them and they had air and fire support.

The resistance had been broken. Chino knew that. He didn't know who was alive or who was dead. Had any been captured? It hadn't looked like CELL were taking prisoners. They had risked checking the Macronet feed when they'd been hiding. There were purges going on all over the word. CELL forces assisted by local police and military were arresting or killing the so-called "terrorists" in every country the resistance operated in. It looked like they had been betrayed. They had put too many of their eggs in one basket. Put too much trust in people they shouldn't have. The operation had been too much about hope and not enough about their actual capabilities. CELL were never going to let them get close to their NY operation. They had far too much to lose here.

And his man Dane hadn't come back from the *Robin Hood*. He wondered if the Brits had fucked him too. Betrayed him. Handed him over to CELL. In the cold nights to come, Chino was going to keep himself warm by thinking about what he would like to do to Captain fucking-Harper of the Royal-fucking-Navy. *What kind of candy-assed outfit calls itself 'royal' anyway*, he wondered bitterly, *delusions of fucking grandeur, is what that is?*

They had spent the day lying low. They had hidden in partially destroyed buildings. It had made Chino nervous. The last time he had been in Manhattan it had been crawling with dangerous alien killing machines. CELL had apparently cleared all the Ceph out. That was their justification for the heavy-duty gun emplacements, not that they really needed an excuse. They owned New York now.

There were eight of them still together, in two inflatable raiding craft. They were making their way down the Bowery heading south for the time being. CELL would expect them to run to the north, so they hadn't. They would either double back or find another exfiltration route when the opportunity presented itself.

Chino was lying across the prow of the IRC, his Marshall pump-action shotgun pointing out from under the scrim they had lain across the top of the boat. The scrim was laced with a type of foil that was supposed to confuse thermal imagery. Chino, however, was not willing to bet his life on it.

Behind him, also lying down on the boat, their weapons just pointing out from under the scrim, were Earl and Hank.

Earl was on the left hand side of the boat, covering the Bowery and over into the Lower East Side. He had to be in his mid-forties at least but the x-Delta sniper had looked after himself. The quiet Missourian was wiry with leathery skin and still carried an ancient M14 rifle. Chino's weird, nanosuited friend, Lazy Dane, went way back with Earl. They had both served in D squadron's recce/sniper troop in Delta Force.

Hank, another southerner, had been 1st Marine. He had known Alcatraz briefly during the evacuation of

New York. Earl had then ended up going to work for CELL. The thoughtful bucktoothed Georgian had witnessed what CELL was like first hand and deserted after finding that the terms and conditions had been altered so much that he was effectively going to end up a lifelong indentured servant of the multinational company. Hank's Mk 60 medium machine gun was pointing out the right side of the boat. Into what had been Chinatown.

Davis was an outspoken self-proclaimed Irish-African American and southie from Boston. He had been part of the Navy's SEAL delivery vehicle team and was the best boatman that Chino had ever seen. He was lying down in the back of the IRC, piloting it via a periscope sticking through the scrim and with the aid of guidance from Chino on the prow.

Davis' suggestion for exfiltration was to head to a dive store he knew in Downtown, scavenge it for working closed circuit or SCUBA diving gear and head to Brooklyn subsurface. As a plan went it wasn't for the fainthearted, and it was problematic in that Earl wasn't dive qualified. Nor were two of the members of Sarah's crew in the other IRC that was trailing them.

Chinatown's getting weird, Chino thought. He'd been in New York when it had been close to a hundred per cent humidity before but the mist was new. The lower part of Manhattan was still under about ten feet of water. It covered the first storey of most of the buildings. Plant life had returned in a big way, flourishing in the moist environment, returning the city to its roots as a swampy island, Chino guessed. Trees, mosses and other climbing plants crept up the side of buildings, obscuring once glowing signs in Hanzi script. It reminded Chino a little of the swamps of Florida and the Bayous of Louisiana. He was half expecting to see an alligator slither out the second storey window of a laundry and swim across in front of them.

The moonlight shining through the thick mist gave the whole place an eerie, haunted feeling. *Haunted would be right,* Chino thought, *a lot of people died on these streets.* He immediately thought back to his brother-resistance fighter, Lazy Dane, and all the dead people the nano-suited soldier saw. He hoped Dane was okay.

Then it sounded like the world was ending. He was soaked as water was kicked up in a line stretching out in front of him. He glanced behind to see Sarah's boat. The IRC looked like it had been folded down the middle. The thirty millimetre tracers from the gun emplacements looked like stars tumbling out of the night sky at them.

Chino heard the muffled outboard engine rev up as Davis took the boat wide out into the Bowery, behind the line of fire, and slewed it right into a tiny alley that Chino was sure it couldn't fit down. The boat was a tight fit, Earl and Hank had to roll off the side and into the well but Davis made the turn and gunned the motor, accelerating as fast as he could.

Behind them the rounds started flying through the walls as the auto-cannons tried to walk their aim in on the flimsy boat. Chino hated this. This wasn't a fight for someone who was basically infantry. All he could do was watch, shout warnings and hope that a thirty millimetre round didn't cut him in two.

Parts of the buildings on one side of the alleyway collapsed into the water under the intensity of the incoming rounds. Chino was almost thrown off the boat as it hit something, probably a sunken truck just under the waterline. The boat jumped but kept going. Davis was sat up now, having pushed the scrim aside. Earl and Hank, like Chino, were just holding on for dear life.

As Davis shot across Elizabeth Street, Chino caught a glance of the incoming tracers again. They were a broken line of lights pointing at them.

Fuck off, Chino silently screamed.

They were in another alley. Rubble raining down on them as the heavy fire all but bisected buildings. The boat bounced off another submerged obstacle and almost went into the wall. Davis fought with it and kept the craft under control. He slewed the craft hard right onto Mott Street and headed up it, past sunken shop fronts and old signs, the undergrowth whipping at their faces, their passage making eddies in the thick mist. Chino glanced back at Davis. The guy couldn't have been able to see further than he could but he hadn't guided them wrong yet.

In the middle of Mott Street the boatman suddenly slewed left, straight towards a building.

'Down!' Davis barked. Chino scrabbled back and lay on the floor, sure they were about to collide with a brick wall. The IRC slid into the building through the top of an arched two-storey window. There wasn't much glass left in the frame but what there was rained down on them. Davis reversed the engine, it howled in protest and they still hit the opposite wall. They found themselves floating quite close to exposed beams, just under the ceiling.

Davis unclipped the outboard and then lifted it up and dumped it into the water.

'What the fuck!?' Hank protested.

'Heat,' Davis told him. 'Don't worry, it's sealed man. We don't die in the next thirty seconds, I'll go down and get it.'

It was only then that Chino realised the firing had stopped.

'If they've lost us then they'll send patrols in,' Chino said, for something to say. His heart was beating very quickly. He wanted to break the tension.

'Patrols we can handle,' Davis said. Davis and Chino were both motor mouths in comparison with the two southerners in their four-man recon team.

Davis was sat on the edge of the boat, looking around at the peeling paint and the creeping plant life of the building they were floating in.

'This used to be a really good restaurant, they did awesome ...' Davis disappeared into the water. Water which was churning up and red now. Part of the front of the boat was missing. Even Earl was surprised. *There's something in the water* was all Chino had time to think before he realised the boat was crumpling up like a used condom and sinking rapidly.

Chino tried to leap up but felt the boat give way underneath him. His fingers just grasped the wood of the exposed ceiling beams, scrabbling for purchase. He felt something brush against his boot and let out an involuntary scream. He swung his legs up, almost kicking Earl in the face, and managed to wrap them around the beam. His shotgun was hanging down on its slung. He felt something grab it and try and pull him back into the water. Chino just reached down and pulled the trigger. The shotgun firing sounded deafening, even after the barrage they had just experienced. The pull on the weapon disappeared, however. The shotgun bucked up and bounced off Chino's body armour. Chino swung himself up onto the beam and readied the shotgun, pointing it down into the water.

Earl had an old H&K .45 in one hand. He was helping Hank up onto the beam with the other.

'What the fuck!?' Chino demanded. The boat had gone and what was left of Davis was a dark cloud of blood spreading on the surface of the water, though limbs and other body parts were starting to bob to the surface.

Something exploded out of the water and grabbed the beam they were all on. Chino fired, worked the shotgun's slide and fired again. He was dimly aware of a .45 being fired faster than he'd ever heard one fired before. The beam broke. The water rushed up to meet him.

Chino broke the surface of the water screaming, with his knife/machete cross in his hand, shaking. He hadn't been able to make out what it was that had leapt out of the water but he knew one thing for certain: it wasn't human.

Earl was on the surface as well. The old guy also had his knife out. *Hank, shit,* Chino thought. The ex-Jarine was weighed down with an MMG and about half a tonne of ammunition.

'Did we get it?' Chino asked.

'Dunno,' Earl said. Chino wasn't sure if Earl was just being calm or was, in fact, adrenalin deficient.

'I'm going down for Hank,' Chino told him. Earl nodded. It was instinct. Get your people out. It was only when he dived under the surface of the bloody water that he realised that he would be in there with ... with whatever the fucking thing that had attacked them was.

It was pitch dark in the water. He grabbed his torch and flicked it on. He saw the ex-marine panicking, trying to unclip his MMG and drag off the belts of ammunition at the same time. He was between two of the tables on the floor of the submerged Chinese restaurant. Chino kicked down quickly. He grabbed Hank a little too hard before realising his mistake, as it just freaked Hank out further. He got the marine's attention, signalled for him to calm down, and then used his thumb to motion upwards.

Chino glanced up. He couldn't see Earl. He helped Hank out of the weighty ammunition, made sure he had hold of his MMG and then pushed him upwards before kicking off himself. As he assisted Hank's ascent he caught the sensation of movement behind him, from somewhere out in the water on Mott Street. He glanced back but all he saw was beams of moonlight refracting through the water.

'Over here!' Earl called as they broke the surface. Earl was on a flight of stairs that led up into another level of the building. Chino was all but dragging Hank with him towards the stairs. He felt something brush against him under the water, panicked and redoubled his pace, swimming in a frenzy towards the steps. He felt Earl grab Hank and pull the marine out of the water. Chino all but crawled up the wooden stairs.

It smashed through the stairs beneath Chino. He felt blades dig into his leg and open his flesh as it tried to drag him under the water. Earl threw himself bodily down the stairs, grabbed Chino as he was being dragged back into the water. Earl's other hand smoothly brought up the H&K Mk 23 pistol. Earl fired the pistol rapidly. The slide went back on an empty magazine. Chino realised there was nothing trying to drag him into the water anymore. He all but climbed over Earl, scrambling up the stairs. He burst through a doorway at the top of the stairs and collapsed on the floor, gasping for breath. Earl appeared in the doorway behind him.

'Grenade,' the Missourian told them and then turned and dropped a fragmentation grenade into the submerged restaurant. There was a subdued explosion and water slopped into the room.

Hank rose up looking furious, and went and stood

in the doorway and started shooting the MMG wildly into the water. Earl put a hand on the ex-marine's shoulder. Hank stopped firing.

'Easy now brother, bullets are no good in water.'

Hank nodded. Chino realised that the Georgian wasn't furious. He was terrified. Hank was shaking like a leaf. Earl ejected the magazine from his Mk 23 and replaced it with a new one, working the slide to chamber a round and then holstering it with the safety off. He started to dry his M14.

'You need to dry your weapons as best you can,' he told them.

'You see what it was?' Chino asked, looking around. It looked like they were in the restaurant's wine storage area. Chino repressed the borderline-hysterical urge to have a drink to steady his nerves. Earl shrugged.

'Alien I guess, don't know, never seen one before, zombies I seen but not aliens.' Hank and Chino stared at Earl. It was one of the longest things Earl had ever said to them that hadn't been strictly operational. 'I'm going to have a look around. You need to look to that leg.' He told Chino. 'And one of you needs to watch the door.'

'I'm on it,' Hank told him, still stood in the doorway, MMG at the ready.

'Move back a little, *ese*, don't silhouette yourself in the doorway,' Chino said. He knew that Hank knew this, just like he knew that the marine was shaken up despite being a New York veteran and, apparently, having seen some shit in Russia whilst working for CELL.

Earl brought the M14 up, took the condom off the end of the barrel and disappeared into the mists.

***

Chino pulled the med kit out of one of the pouches on his webbing. He cleaned and then dressed the wounds. His leg hurt like a *sonofabitch* and one of the wounds was a through-and-through but he had got lucky, or at least as lucky as you can get when having sharp things pushed through your flesh. Whatever had attacked them had only pierced meat. It hadn't got anything vital and Chino would still be able to move.

Keeping one eye on Hank and the doorway, Chino dried off his shotgun and the Majestic revolver, which wasn't waterproofed. He oiled both weapons as best he could but he didn't have the time to strip and clean them.

'Did you recognise it?' Hank finally asked.

'Didn't see enough of it, you?'

Hank shook his head. 'It was fast, though. Definitely Ceph, you think?'

Chino laughed humourlessly. 'Man, I don't even want to think about there being another fucked-up alien species in New York.'

'I guess CELL didn't kill them all after all,' Hank mused.

'CELL lie? Say it ain't so.'

Hank let out a little laugh. There wasn't much humour in it. Chino slid two shells into the shotgun to replace the ones he'd fired. He worked the slide to make sure there was a round in the pipe. He heard the whistle and looked around. Earl came stalking out of the mist.

'What you see, what you hear man?' Chino asked. Hank glanced around and then went back to keeping watch. Earl put a finger over his lips and then touched his ear.

Chino listened. He could hear the lapping of the water, a slight breeze through the branches of the trees outside. He started to shake his head and then he heard it. It sounded like a hiccough followed by a series of clicks. He opened his mouth to say something, but Earl held his finger over his lips again. There was an answering hooting noise coming from somewhere else but both had been close by.

'We're being hunted,' Earl told him. Chino felt himself go cold. Somehow it was the more chilling because it was Earl who was telling him this. If rumours were true then Earl had spent the last ten years off the grid, living in the wilds, self-sufficient. 'If'n we want to move then we either go up onto the roof or back into the water, those are our choices.'

'We go onto the roof then we'll get picked off by the guns,' Hank said.

'Only if we draw attention to ourselves,' Chino pointed out. 'If we keep hidden then we'll be OK.'

'And if we meet those things up there?'

'So you want to go back into the water then?'

Hank gave this some thought. 'Let's head up to the roof.'

There was the sound of breaking glass from above them. The three soldiers looked at each other. Earl turned and led the way, heading back the direction he had come from, his weapon at the ready. Hank fell in behind him, the butt of the MMG nestled against his shoulder. Chino followed. Checking behind them all the way.

***

Three floors up they found the stairway had collapsed. Earl didn't waste time examining it, he just opened the next door he found, taking them out into an open plan office space.

They saw half a skeleton lying close to one of the windows. Chino guessed that it had been a victim of the Manhattan Virus that had only partially liquefied. There wasn't even much in the way of damage, though the plant life was starting to creep in and the broken windows let in tendrils of the creeping mist.

Chino thought he heard movement below them.

'Earl,' Chino said quietly. There was *definitely* movement below them. He heard a crash. Now that they knew what to listen for they had been hearing more of the clicks and hooting noises. They had seemed to be getting closer, and it sounded like they were all around them now. 'As much as I appreciate and support your one shot, one kill ethos ...' There was a sound behind them. Chino spun around, shotgun at the ready. 'If you've not fought these things before then I think you should know that it might take more than one shot ...'

Chino caught movement out of the corner of his eye. He spun around but there was nothing. Something fell over to his left. He spun around and caught more movement but no viable target.

The door they had just came through slammed open. Chino spun back to it. He caught the shadow of a figure moving behind a partition. His finger tightened around the shotgun's trigger but there was still no viable target.

Behind him Earl started firing the M14 single shot, steadily and repeatedly. Next to him Hank started firing the MMG.

There, Chino saw it! It was a tall, thin, jagged, misshapen figure, still hidden by the darkness. It looked like it was made of sharp angles. Even in the darkness, as it ran through the tendrils of mist, he could make out the swaying tentacle. It looked like a massive rubbery tail sticking out the centre of its back.

Chino squeezed the trigger. The shotgun bucked. He was working the slide already. The creature staggered, bits flew off it. Another round chambered. The shotgun's muzzle flash flared again. The creature staggered but kept running. And again. The creature hit the ground and slid towards Chino, dead on the floor.

There were more sprinting at him. Chino shifted aim to his right, firing once, then again. The Ceph staggered with the impact of the first shot and the second shot knocked it out the window. He swung to his left. Two more of the things were trying to flank them. The muzzle flash from the MMG made the aliens look like they were caught in a strobe light.

Chino fired another three rounds and the closest one dropped. He fired two more rounds from the shotgun, one hit staggering the Ceph, the other missing. Chino let the empty shotgun drop on its sling. He moved forwards, drawing the big Majestic revolver from its holster. Aiming carefully, he squeezed the trigger. The revolver bucked in his hand. About two foot of muzzle flash leapt out of the end of the barrel. The .50 calibre compact round hit the soft part of the Ceph and then exploded.

***

He hung off the gargoyle one handed, his feet against the stone of the old building. He could see the flickering light and hear the sounds. The flashes threw grotesque shadows in their brief but repeated moments of existence. He too wanted to hunt. He wanted to hunt like a shikari, *but he needed to find a place to worship the night sun. He wanted to see the sky burn again. He looked around at his brothers, sadly.*

***

'Clear!' Hank shouted.

'Not fucking here it isn't!' Chino shouted as he fired the last shot from the Majestic. Both he and Hank spun round, exchanging positions. Hank started firing the MMG again immediately. The machine gun's rounds were blowing chunks out of the creatures as they leapt from desk to desk or just powered through them.

Chino flipped out the revolver's wheel, grabbing a speed loader with six of the huge .50 calibre explosive rounds. It was faster to reload the revolver than it was the shotgun.

Earl let the M14 drop on its sling and fast drew the Mk. 23, already firing as he brought it up to eye level in a two-handed grip. In front of the sniper, five of the things lay dead or twitching on the ground.

Chino watched in horror as Earl's pistol rounds sparked off the charging Ceph's armour. He flipped the revolver's wheel closed. He knew he was going to be too slow as the Ceph closed with Earl. It was like it was happening in slow motion. He watched the creature raise its bone-like arm blade. Earl was still firing. Chino was raising the Majestic. The alien's bone blade took Earl straight through the centre of his head. It shot out the back of the sniper's skull in an explosion of bone, blood and brain matter, splattering Hank. Chino all but put the Majestic up against the soft matter on the creature's back and pulled the trigger. The Ceph bioform hit the ground, taking Earl's corpse down with him and battering the body into Hank.

Chino wanted to cry, freak out, but he'd seen this before. He knew what happened when humans tried to fight these things up close and personal. They needed to be like Dane or Alcatraz if they were going to have a chance. If he wanted to live they needed to move. He couldn't see an exit from this floor other than the one he'd come through, and yet more Ceph were gathering there. He fired the massive revolver twice and one of them went down, staggering and then stumbling out the window.

He knew what they were now. The grunts had nick-named them Stalkers. Fast-moving, close-in killers. But these ones looked different. Devolved somehow, feral. Purer. It seemed they had lost their ability to think tactically, but now, if anything, they were faster, and hunting like a pack, albeit one with deeply suicidal tendencies.

Chino had a really stupid idea.

'Hank, I need you to trust me and follow me!' he shouted.

'Where we going?' Hank shouted back and then continued firing burst after burst.

'Out the window. We're going to jump to the building opposite, it's really close,' Chino lied. Hank didn't answer.

Chino ran at one of the broken full-length windows. He fired the Majestic one-handed, as he ran, at the Stalker close to the window. The first shot missed. He had a moment to reflect on the stupidity of basically charging one of these things and fired the second shot when he was practically on top of the thing. The muzzle flash illuminated its alien countenance. It staggered back but didn't go down, swung at Chino with its bone blade. The blade tore into Chino's arm as he left the ground, turning him slightly in the air. His blood flew out of the wound in an arc, looking black in the moonlight.

He was in the air, jumping through the mist. He had no idea if there was a building nearby. He knew that many of the streets and alleys in Chinatown were narrow. He knew that many of the buildings were lower than the one he had jumped from and had flat roofs. And he knew that if there was no roof then the streets below him were submerged under ten feet of water. Falling through the air didn't seem quite the calculated risk it had moments before, when he was about to get torn apart by the stalkers.

The roof hit him hard. He screamed as he went down on his already injured leg and collapsed onto the surface of the roof, losing more skin from his arms as he slid and tumbled across it.

He sat up and looked behind him. The building he'd just jumped from was obscured in the mist. It even distorted the constant staccato hammering of Hank's MMG. All Chino could see was the muzzle flash from the Georgian's weapon illuminating the mist from within whenever it fired.

'C'mon man!' Chino shouted, mostly to himself. 'Jump, bitch!'

He had holstered his Majestic and was sliding a shell into his shotgun when the firing stopped. He heard Hank screaming. It was getting closer. Chino saw the ex-marine appear through the mist. He impacted at chest height against the edge of the building, spitting out blood. Chino reached for him. A Stalker appeared out of the mist right behind him, flying towards them.

Chino brought the shotgun up one-handed and fired the only round the weapon had in it. The recoil almost took his arm off. The blast caught the Stalker, spinning it in mid air. It hit the side of the building and bounced. Chino reached for Hank, who in turn was reaching for him. The second Stalker practically landed on Hank's back. Chino let the shotgun drop on its sling and drew the Majestic. The Stalker was repeatedly stabbing Hank with its blades, holding onto him with its strangely jointed legs. Hank let go of the building. Chino moved to the edge. He saw his buddy disappear into the mist below, the Stalker still savaging him. He didn't even hear the splash.

Part of the building seemed to explode, throwing fragments into the air that tore into Chino's exposed flesh on his arms and face. The heavy calibre tracers looked slow far away, but a trick of perception made them seem to accelerate the closer they got. More than one gun emplacement was targeting the roof he was on. Chino staggered to his feet and took off at a limping run, parts of the roof collapsing behind him.

'Give me a break, you fuckers!' Chino reached the other side of the roof and jumped.

***

The fire was daring the lesser gods to strike him down. They didn't. He smeared the ash on his face, covering it. Making it grey. He would become one of the dead.

His prey hung from the partially destroyed false ceiling of the open plan office he'd found. He pushed the knife into exposed flesh and forced it down, trying to gut it like it was Earthly, though its kind had been here longer than humanity.

The blood wasn't a different colour to his but it was thicker somehow, more viscous. He collected it in an oversized novelty NYC mug.

'Sorry, brother,' he told his prey. 'I need to take your spirit so I can hunt.'

As he used the blood to make a horizontal line across the ash on his face, over his eyes, he saw them. The dead surrounded him. Those he'd seen die, those he'd killed, human, Ceph, it didn't matter. Aztec and Jester stood at the fore. They said nothing, they just watched him.

'There's still shackles on the human spirit, brothers. Our enemy's hiding in the same place it always has. Inside.' They said nothing, watching him, judging him. Dane looked away first. 'I'm waiting for the Sun King,' he told them. He knew it wasn't enough, though he'd seen the sky catch fire.

***

Chino reflected on the training that kept him fighting against inevitability.

He'd jumped, blindly, fallen about five storeys into water. The water had slowed him significantly but he'd still hit the street under it hard. Pain had shot through his already wounded leg and he'd all but kneed himself in the jaw.

He found a place to lie low but he could still hear the

hooting and the clicking. There was movement in the water and movement through the surrounding buildings. They were still hunting him.

But they're a pack, he told himself, *packs are finite.*

He had dried, stripped, cleaned and reloaded the Marshall shotgun and the Majestic revolver. Then, moving as stealthily as he could, he had gone looking for a place for his last stand.

What he'd found, tactically speaking, was a shit place for a last stand. It was surrounded on all sides by high buildings. Chino was hoping that the narrow street would shield him from the CELL gun emplacements.

He slid into the water quietly. *I'm the alligator,* he thought inanely, overcoming the urge to giggle brought on by tension. He did the breaststroke out to the submerged delivery van. Most of it was under the water. Only the roof showed over the surface. *By using this at least I have a moat,* he thought. The Stalkers would have to swim to him, *or jump,* he thought. During the New York incursion the Stalkers had had some kind of ranged weapon. He hadn't seen these new ones use it yet. Either they'd run out of ammunition or this purer form preferred the blades. He was banking on that. If they could engage him at range he was screwed.

'Let's get this over and done with,' Chino muttered to himself. He lit two road flares and held them up high. They illuminated the dark, narrow, Chinatown street with their phosphorescent, flickering, red glare.

Whatever happens tonight some other motherfuckers are dying with me, he thought.

226

He looked up, searching for the moon, and howled at the broken cityscape.

Then he waited, listened and watched.

He heard the clicking and the hooting first. Then the sound of water gently rippling against the side of the sunken delivery van. Then the sound of blades scraping against stone. He could see them now, dark shapes in the water. Dark shapes clinging to the side of buildings, moving towards him.

He dropped one of the road flares into the water. It spiralled down to the bottom, illuminating alien shapes moving sinuously towards the submerged delivery van.

Chino took an M17 fragmentation grenade out of one of the pouches on his webbing. He removed the pin and let the spoon flip off. He started counting. On three-Mississippi he tossed the second flare into the water on the other side of the van. It illuminated more shapes in the water. He needed them out of the water, ballistics were for shit in liquids. On four-Mississippi he held the grenade just a bit longer. For a less than a moment he remembered playing softball in the park with his brothers and sisters in East LA during family cookouts. Then he threw.

With less than a second left on the fuse, the grenade exploded in the air. Fragments tore into alien flesh. Concussive force battered and broke their forms, bounced them off the wall and into the water.

Chino had turned his back and put his hand over the back of his head. Fragments imbedded themselves in his body armour and tore into his arm, but he barely felt it. The force of the explosion staggered him. He went down on one knee.

One of them shot out of the water next to him. The barrel of the shotgun was almost touching the fleshy matter behind its jagged biosteel head and shoulder armour. He pulled the trigger. The alien flesh exploded. Chino stood up and helped the Stalker back into the water with the toe of his boot, as he worked the slide on his shotgun. He felt calm.

Another Stalker burst out of the water at the opposite end of the van. He raised the shotgun, aimed for flesh. Shot sparked off armour as he worked the slide again. He fired. The Stalker fell back into the water. Another shot out of the water to his left. He walked at it, taking his time, aiming the shotgun. He felt its bone blade hit his armour. He shot it at point blank range. It flew backwards, the dark water engulfing it.

One of them stabbed at him from the water, over-extending itself. He stepped back, pushed the shotgun against its tentacled back hump and pulled the trigger.

For a moment he was on top of the van on his own. He took a moment to fire four rounds at the dark shapes crawling across the sides of the nearest building. One of them fell off. Others started leaping. The shotgun was empty.

Now it gets interesting.

He let the shotgun drop on its sling and drew the Majestic. He was peripherally aware of the gun emplacements firing again, more than one of them. There was tracer fire raining in from multiple directions. Chunks of the buildings were being blown off. Rents were torn through concrete and brick by the heavy calibre fire, but it was inaccurate. They had no eyes on the target, not when the target was down between the buildings on a street this narrow. It was just a fireworks display. The backdrop for his death.

***

It was beautiful. Yesterday he had seen the sun fall from the sky. Now it was the stars.

***

One and then another landed on the roof. Chino moved at them, firing. Two shots and the first fell, the huge .50 calibre rounds exploding inside it. The second he killed with just one round. He swung on a third. Its head exploded as he raised the revolver. He didn't have a moment to be surprised. More of them were landing on the van and climbing out of the water. After all, they were a reactive species. They'd worked out that they could get him in a rush.

The next one he killed by putting the barrel of the big revolver against its flesh and pulling the trigger. Then something heavy and sharp hit him. Took him down onto the roof of the van. He angled the revolver up and almost broke his wrist firing the final two shots. He dropped the revolver and rolled into a crouch. Another died charging him, shot through the head by someone unseen, giving him the moment he needed to draw his large knife.

***

He looked through the tech scope at the Stalkers clambering onto the roof of the sunken delivery van. He squeezed the trigger. The electromagnetic field generated by the coils shot the ten-millimetre armour piercing solid slug out of the barrel of the gauss sniper rifle at hypersonic speeds. The slug shot though the armour and then the flesh of a Stalker. It was dropping as he moved to the next target. That one fell. Then the next. Reload.

His goat was doing well, he reflected, or at least his goat was still alive.

***

Another one died before it reached him. A Stalker threw itself at Chino and he rolled with it, coming up on top. Screaming, he repeatedly stabbed at the creature with his knife. Alien blood spattered all over him. He could taste it.

I killed one hand-to-hand he exulted, then he was torn off his victim. Chino screamed as he was lifted high into the air, a bone blade through his left arm and another through his right side.

***

He was moving now. Running through the falling stars' impacts.

He was an invisible ghost. He saw his goat lifted high up into the air. He stopped and fired.

***

The Stalker lifting him up collapsed under him. Chino did some screaming as the bone blades moved in his flesh. He was stuck, impaled. More of them were climbing out of the water and another landed on the roof. They towered over the ex-marine as they moved towards him.

'Yeah, fuck you! I killed more of you than you killed of me!'

He should be in agony, he knew, but there was only anger and tears of frustration. He'd fought too hard. He didn't deserve this.

Something landed on the roof of the submerged delivery van. The night air moved strangely behind one of the Stalkers. The Ceph stopped and seemed to shake. The bloody point of a knife appeared through its flesh. The armoured figure appeared behind it and threw the dying creature against the wall of one of the buildings that lined the narrow street. *It's like watching a demigod move amongst mortals and monsters*, Chino thought.

One of the Stalkers swung at Dane. Dane stepped back and then rammed his bloody knife into a soft part of the alien. He left the knife there. He kicked the alien, knocking it back and then drawing his Hammer II automatic, which he shot twice at point blank range. The Stalker hit the roof of the van and slid into the water.

Chino could feel the pain now. His vision was getting hazy but it looked like Dane was fighting with his visor down. He had painted his face like a corpse and smeared blood across it. Dane turned round and grabbed a bone blade that had been thrust at him, broke the blade, and then shot the Ceph three times. Chino could see that there was something wrong with the back of Dane's armour. It looked like it had been partially melted, somehow, and had only been able to repair some of the damage.

Dane made the killing of the remaining Stalker look very casual.

Chino blacked out.

He came to with Dane's bizarre visage leaning over him.

'I've got to lift you off its blades. Sorry, brother, this is going to hurt.'

He hadn't lied. Chino did some screaming and then passed out.

***

There was a fire. It didn't smell good. It had the sort of acrid quality to it that came with burning man-made fibres. There was still a lot of pain. Chino was hoping he was stabilised, as he had some morphine ampules in his med kit that he was going to treat himself to.

Even looking around was painful. He broke into a cold sweat. They were on one of the higher floors of a skyscraper somewhere in Midtown. He could see the glow of the lights from CELL's various construction sites around the ruined city. The rest of what was left of New York was quiet and dark.

Dane was sat around a campfire he'd made in the centre of an open plan office. There was a gutted Stalker hanging down from the ceiling. That stank as well.

'The guns, they'll see the fire, man,' Chino managed. 'Fucking Psycho. Where is he?'

Dane shook his head sadly.

'Psycho's gone, man, somewhere I can't see or reach.' The armoured figure moved over and knelt by Chino.

'I've bound your wounds. You're messed up, but you'll live.'

'What happened? Where were you, man?'

Dane looked at him as if making a decision.

'I saw the sky catch fire,' he finally told Chino.

More crazy Lazy Dane shit, Chino thought.

'The fucking Brits sold us out,' Chino said, pained. Dane was shaking his head.

'No, they were true, righteous. The sun fell to Earth. They walk with me now.'

Chino tried to make sense of this.

'Shit,' he finally said. 'It's over then.'

Dane shrugged.

'Nothing's ever over man, we just change state.'

Chino closed his eyes. It had all been for nothing, the fighting, the pain, all the dead. CELL would win. The world was theirs now. It probably had been for a while.

233

'You know what this place is?'

'A graveyard?' Chino suggested, giving into his pain and the despair.

'It's a necropolis. All of them. Our guys, CELL, the victims of the disease and everyone back to when this was a swamp and it belonged to the first people. They're all still here. Ceph too, human and alien living together, it's beautiful man. It's dead and it's beautiful.'

Chino said nothing. There wasn't much he could say to a crazy person's ramblings.

'Thank you,' Dane said.

'For what, man? You saved me.'

'For being my goat.'

Chino stared at him. 'Your what?'

'When a *shikari* hunts a tiger he ...'

'Tethers a goat to a tree and bleeds it a little to get the tiger's attention.'

Dane nodded. Chino stared at him. *He doesn't think he's one of us anymore. He thinks we're playthings, mere mortals.*

Chino spat in his face.

***

Maybe if the nanosuit hadn't been so badly damaged Dane would have heard their comms. If Chino hadn't been so badly hurt, if both of them had been alert, then maybe they would have heard them moving around beneath them.

They had been pinpointed by thermographics. The fire hadn't helped.

The floor of the open plan office exploded in a circle around Dane and Chino. They fell through to the floor below them. The impact made Chino scream as multiple wounds were badly jarred and he started to piss blood again. The campfire exploded in a shower of sparks.

Dane was moving. Disappearing, becoming transparent, fading into the background. Then he was wreathed in lighting. Electrostatically charged pellets fired from K-Volt weapons stuck to Lazy Dane's suit. The pellets dropped the cloak, making him visible. More and more of the pellets stuck to him. The voltage he was receiving grew and grew. The damaged suit's systems were overloaded. They started shutting down. The pellets were electrocuting Dane as he tried to move. There were four members of the CELL spec ops armed with K-volts. They continued laying on the fire.

Dane looked like he was made of electricity as he stood up. Members of the spec ops team took a step back.

Chino saw his Majestic. He was reaching for his big revolver when someone stood on his hand and then kicked him in the face, hard. He saw lights and felt sick. He felt darkness swimming up to claim him.

'Reloading,' the first K-Volt gunner said as he ran out of pellets. There was only a hint of panic in the man's voice. He swapped out the magazine as the next, and then the next gunner, ran out of pellets as well. Dane took a step forwards.

Reloaded, they started firing again. Dane took another step forwards through the electricity crackling all around him and then toppled over.

'Don't stop firing, the Commander ordered.' They didn't.

*****

Chino came to again. He glanced over and saw Dane being dragged out. A VTOL was circling the building, using its spotlight to provide light for the spec ops team. Chino wasn't sure he'd ever seen someone so singularly bound with restraints as Lazy Dane.

'Commander, he's awake,' a CELL commando standing over Chino said. The Commander of the Spec Ops team turned to look at her subordinate. She shrugged.

'He's surplus to requirement.'

Chino looked up at the gun barrel. He saw the finger tightening around the trigger.

He felt calm.

A Foreign Country

Screaming. Agony. Then nothingness.

London, 2016

Jab, jab, hook, cross, move your fucking feet. Mike reflected that the less he had trained, the more out of shape he'd gotten, the more he hit the drink, the food, certain recreational pharmaceuticals, the more he'd been fighting. *I said move your fucking feet, not mince around like a fairy!* Mike bobbed left and right, weaving rapidly, and threw another combination of punches at the heavy bag.

When he'd thought of himself as a fighter, in the streets – stupid shit – as a nipper, or in pubs, clubs, he'd been lying to himself. There had been no discipline to it, no real effort, just the excitement but it wasn't the rush he felt in the ring. There certainly wasn't the feeling of satisfaction that there was in winning a match.

Speedball next, then pull-ups and then skipping to warm down. No showers in this gym, just the smell of leather and the stench of more than a hundred years of sweat. Then back to walking the streets looking for work.

It had been another morning with nothing to show for it but sore feet. He glanced at the sandwich board outside the newsagent as he made for the *Blind Beggar*. It was a headline from a newspaper he liked to think of as the *Daily Fail*, trumpeting the passing of the controversial Offenders Conscription Act. Mike just shook his head as he pushed the door open to the *Beggar* and the welcoming smell of his local.

***

He took another sip of his pint. He found it easy to waste away the afternoon in the pub, but Sarah had said he should only have one during the day, when he was trying to find work. He wanted to savour it. He stared at the sparse list of jobs in the local paper, willing himself to be qualified for one of them. *As what?* He remembered Sarah telling him *you can't think like that*. He thought about how his world had changed. He used to be all about wanting a life like he saw on telly, a rich easy life. Now he'd settle for a job in a warehouse. The news was talking about another dip, a triple dip. Mike was of the opinion that this was just the way things were going to be for the foreseeable future. People needed to get used to it.

'Hello, Psycho.' The voice was so gravelly it sounded a cigarette away from full-blown throat cancer. *Don't call me that,* but you didn't tell Jack Hamilton anything. Mike looked up and pretended to be pleased to see Hamilton. In truth he liked the man, and always had done. He had been a good friend to Mike's dad. Mike had looked up to him, and Jack had done right by his mother after his dad had died over some stupid shit in a pub.

Hamilton was tall and still had a thick, full head of hair for a man in his late sixties, though it was white now. Jack had never been a pretty man. He had a flat face and a nose that had been repeatedly broken in his youth. He did, however, have an undeniable charisma.

'Well, well, if it isn't Jack Hamilton, last of the great white gangsters,' Mike said, smiling.

'You always were a cheeky cunt, weren't you?' Hamilton said, smiling indulgently. 'How's your mum?'

Mike shrugged.

'She's keeping alright. Needs to get out a bit more.'

'Real looker in her day, your mum.'

'Jack ...' Mike started. Hamilton hit him on the shoulder.

'You know I don't mean nothing by it.' Hamilton sat down at the stool next to Mike and lit up a cigarette.

'Jack, you're going to get my licence taken away,' Jean screeched at Hamilton. Some of the pub's punters were of the opinion that the sharp-tongued undisputed matriarch of the *Beggar* had been here before the pub, just waiting for it to be built around her. She'd always reminded Mike of the harpies that Zeus had sent to torment Phineus, but in a good way.

'I think we both know that'll never happen, darlin'. Two triple brandies, love, it's lunch time after all.' Mike started to protest. He started to protest because it sounded really, really good. Jack let him know that to refuse would insult him. Mike sighed, nodded and thanked the older man.

'What's this shit?' Hamilton said tapping the paper open at the wanted ads. *Here we go*, Mike thought.

'Looking for work, ain't I,' Mike said.

'Mikey, all you have to do is ...'

'Please, Jack ...' Mike said. He didn't want to offend the older man and it wasn't because he was a dangerous individual. He just didn't want to hurt the gangster's feelings.

'Sarah?'

'Yeah, no. Sort of. I need to get away from all of that. She ... we want a family and I just remember when I was a kid, my dad ...'

'Your dad was a good man,' Hamilton said seriously.

'He was. Could have been a better dad.'

Hamilton thought about this. It looked to Mike like his dad's old friend was about to stand up for his dad.

'I can see that,' Hamilton finally said. 'One of the reasons I never had kids.'

'That and you're still shagging twenty-one year old lap-dancers, if what I hear is right.'

Hamilton's growling laughter made Mike think of a dog drowning.

'Rank has its privileges, son,' Hamilton told him.

'Some of the work what I've got is legit,' he said changing subject.

'Jack, I appreciate it, I really do but ...'

'S'alright, I understand, I get it. I know you need some distance, but I don't want to lose contact. Why don't you and Sarah join me and ...' Hamilton stopped, a look of concentration spreading over his face.

'You can't remember your girlfriend's name, can you?' Mike said, grinning. Hamilton was shaking his head.

'I'm getting fucking old. I can picture her. Great tits, fucks like a wolverine sewn into a sack.'

'Nice,' Mike said nodding.

'You watch your mouth, Jack Hamilton!' Jean howled at Hamilton. 'I don't care who you are out there!'

'I'm sorry Jeanie, you know I've only got eyes for you, but you should see this girl's tits.'

Mike was laughing now as he took another sip of brandy.

'I will fucking bar you, you cheeky little bastard!'

Hamilton was laughing as well. Winding up Jean was a time-honoured tradition of the punters in the *Beggar*.

'Seriously though, one Sunday, the four of us can go out to Epping Forest, have a walk, spot of Sunday lunch. My treat.'

Mike nodded, grateful. He did like Hamilton's company, but he could never shake the picture of the number of times he'd seen the older man with blood on his hands. That was why Hamilton still ran this manor.

That was why all the little fresh-faced, gun-toting gangster-wannabes left him alone. He wasn't greedy, he just wanted his patch, but if you fucked around then he took care of business. Personally.

'Now let's have another drink.'

'Jack, seriously …'

***

Sarah's going to fucking kill me, Mike thought, *I am well hammered.*

'… so he comes back in, looks in the quilt cover and then back at me and says: "Jack, why's there a dead dog in my quilt cover?" Now Richardson was a hard fucker and you had to respect him, but I couldn't help myself, I got all aggrieved and said: "Where did you want me to put it?" Oh, he gave me such a kicking. He was proper furious.'

Mike had heard the story before but he was still laughing. Jack's face became serious again.

'You picked a shitty time to become a civilian, Mikey, even the fucking yuppies are moving out. You hear about the body of that girl they found?'

Mike shrugged. 'It's the Jack the Ripper theme park, isn't it?' he replied. 'Every nutjob in the fucking country wants to pay tribute.'

Jack was looking at him thoughtfully, nodding.

'I like that. That's, what-cha-call-it …?'

'Profound?' Mike asked, his heart sinking. He saw where this was going.

'Yeah, profound. Good word. Where is it, Mikey?'

'Jack, don't do this,' Mike said shaking his head. Hamilton had his hand out.

Mike sighed, reached into the pocket of his battered leather jacket and handed Hamilton the book. Hamilton looked at the cover, frowned and then reached into the breast pocket of his suit and took out a pair of reading glasses and held them in front of his face. *Those are new,* Mike thought.

'Who's Descartes then? Sounds like a frog.' Hamilton put the book down on the bar. *Here it comes,* Mike thought.

'Wish I'd read more,' Hamilton said quietly. 'Particularly history, I love that stuff. You know I heard once that down here, in Victorian times, everyone was a criminal. I mean they all had legit jobs but everyone, and I mean everyone, had something on the side. Had to, if they wanted to feed their family. Know what a dollymop is?' Mike did, but he shook his head. 'A part-time prostitute. You think on that. Imagine you're a wife and a mother but sometimes you have to go out and sell yourself just to make ends meet. It's going to get like that again, I reckon. You keep your Sarah close and you look after her. She's a good one, son. You needed sorting out. You were breaking your mother's heart. I almost had to step in, know what I mean?' Mike swallowed hard. Thinking about his mum. The guilt. 'You're lucky Sarah saw something in you. Took the time. She may not like me or what I am ...' Mike started to protest. 'Quiet. Sometimes I don't like what

I am. But you need anything, either of you, you just have to ask.'

Mike nodded.

'Thanks Jack, that means a lot.'

'And don't you worry. I've texted her to let her know you'll be late and that you're with me.' Then Jack started laughing. Mike felt his heart sink. *I am so dead.*

'Hello Psycho, what's this faggot shit?' Mike bristled at the sound of the voice. He looked up as Davey Falconer picked up his book. Falconer was whip thin, with amphetamine eyes that looked yellow to Mike and a constantly moving jaw. His hair was slicked down with too much gel and, presumably aping Hamilton, he wore an expensive tailored suit. *Saville Row can't hide what a vicious little prick Davey Falconer is,* Mike thought.

Falconer's most defining feature, however, was the jagged scar on the right side of his face that climbed up his cheek to his temple. He'd tried to get people to call him Scarface, but it hadn't taken. Mike was of the opinion that Davey wanted to take that scar out on the world.

'Yeah, nothing screams homosexuality like literacy,' Mike muttered.

'What's that supposed to fucking mean?' Davey demanded. Hamilton was laughing. Mike just shook his head. 'How much longer do I have to wait in the Jag, boss?' Davey all but demanded.

'Until I'm finished you cheeky little bastard,' Hamilton told him, less than pleased. 'I'm having a drink with young Mikey here.'

Davey looked at Mike. Mike could feel the other man's resentful glare. He didn't even want to look at him. His fingers tightened around the brandy glass.

'I hear you've become a pussy now.'

'That's enough, Davey, go wait out in the car,' Jack told the younger man.

'You're Sarah MacFadden's wife now, yeah? Not a pussy, pussy-whipped more like.'

'Davey, shut the fuck up. I'm not going to tell you again. What is it with you two? Did you give him the scar or something?' Hamilton asked, angry that his pleasant afternoon was being ruined.

No, that was his dad, Mike thought.

'I used to pick on him at school,' Mike said. *What're you doing, Mike, just let it go.* 'If I'd known what a whiney little cunt he was going to turn into I wouldn't have fucking bothered.'

Davey was just nodding, smiling a vicious little smile.

'Here, Hamilton, his Sarah might be a good little girl now but at school, my goodness, did that girl get around.'

'Well you wouldn't know, would you?' Mike said. 'Fucking cock-less virgin.'

'Alright lads, we're all friends here,' Hamilton growled.

No, we're really fucking not, Mike thought.

Davey had bristled at Mike's insults but swallowed it and turned back to Hamilton, buoyed by the presence of his boss.

'She'd do all sorts of dirty shit, five or six cocks at the same time ...'

'Alright, you're bang out of order. Fuck off Davey. Now.' Hamilton told him.

'She looked so good looking up at you, her mouth round your ...'

Mike was on his feet. He hadn't even thought about it on a conscious level. He had grabbed the front of Davey's suit. His fist pulled back, then it shot forwards again and again into the terrified face. He felt bone and gristle giving under his knuckles. Davey went down. Mike didn't stop punching. He wasn't even aware of the screaming.

Someone grabbed him. Mike's head shot round. His face a mask of rage. He was looking for the next victim. His fist coming up. Ready to punch.

'Mikey!' Hamilton shouted. Shaken, Mike realised that he was about to punch Hamilton. For a moment he realised how old the other man looked. He felt the rage drain from him. He turned and looked down at Davey. He was curled up on the floor, sobbing. He'd wet himself, at least. He'd seen his murder in Mike's eyes. Mike looked down at the blood on his calloused knuckles.

'Shit!' Mike shouted. Jean was staring at him. 'You need to get out of here,' she told him.

'What were you thinking?' Hamilton said to Davey. He was looking down at the younger man, shaking his head. 'He's a fighter, you're just a thug.' He turned around to Mike. 'I'll clean this up. You get out of here, alright.'

Mike nodded, shaking. Davey wasn't the only person Mike had frightened.

***

Am very angry, have gone out with Karen. Give a lot of thought to how you're going to make up for this. Mike looked down at the note. She was pissed off, but she understood. It just made him feel worse, somehow.

He put on some music. Poured himself a brandy and then sat in his chair in the dark, putting his fist into a bowl of ice. He checked his phone. Still nothing from Sarah, which was always a sign of how angry she was with him.

***

The sound of the phone ringing woke him. His head was killing him, a proper spirits hangover. He'd spilled his glass and there was brandy all over the floor. *We're not getting tired of fucking up today, are we?* He glanced at the phone. It was Karen calling. Something cold uncoiled inside him.

'Hello?'

Karen was crying.

***

He ran into A&E. He pushed to the front of the reception desk, oblivious to the angry complaints of the people in the queue. He demanded to know where she was. There was more shouting, complaining from the queue, but they told him where she was. He was running again.

Karen in a short dress, her face streaked with tear-stained mascara. Both her arms bandaged from where she'd tried to get in the way. She was speaking to him, telling him what happened as tears ran down his face. Sarah's face was completely covered with the surgical dressing. He'd cut her a lot. She was out now, sedated.

Karen was on her knees on the hospital floor, screaming at him to come back as he headed for the exit. He heard her shout the last thing Sarah had said to her before she passed out. *Don't let Mike go after him.*

***

On the phone now.

'Where is he! Tell me where the fuck he is or I'm coming after you!'

You don't speak to Jack Hamilton like this, ever. Hamilton tells him what he wants to know.

***

Hamilton stared at the phone. He hadn't told him because of the threat, though he had no doubt that right now, like this, Mikey would have walked through his people and beaten him to death.

Maybe in my youth I could have taken him, Hamilton

thought, but he knew he was fooling himself. He knew what little pricks like Davey Falconer would never properly understand. For the likes of Falconer violence was power, which was why they hurt other people, to make them feel better about themselves. Hamilton knew something that not even Mikey had admitted to himself. Mikey just liked fighting. For the rush. A lot of people didn't understand the difference. Hamilton did. *The only thing stopping that boy from being a complete monster is his own morals and Sarah. Now that stupid little prick has tried to take one of those things away.*

Hamilton had told Mikey what he wanted to know because someone was going to get hurt tonight. Hamilton was of the opinion that it might as well be the little cunt that was actually responsible. He had told Mikey what he had wanted to know because at some level he knew he himself was responsible. So he told him, and he knew he'd damned his old friend's son.

Everyone else thought he ran the manor because he would fix things, people if needed, with his own hands. *He* knew he ran the manor because he understood what it was. At its heart it was a web of loyalty, obligations, relationships, respect and even friendships. He also knew that it wasn't going to stay that way for much longer.

***

You do something stupid. You hurt someone you shouldn't have. You get the wrong person angry at you, and then you have a choice. You either run, hide and stay hidden, or you get out in the open. Lots of witnesses. Lots of people to get between you and the other guy. Lots of people who will phone the police. Davey had made the wrong decision. Mike almost tore the door off the West End bar. He was screaming.

***

'Mr Sykes, you hospitalised six people, including two police officers, and left several more in need of medical attention. Mr Falconer only lived due to the quick thinking and medical expertise of the ambulance service. He has, however, been left wheelchair-bound and blind in one eye. Whilst I understand that you had provocation, you also have a history of violence. It seems that despite your time spent in youth correctional facilities, and indeed at Her Majesty's pleasure, you still have not learnt your lesson. With this in mind, I have chosen a sentence for you that will hopefully channel your aggression, allow you to contribute to your country and, most importantly, teach you discipline. Mr Sykes, are you listening to me?'

He wasn't. It didn't matter what the judge had to say. He was thinking about the last time he had seen Sarah.

***

He was on his knees next to the bed, holding her hand. Looking at her face, still covered in bandages. Covering where he'd cut her. Punched her a bit to soften her up, because she was a fighter, and then laced her with a Stanley knife, just like his dad had taught him. Did it twice. He had given her twice as many scars as he had.

'You weren't here when I woke up,' was all she said.

'I ... got him ...' was all he managed. It was then he realised that it meant nothing. Her look was enough. She knew that what he'd done to Falconer hadn't been for her. It had been for him. She pulled her hand out of his and rolled away from him. He never saw her again.

***

The prisoner transport rolled into Depot Para in Catterick, North Yorkshire. They'd been all but dragged out of the secure vehicle, and then the shouting had started.

'The pampered Etonian homosexuals in Whitehall, who we have the misfortune to serve, have, in their wisdom, chosen to turn my beloved 2 Para into a penal legion! That's penal as in penitent, not as in penis! You are amongst the first low-life parasitical scum who have been sent to befoul my beloved battalion! We normally have nothing but contempt for recruits stupid enough to join this regiment! You! We actually hate! We hate you more than the French! I congratulate you on your stunning achievement on making the entire of 2 Para hate you! You will not be here long! We will break you! You will have training accidents! Terrible things will happen to you at the hands of trained killers! You will come to me, begging to me to be allowed back to Wormwood Scrubs so large unpleasant gentlemen can get at your tight little bottoms! What you will not be doing is joining the parachute regiment! Is that understood!?' There were a few mumbled replies. 'The proper reply, scum, is, "Yes, Sergeant"!'

'Here, do you think you're hard or something?' Psycho asked. The training sergeant turned to look at the squat, muscular, shaven-headed item who had spoken.

'Oh, well volunteered ...' the training sergeant started. Psycho laid him out with one punch.

***

He thought he had been tortured before. He hadn't. He didn't really know what it was. He thought he could withstand torture. He couldn't. He'd tell them anything as long as they stopped. No, that wasn't true, he'd tell them anything if they ended it and killed him. Except they weren't asking any questions.

South London, 2017

Four hot days in summer and the riot season was upon them again, but this time it had been different. This time people, who were normally killing each other over which postcode they lived in, were armed, organised and had had at least rudimentary training.

To Psycho, looking down the barrel of his Minimi, there was a degree of inevitability to this. It was going to happen eventually in any society where the gap between the rich and the poor was so well-defined and widening. When you had a society that penalised the least fortunate for the excesses of the most fortunate, it was only a matter of time before the unfortunates at the bottom, who were used to desperation and fighting each other, finally turned on the people that were actually screwing them over. He'd said as much to the squad. Perkins had called him a communist. It wasn't politics. It wasn't economics. It was common sense. Cause and effect. You beat a dog often enough, it'll get round to biting you. And frankly, as far as Psycho was concerned, if you hadn't done anything about the reasons why these things were happening then you couldn't complain when your capital city burnt.

Psycho had heard a couple of the old boys, ex-2 Para, talk about how the LCZ looked like Belfast during the 1980's now. The police had very quickly been overwhelmed. The TA had gone in. A lot of them had been killed. Car bombs, rocket and mortar attacks and just good old-fashioned street fighting. Then the Paras had been called in. *Yeah, because 1 Para had really cooled things off in Northern Ireland, hadn't they?* Psycho thought. The Royal Navy were also involved. The Frigate HMS *Anguish* was anchored in the Thames less than a mile away from where Psycho was in cover behind sandbags.

The problem was, the kids with the AKs had taken over a number of tower blocks. They were well provisioned. Knew the area. They seemed to have endless amounts of ammunition. Even for people who knew what they were doing when it came to fighting, the prospect of going in and rooting them out did not appeal. The same architecture that turned these tower blocks into rat-infested warrens was the same architecture that would turn them into death-traps that would have to be cleared room by room. Their ROE were to engage them in the street or if fired upon, but otherwise to patrol and contain while the politicians and the police negotiated.

The gunmen may have been organised to a degree, at least when it came to fighting, but they didn't even have a name. It had just steadily escalated, kicking off with a policeman killed in revenge for shooting an unarmed kid. The gunmen and women wanted fairness, an even playing field, but lacked the vocabulary to express it in terms that politicians would understand. *Fat chance*, Psycho thought. Nobody with a vested interest wanted an even playing field and the negotiators were trying to buy them off with training shoes, X-Factor and PlayStations. After all, it had worked in the past.

It hadn't taken much: a number of the older kids who'd been trained by the army, under the Offenders Conscription Act. Someone with contacts in the Eastern European mob for weapons. They would have gotten seed money from who-knows-where and then all it took was for someone to push them just a little too hard.

This was how Psycho found himself looking down the barrel of a Minimi behind a pile of sandbags in his hometown. Admittedly he was south of the river. He was probably shooting at Chelsea fans. He still couldn't shake the feeling that he was on the wrong side.

They were stationed at a road junction, looking at one of the tower blocks. The six-wheeled Coyote tactical support vehicle was parked up behind them. The TSV's mounted .50 calibre heavy machine gun was pointed at the block, the mounted general purpose machine gun, or jimpy, covering the road behind them.

'Come on, you little shit, show yourself,' Perkins muttered. He was looking through the scope of the L129A1 sharpshooter rifle. The corporal was one of the body-beautiful types, who somehow managed to hit the gym even after all the PT he did. An attractive guy who knew it, but his good looks couldn't hide the vicious cast to his features. He knew who to brown nose above and who to victimise below. As far as Psycho was concerned he was a nasty piece of work.

'Perkins, why don't you wind your neck in? Things are quiet. Let's just leave it,' Psycho told him. He could see Lumley nodding in agreement. There was only one thing that career soldiers hated more than the offender conscripts: the fully integrated front-line female soldiers. This had led to a strange alliance between the women and the offender conscripts in infantry units. Psycho also knew that Lumley, a stocky girl from Derby, was harder than half the guys in his section. She'd had to be, to get where she was.

'That would be Corporal Perkins, right, Private Sykes?' Perkins asked, looking up from the scope.

It'll be Corporal Wanker, Sykes managed not to say.

'ROE, corp,' Psycho told him.

'The rules of engagement say that we may return fire if fired upon. I assure you that if I slot the fucker he will have shot first. Isn't that right, Geordie?'

'Aye, too right, corp,' Geordie, the thickly-set Lance Corporal manning the TSV's .50 cal said in his thick Newcastle accent. To Psycho it seemed that every squad in the British army had to come with someone called Geordie in it. Geordie was Perkin's henchman in the squad.

'Walker?'

'Aye, corp,' the massively built Afro-Caribbean private from Birmingham said.

'Wally?'

Walowski was a wiry Pole who had somehow also managed to end up in 2 Para as part of the Offenders Conscription Act. The Pole hesitated.

Psycho got on well with Walowski. The Pole seemed to be constantly surprised at finding himself in the British army.

Perkins turned to glare at Walowski.

'Yes, Corporal,' the Pole finally answered.

'Private Lumley?' Lumley just stared fixedly ahead, watching her sector. 'I said "Private Lumley"?' Lumley ignored him. 'Stupid bitch, probably deaf as well as frigid.' There was laughter from Walker and Geordie. 'You know what you need, Lumley?'

'A corporal who isn't a wanker?' Psycho suggested. Lumley and Walowski tried not to smile.

'Right, Sykes, you're going on report.'

'Fine, I live on report. I haven't, however, been to the

256

Glasshouse in a while. Want to keep talking?' Psycho was still looking down the barrel of the Minimi, watching his section, but he could feel Perkins glaring at the back of his head. He felt a glare from another quarter as well. He glanced over at Lumley. She was looking less than pleased. Psycho sighed internally. She was right to be pissed off at him. If she wanted to be accepted then she would have to stand up for herself, otherwise ...

'Is it love?' Perkins asked. 'Aw, isn't that sweet. Thing is, I'm not sure that Lumley's much more of a looker than the scarred-up tart who dumped you.'

He heard Lumley's sharp intake of breath. Wally was desperately looking elsewhere. Psycho's knuckles whitened around the Minimi's grip. He was going back in the Glasshouse, he decided, *but not until we're out of the line of fire*. He would get Perkins when they were back at the forward operating base at Battersea Power Station.

'What, the East End hard-man got nothing to say?' Perkins mocked.

'See those guys over there?' Lumley asked, trying to ignore Perkins. Psycho nodded. He'd been watching the two men in dark civilian clothes carrying high-end military gear. They were crouched behind a car about two hundred metres to their left. One of them was observing the same tower block that Perkins' squad had been assigned to watch through a pair of binoculars. He had a boxy device slung across his shoulder. Psycho recognised the device as a laser designator. The other man was covering him whilst speaking into a radio headset. Presumably relaying the instructions being given to him by the observer.

'Special forces,' Psycho muttered. Lumley nodded.

'They'll be forward observing for the *Anguish*,' Lumley said. Psycho nodded in agreement. That made him very nervous indeed. It was one thing to exchange gunfire in the streets with these kids. It was another altogether to start lobbing ordinance into south London.

'Corporal,' Walker said. There was something wrong with the brummie's voice. Psycho glanced round. Walker looked shocked. He had the headset for the TSV's radio on.

'What is it, Walker?' Perkins asked, concerned.

'Someone's just fired ten LAW 80 rockets into the Houses of Parliament,' Walker told them. Psycho and Lumley glanced round at him. The rest of the squad were staring at Walker, appalled.

'Fuck,' Perkins said.

'They're pulling us back to the FOB,' Walker said.

'Fucking little cunts,' Perkins spat. He had the marksman's rifle up and was scanning the front of the tower again.

'Perkins, what're you doing?' Psycho asked. Perkins turned on the Londoner.

'Shut your mouth, you disloyal little bastard!' Perkins went back to scanning the front of the tower block. Lumley glanced around, looking up at the corporal, worried, and then went back to covering her section through the optical sight of her SA80.

'Orders?' Psycho asked the Corporal.

258

'When have you ever given a fuck about orders?'

The sound of the marksman rifle firing echoed around the canyons made by the surrounding tower blocks. Psycho felt his blood run cold. He noticed that the two special forces troopers turned to stare appalled at the Para squad. Psycho saw someone drop on one of the tower block landings.

'What the fuck're you doing!?' Psycho demanded, not turning round, keeping up observation of the front of the tower block, his Minimi at the ready.

'That was a kid, he wasn't even armed!' Lumley said. She was also scanning her section.

'No, it wasn't ...' Perkins started. Psycho could hear the panic in the Corporal's voice.

Then it looked like the entire front of the tower block opened up on them. Gunmen and women appeared from almost every apartment. Fire was pouring down on them. Most of it was inaccurate, but there were a few people in the tower block that knew what they were doing. *Thank you, the Offenders Conscription Act,* Psycho thought. He, like Lumley, was just hunkering down behind the sandbags as bullets rained down, sparking off the streets.

'Contact, contact!' Perkins was screaming.

'Smoke!' Psycho shouted. Nothing happened. 'Walker, smoke!' *Where was Geordie on the .50?* Psycho wondered. He glanced around. Geordie and Walker were taking cover as bullets sparked off the TSV's superstructure. He couldn't see Walowski. Perkins was all but lying in the vehicle's footwell, trying to start it up.

Lumley fired the SA8o's underslung grenade launcher blindly over the top of the sandbag. The tear-gas grenade wouldn't provide them with as much cover as the smoke projectors on the TSV, but it was a start.

'Under the wagon and get the .50 up?' Psycho shouted at her. Lumley nodded. Psycho popped up and started firing long bursts from the Minimi, hoping to keep people's heads down. Lumley scrambled across the floor under the TSV and up onto the back of the vehicle. Psycho then had a chance to realise the stupidity of drawing attention to himself in this situation. It felt like everyone in the world was firing at him. He curled up behind the sandbags and tried not to get shot through pure positive mental attitude. It didn't work. His body armour was taking hits. Each one felt like he'd been hit with a baseball bat. He was glad that he'd upgraded his body armour out of his own pocket.

On the back of the TSV Lumley dragged Geordie out of the way of the .50 cal, racked the heavy machine-gun's bolt and turned it on the front of the tower block.

Psycho was pretty sure that the slow, rhythmic hammering of the .50 cal was the most beautiful sound he'd ever heard. The fire slackened off as large holes started appearing in the tower block in explosions of powdered concrete. He was aware of an SA8o firing and then the jimpy started firing as well.

'Stop firing!' Perkins screamed at Lumley from the footwell of the TSV. 'You'll draw their fire. Stop firing, you stupid bitch, that's a fucking order!' Lumley ignored him. 'I'll fucking have you shot for this!'

Psycho saw the tracers from the .50 cal and the jimpy flying overhead. Keeping low, he started back towards the TSV, firing bust after burst from the Minimi anywhere he saw muzzle flashes.

Psycho reached the TSV and found Perkins in the footwell on the driver's side, still trying to start the vehicle blindly. Psycho hit the button for the driver's side smoke projectors. Four smoke canisters popped out of the tubes angled away from the vehicle. They hit the street and started emitting thick smoke. He grabbed Perkins and dragged him bodily out of the vehicle. Perkins scrambled under the TSV. Psycho unclipped the Minimi from its sling and tossed it into the back of the vehicle and then climbed into the driver's seat.

Smoke was rapidly filling the street, obscuring the tower block's view of the TSV.

'Cease fire!' Psycho shouted as he started up the engine. If they lit up the smoke with muzzle flashes then the people with guns would know where they were. Lumley and Walker stopped firing and immediately hunkered down as rounds were still sparking off the superstructure. Perkins threw himself into the back of TSV.

'Drive! Get this vehicle moving, Private Sykes!' Perkins screamed at him. Psycho put the vehicle into reverse, swung it around ninety degrees and then headed down the street. 'Walker, Lumley, I need you on the MGs now,' Psycho shouted. Both of them got up, Walker reluctantly. Lumley swung the .50 round so it was aiming back up the way they had come at the street full of thick smoke.

All of them were thrown forwards as Psycho slammed on the brakes.

'What the fuck are you doing!?' Perkins screamed from where he was lying in the back of the TSV. 'Get this vehicle moving now!'

The two special forces troopers leapt into the back of the vehicle.

'Appreciate it,' one of the special forces guys said and started covering out the back of the TSV.

'I think your friends have had it,' the other one said. Psycho looked behind him. The top of Walowski's head was missing. He couldn't see the wound that had killed Geordie, he just saw the man's dead eyes staring up at the night sky. Perkins was still screaming at him. One of the special forces guys put their hand on his shoulder.

'Mate, trust me on this, you need to start driving, okay?'

Psycho nodded and started heading for the FOB. He could see the unmistakable silhouette of the derelict power station ahead of him as he watched the light from the missile's engines rise into the sky beyond the FOB.

'Look, we say nothing about it kicking off, okay,' Perkins said. Nobody answered.

Yeah right, Psycho thought, *who would have thought Mrs Sykes' little boy was going to turn grass?*

The ground shook and the horizon behind them

turned to fire. Psycho glanced behind. It was only then he realised how beautiful it all was. It was only then he realised how much he'd enjoyed the firefight.

***

He can hear a voice.

'I'm not sure how much more the subject can take of this, physiologically speaking,'

None, I can't take any more, please, you have to kill me, *he thinks. He wants to scream this at them but he can't.*

Another voice now: 'This is not what we intended. We're not sadists.'

'I'm not sure that this poor bastard would know it.'

2017, Stirling Lines, Hereford

Dragged out of the back of the wagon. He hit the floor and was given a bit of a kicking. Psycho curled up into a ball. He'd had worse, frankly. He was hungry, he'd had little to eat over the last week, but it was how tired he was that got to him. Not just lack of sleep, not the solid mass of aches that was his body, it was the physical and mental fatigue that made him feel that he was just stumbling through a half-world.

'Get up, maggot!' More kicking.

The Special Forces Support Group had been the hunters on the week-long escape and evasion exercise. Psycho and the other hopefuls who had made it this far had been given a World War 2 era greatcoat and

263

a tin with some bits of survival kit in it. Basically he'd been living rough for the better part of the week. He'd made it as far as Bristol and had hid out amongst the homeless camps there. He had thought about trying to jump a train and heading back to London, but decided against it.

He had turned himself in at the end of week for the final part of Special Forces selection: RTI, or resistance to interrogation training. This would also be conducted by the SFSG, many of whom were Royal Marines, RAF Regiment and Paras, Psycho's regiment, all performing under the watchful eye of instructors from the SAS, SBS and Special Reconnaissance Regiment.

'Get up, you piece of filth!' And the boots came in again.

Sorry mate, as cold and wet as the ground is, I like it down here, even with you kicking me, Psycho thought. He was pretty sure that even with them kicking him he could go to sleep on the ground. *You want me up, you're going to have to …*

He felt himself being dragged to his feet. His legs threatened to buckle.

'What unit are you with?! Where are the rest of your men?' someone who'd been eating curry recently screamed in his face. He wanted to give them his name, rank and number, he really did, he tried but it came out a slurred mess. The punch to the stomach doubled him over. Made him retch up his last meal.

'Disgusting!'

Psycho tried to collapse but arms grabbed him and

pulled him to his feet before dragging him towards a set of Quonset huts.

***

It seemed pointless to Psycho. He was so tired he wanted to cry, but it didn't make him want to talk. He was so tired he didn't think he could talk. He just nodded off when he could and was woken up by shouting or by collapsing to the ground.

All the shouting felt like it was coming to him through cotton wool. He didn't really understand what most of it was about. They had him standing in stress positions, but he kept on falling out of them as he faded towards sleep. It was cold because they had stripped him, but even that didn't stop him from falling asleep on his feet. They'd had a female soldier come in and make fun of his genitalia. That had just seemed weird. So weird, in fact, that it had set him off with hysterical giggling that had earned him a bit of a kicking.

He'd managed to give them his name and rank a few times but he could not remember his number. It wasn't that he was tougher than any of the other recruits that had made it this far in the selection. It was just that his brain handled this sort of thing by drifting off. Tired as he was, it all seemed to be happening so far away. The only times that he was brought back into reality was when they hit him. On the other hand, he'd taken lots of beating in the past.

They were trying to get him to stand up but he was

a dead weight. His lack of co-operation was getting him another beating. He managed to stand up, leaning forwards against the wall in a stress position. He collapsed and blacked out as he slid his face down the wall.

***

That fucking hurt! He was wide-awake now. He threw up down himself. Something very hard had hit him in the kidneys. Bitter experience told him he'd be pissing blood for the next week.

'Sarge?' The voice sounded unsure.

'Shut up.' Psycho recognised the voice but he couldn't place it. It sounded like it was coming from far away, through a thick fog. 'We're supposed to break them, aren't we?'

Psycho screamed. Something had hit his right hand and he'd felt the bones break inside.

'I think he felt that,' Perkins said. 'Ironic, taking out the biggest wanker I've ever met's wanking hand.'

Even through the pain it was so difficult to open his eyes. He recognised Perkins' voice, though. He felt something cold run through his body. He wanted to fight, but even had he been able to move, and he didn't think he was, he was cable-tied to a chair.

'H-how …?' Psycho tried to ask. Perkins grabbed him by the hair and bent Psycho's head back. *How did you get into the SFSG?* Psycho wanted to ask. He had reported Perkins for what had happened in the LCZ but the army didn't want to do anything about it. It got lost in the furore of the HMS *Anguish*'s missile attack. It had been made clear, however, that Perkins was finished in the paras one way or another. Now it seemed that he had been promoted to sergeant and had made it into the SFSG.

'You always knew how to play the game,' Psycho tried to say. Instead he mostly mumbled and drooled on himself.

'What's that?' Perkins asked and then swung the collapsible baton into Psycho's balls. Psycho howled and then passed out.

***

'See, this little prick can't be allowed into the SAS. Know what he did? Know what he fucking did!? Only killed an unarmed kid in the LCZ, dropped us right in it and then shat himself when they returned fire. He's a fucking coward and a liability!'

Not true, some part of Psycho was screaming. He felt sick. His hand and his balls were agony. His hair was grabbed again.

'Tell them! Tell them what you fucking did!' Perkins was screaming at him, spraying him with saliva.

'N … n … no,' Psycho managed. Perkins started hitting Psycho's arm as hard as he could, over and over again. Psycho was screaming with every blow.

'Tell them what you did! Tell them and I'll stop!'

'P … please …'

Perkins stopped hitting him.

'Sarge, I don't think ...' Psycho had no idea who the other voice was. He sounded young, frightened.

'Tell them about the kid you killed,' Perkins said, softly now.

He sounds like he believes it. Maybe he's right. Maybe I've got it wrong in my head, so tired.

'Wasn't ... me ...' Psycho managed.

Perkins started hitting him in the arm again. Psycho screamed until he passed out.

***

He came to again. This had to stop now. He couldn't go through any more. He looked down at his pulped left arm. There was bone sticking through the skin.

Someone was whispering to him.

'They've got Lumley next door. Stupid bitch thought she could make it through selection. Unless you tell them about how you killed that kid and then shit yourself, that you're a coward, she's going to get raped. Do you understand me?' Psycho was crying now, nodding numbly. 'Are you going to tell them?' Psycho didn't answer. 'Tell them.' Perkins voice was getting louder. Psycho didn't look up. He just kept his eyes closed. His head down.

He remembered the LCZ. He remembered the shooting. The missile strike. He saw a figure, he couldn't make out his features, pointing the marksman's rifle at the tower block. Pulling the trigger, the kid dropping.

He saw the same figure curled up in the foot well of the TSV.

He felt the metal head of the baton being run up his right leg. *He's going to break my legs,* Psycho knew. It wasn't the thought of the damage, that was irrelevant now, it was the thought of the pain. He just couldn't take any more pain.

'You put the rifle to your shoulder, you saw the kid through the scope, knew he wasn't armed and ...'

He was looking through the scope of the rifle. He saw the kid. So easy, so easy to kill, just squeeze the trigger.

'Because you're an animal ... .'

Stood over Davey Falconer, his face so much pulped meat. He hadn't stopped hitting him. He could hear people screaming the word "animal" at him. He was an animal.

'Tell them what you did,' Perkins whispered to him. It was intimate, like a lover. He had let the tip of the baton rest against Psycho's compound-fractured arm.

It was him. He'd pulled the trigger. He'd killed the kid. He'd been the one cowering, hiding in the TCV.

'Tell them and all the pain goes away.'

It took every bit of effort he had. He spat in Perkins' face. He regretted it the moment he'd done it as fear of the pain overwhelmed him again. Perkins raised the baton and brought it down on his leg. This time Psycho knew it wasn't him who was screaming. He was too far away. Whatever was making the noise wasn't human. It was a wounded animal.

***

He was going to say what Perkins wanted him to say. He couldn't get hit again. He couldn't take the pain. He would beg him if he had to, anything, but Perkins had to stop hitting him.

He opened his eyes to pain and light. But not as much pain as he had expected. He was lying in a hospital bed. His right hand was bandaged. His left arm and right leg were both in casts and held in traction.

'You're in a bit of a mess,' a voice said. A shadow sat in the seat in front of the window. It was a sunny day. Even seeing hurt. Psycho tried nodding, but that hurt too.

'Obviously Sergeant Perkins exceeded his brief,' the figure said. The figure was starting to come into focus now. He was a little guy, wiry. Psycho had seen him before but couldn't place where.

'No ... shit ...' Psycho managed. His mouth was dry.

'I remembered him, but not at first. I knew I'd seen him before but couldn't place him. He's the wanker who fired on the tower block, really stirred them up.'

'I remember you. You got a lot of people killed,' he told the special forces soldier. He had been one of the forward observers he'd seen in the LCZ, one of the ones who had guided the *Anguish*'s attack. The man stared at Psycho coldly. Assessing him.

'I remember you stopping for us.'

'Lumley?'

'She made it, first fully-operational female member of the regiment. Made a few of the boys uncomfortable during RTI, but I've seen lads go from being staunchly against women in the regiment to being really proud of her.'

Psycho nodded. He couldn't feel much about Lumley or anything else at the moment.

'What're you doing here?' He was only beginning to understand the ramifications of just how messed up he was. Even through the drugs, the pain was nearly overwhelming.

'I came to apologise. I took an interest in you. I was overseeing the RTI.'

'You did a really good job.'

'I stepped out, no excuse. For what it's worth, I'm guessing not very much, I'm sorry.'

'Fuck you,' Psycho said quietly. The special forces trooper nodded as if it had been a reasonable response. He stood up and made for the door.

'Perkins?'

The trooper stopped and looked back at Psycho.

'He had several accidents on his way out of the army. Look, we can deal with …'

'No.' The trooper nodded. 'Selection?' The trooper looked troubled. 'I fucking passed!' Psycho spat. The SAS man nodded.

'Yes, you did, but you can't go operational. With those injuries we don't even know if you'll heal fully, then there's rehabilitation. You'll be lucky if you can go back to 2 Para. Not to mention … RTI's not about surviving it. Given enough time, everyone breaks. It's how you're able to cope with it, rationalise it afterwards.'

Psycho was just staring at him.

'Get the fuck out of my room.'

The man nodded and then walked out.

*****

The man that Perkins had hurt, that was someone else. A different piece of screaming meat. It had been nothing. He hadn't known anything about pain then.

2018, Stirling Lines, Hereford

'What unit are you with!? Where's the rest of your people?'

Say nothing, head down, passive, don't make eye contact, and never encourage them by being a smart arse. This last had been a hard-learned lesson. He received a solid punch to the stomach. It knocked over the chair he was tied to. Then the boots came in.

'Corporal, that's enough,' the SAS man said. The SFSG corporal stopped kicking him and helped him up.

'Sorry mate,' the corporal said.

Psycho looked at the SAS man.

'Exercise over?' he asked. The SAS man nodded. Psycho turned back to the corporal. 'You are such a fucking pussy.'

The corporal laughed.

'Don't blame me,' he pointed at the SAS man. 'He told me to be particularly hard on you.'

Psycho looked at the SAS man and nodded.

'I don't think I like you very much.'

The SAS man smiled and helped him out of the Quonset hut. Lumley was waiting for him in the yard.

'You look like you need a brew and smell like you need a shower,' she told him.

'I need two ampules of morphine and my bed, is what I need,' Psycho told her.

2019, Stirling Lines, Hereford

Psycho was stood in front of the CO's desk, at ease. Psycho was in civvies. The "Old Man" was in fatigues.

'You've always been an insubordinate little fucker, haven't you, Sykes?' the Colonel asked.

'Yes boss, thank you,' Psycho said, in a smug enough tone to warrant a warning glare from the CO.

'Commandeering an RAF helicopter and taking it into the middle of an air strike. You've outdone yourself this time. I want to RTU so much I have an erection.'

Suddenly Psycho was taking this seriously. He did not want to be returned-to-unit.

'Boss, I'm not going back to 2 Para.'

The Old Man looked up from the desk to glare at Psycho.

'You don't have a choice, Sykes, you haven't served out your court-appointed term yet. If I drum you out of the Regiment, I assure you, you *will* be going back to 2 Para.'

'Any options, boss?' Psycho asked, worried.

The Old Man just continued glaring at him.

'Well, it seems your little stunt impressed our American friends,' the Colonel said, finally. He tapped a folder on the desk. 'It's RTU or this.'

Psycho glanced at the folder. It had the words "Raptor Team" printed on the front.

2020, Nellis AFB, Nevada

'Well, you look a lot better than you did the last time I saw you,' Psycho said.

Barnes shielded his eyes from the glaring desert sun with his hand. He was surprised to see the Brit still wearing a leather jacket in this heat.

'I wanted to say thank you,' Barnes said.

'No issues, mate. Call sign Prophet, right?' Psycho asked. Barnes nodded.

'I think it's someone's idea of a sick joke,' Barnes said. He was sure the nickname had come from his now highly-classified after-action report from Columbia. 'Nice tattoo. Very subtle.'

Psycho ran his fingers over the highly-stylised winged dagger tattooed on the back of his shaven head. It had only just finished healing.

'Thought I'd wave the flag, y'know, whilst I'm over here on secondment with Delta Farce.'

Barnes nodded, smiling.

'I'm sure we can find some way to impress Supply And Services.'

'Should be a laugh this, though, right?'

'Michael? I'm going to see if I can help you,' The voice said.

You can, *the wretched thing that had once been Michael Sykes thought.* You can kill me.

Chance – Part 2

Rovesky Township, upper Podkamennaya Tunguska River, Krasnoyarsk Krai, Siberia, Russian Federation, 2025

Prophet leapt out into the cold Siberian air, high over the frozen street. Searchlights from the VTOLs tracked him in the air. There were so many lines of light on the suit's Heads-Up Display from the threat tracer, showing possible bullet trajectories, that his vision was almost washed out. He shut down the suit's proximity alarm in mid-air due to information overload. With a thought he wrapped the lensing field of the suit's stealth system around himself. To the CELL gunmen in the street it looked like he'd disappeared. Then they opened fire.

***

That's it, you draw their fire my son, Psycho thought as he dropped out of the attic window stealthed. Above him he could hear the spec ops team they'd sent into the attic find the line of claymores he'd set at head height. He landed on the street hard and noisy. He needed a moment while the suit's systems stabilised him. The noise of his impact hadn't mattered so much. Everyone in the street was looking up and firing at Prophet's aerial show. Above him he saw one of the VTOLs drift over the brothel. Dealing with the pain, he squeezed the detonator for the remote explosive charges they had set in the roof.

***

Prophet had a moment to register just how much he was getting shot when the roof of the brothel exploded. The fireball and debris shot into the air, engulfing one of the CELL VTOLs. The overpressure wave from the force of the explosion hit him in the back with the force of a steam-hammer, as the burning wreckage of the CELL VTOL dropped through the brothel. The explosion's concussion wave drove Prophet through the wall of the building opposite. The suit's ionic electroactive polymer liquid armour, incorporating colloidal-doped ceramics and a copper nanolattice in an ethylene-glycol bucky-ball matrix not withstanding, and his dead flesh not withstanding, being hammered through a wall had really hurt.

He was in a large dormitory room filled with beds. The room was illuminated by the searchlight shining through the windows from one of the remaining VTOLs as it hovered outside. As Prophet staggered to his feet, the suit starting to mend the damage he'd just received, the furniture and much of the floor disintegrated in front of his eyes as it was torn apart by the VTOL's cannon fire. Visible now, Prophet started to run. The VTOL was keeping pace with him, firing as fast as it could. It looked like the walls themselves were being eaten away by the cannon fire.

***

Psycho was keeping an eye on his energy as he continued moving stealthed. He reached under the APC and attached a REX. All eyes were on the VTOL firing round after round into the building opposite the collapsing brothel. He moved rapidly to the next APC and then did the same. At the third APC he was kneeling down next to it attaching the REX when the lensing field failed and he became visible. He stood up to find a terrified-looking CELL gunman staring at him.

'Yeah, there's two of us, sunshine,' Psycho said as he crossed the distance between them, quickly drawing his combat knife.

***

Getting hit by the VTOL's cannon felt like death. It felt like it should have burst his body and scattered it around the building disintegrating around him. It spun him around. Red warning signs from the HUD told Prophet he couldn't take another series of hits like that. Prophet reached the hole in the wall where a window used to be and jumped out over the street. He had a moment to register the look of panic on the VTOL pilot's face. The floor of the building he'd just jumped out of collapsed from the cannon fire, and clouds of dust and powdered debris shot out into the night air.

Prophet landed on the armoured glass of the VTOL's cockpit and immediately started slipping off. He pulled his fist back and hammered it into the glass with all the power the suit could muster. He punched through the windshield and opened his fist. The now slightly-misshapen grenade fell out of his hand and into the cockpit. Prophet slid off the front of the VTOL.

***

The kid had died quickly at Psycho's hands, knowing the terror of inevitability in his last few moments as he had desperately tried to bring his Feline SMG to bear. The kid's death had left the nearby CELL soldiers in no doubt as to Psycho's presence.

A number of them were turning towards Psycho. There was a Bulldog light transport vehicle in the middle of the street. Its heavy machine gun was being turned towards him. Then one of the VTOL's exploded in mid air. For a moment the CELL soldiers were distracted. Psycho leapt high into the air, squeezing the detonator for the REX charges.

***

Prophet landed on the frozen mud street in trouble. The suit was still trying to fix him. Fortunately the CELL troopers, like him, were more concerned with scrambling out of the way of the VTOL that he'd just dropped a grenade into. He ran and threw himself forwards as the wrecked VTOL hit the ground. Secondary explosions blew CELL personnel into the air. Flying debris tore more apart.

The force of the explosions sent Prophet tumbling across the street into the side of a Bulldog LTV. There were more red warning signs from the suit. He was taking fire again. His speeded-up perception, provided by the suit's systems, made the HMG tracer fire coming at him look like a slow and graceful arcing light show.

Then further down the street, next to the burning brothel, three of the CELL APCs exploded.

***

Psycho was in the air as the three APCs exploded. He'd placed the three charges on one side of the vehicles. The force of the explosion flipped them. Sent them tumbling into the street, crushing more CELL personnel and damaging other vehicles.

I live for this Psycho thought as he landed in the back of the Bulldog LTV. Air-stomping it. Hammering his power-assisted foot down so hard it broke the back of the vehicle's chassis. Two of the six CELL troopers in the back of the Bulldog were catapulted out of the vehicle and into the street. Psycho grabbed one of the remaining CELL troopers and threw her across the street into a wall, hard enough to break her back. He kicked another one. The force of the power-assisted blow powdered the trooper's rib cage and sent him flying over the side of the Bulldog, his body tumbling like a rag doll. One of them scrambled over the front of the Bulldog to get away from the nanosuited killer. The fourth one was too slow. Psycho punched him in the base of the back as he was trying to escape. He couldn't hear the spine snapping over the gunfire and screams.

***

I need time Prophet thought as he scrambled to his feet and ran towards a mining supply store that fronted onto the frozen street. There was a Bulldog parked in front of it. Prophet could see the gunner had recovered from the explosion and was trying to bring the vehicle's HMG to bear. All around him the ground was being torn up and CELL troopers were literally exploding, victims of friendly fire, as one of the two remaining VTOLs tried to target Prophet with its cannon.

Prophet increased his speed and power-kicked the Bulldog. The force of the kick slid the vehicle round more than ninety degrees and through the window of the mining supply store. Prophet grabbed a motorbike that had been lying on the ground and spun around, throwing it at the VTOL. The motorbike circled lazily through the air. The pilot added thrust, moving the

VTOL sharply out of the way of the spinning machine. Prophet used the momentary distraction to disappear into the store.

***

Armour mode. The CryFibril nanomuscle tightened the suit's outer weave, increasing the armour's density. Psycho grabbed the HMG and tore it off its pintle mount. He could see the driver and the gunwoman in the Bulldog's passenger seat turning around, trying to bring weapons to bear. Psycho lowered the HMG's barrel and pulled the trigger. The HMG's .50 calibre rounds hit them at such close range it looked like the two CELL soldiers had just vaporised.

Psycho was vaguely aware of taking fire on his back. He turned around and saw that the two CELL gunmen who'd been catapulted off the Bulldog were firing at him. He fired the HMG back at them. The large rounds churned up the gunmen's flesh, sent them tumbling across the frozen mud.

Psycho leapt over the side of the Bulldog in a hail of fire, bullets and fragments of brick sparking off his reinforced armour. He started killing with the HMG.

'Get some, you slags!' He wanted the CELL forces to know that gods of war walked amongst them.

***

Everyone was shooting at the mining supply store as Prophet scrambled through it. The threat tracer showed bullet trajectories all around him. It looked like a bullet was travelling through every square inch of air in the store. He could see tracer fire from HMGs and Mk 60s, then chunks of the ceiling exploded as another VTOL started firing down through the building. A grenade landed behind him and exploded. The force threw him into the air and through a wooden partition wall at the back of the shop.

He felt it. He felt every last impact, every explosion. He still felt the pain. Prophet got to his feet. He had found the stairs. He scrambled up them as they started to disintegrate around him. He activated the stealth mode. The lensing field wrapped around him. He took a moment. Just a moment. He wasn't fighting for breath. He had no need of that anymore. He just needed a bit of time for the partially-alien technology of his suit and his melded flesh to fix the damage.

The floor above the storefront was an apartment. He could see the remains of an old couple, torn apart by stray rounds.

I'm sorry, his remaining humanity thought and then it was business.

They were still concentrating their fire on the ground floor. The rounds were eating away at the mostly wooden building. He could feel it shift beneath him as he walked to the window. Prophet removed the L-Tag grenade launcher from its clip on the back of his armour. He could see one of the VTOLs outside. They couldn't see him. He was as invisible as Ceph-derived human technology could make him.

He raised the L-Tag to his shoulder and fired. Worked the pump. Fired again. Two sixty millimetre smart grenades flew at the VTOL. The grenades exploded in an airburst next to the aircraft, battering it around. It wasn't nearly enough to destroy the armoured VTOL, Prophet knew, but it panicked the pilot. He banked hard, clipping a building as he frantically tried to gain height.

Down in the street Prophet could see Psycho using an HMG like a scythe. *Good soldier*, he thought. Then he started firing the L-Tag again. He used two grenades to clear the streets out in front of the mining store. Then the remaining three he dropped in above the most concentrated areas of fire shooting at Psycho. The smart grenades exploded in the air. Force battered the CELL troops to the ground as fragments tore into their battered and concussive-force ruptured bodies.

Now it was time to go and make a stand with Psycho out in the street. They might die, but they wouldn't be alone.

***

All around the room board members watched the images in horror. None of them had problems making decisions that would kill thousands of people, sometimes tens of thousands, but somehow the immediacy of the carnage unfolding in front of them appalled in a way they weren't used to. Or perhaps, as people who considered themselves powerful, it was the rawness of the physical power being displayed by the two nanosuit operators that was affecting them.

They watched the screens as grenades exploded over the heads of their troops and more were cut down by machine gunfire. The cost in vehicles, and medical and death benefits alone, would be astronomical.

'It's like New York all over again.'

'We have a counter measure in place.'

'Which would significantly damage the infrastructure of the ...'

'What infrastructure? It's fucking Siberia.'

'Chairman, you have the deciding vote. Should we initiate the Cold Protocol?'

'Do it. Bring the cold.'

***

Walker kept his head down, hunkered behind a Bulldog that had been riddled with fire. He had seen the thing coming towards him. It was an armoured figure, impervious to their fire like something out of a comic book or a myth. There was nothing they could do but wait for it to kill them. Not even the drugs could control his fear. He thought of Carlotta and Elsa. He could hear it coming closer. It was going to kill him anyway.

***

The CELL soldier popped up from behind the wrecked Bulldog. He started firing his Scarab at Psycho. The rounds sparking off his armour like all the others. Psycho turned to face him. There was a moment. A spark of recognition. It was gone as HMG rounds sent the CELL soldier dancing backwards.

An auto-cannon round staggered Psycho, put him on one knee. He had no idea where it had come from. The next one almost knocked him over. Only the fact that he was in armour mode saved him. He staggered sideways towards the wreckage of one of the APCs he'd blown up. Its armoured body would provide him with a modicum of cover.

He continued firing the HMG. Mowing people down. He let it be known, through action, that anyone shooting at him would be killed. Anyone who wanted to run, could.

More cannon fire sparked off the carcass of the APC as the VTOL that had been firing at him hove into view above him. Psycho angled the HMG up and sent tracers arcing up at the aircraft. He could hear the rumble of an APC heading towards him. Another cannon round from the VTOL hit him.

***

They'd brought too many people with them. They had provided too much of a target rich environment. Some sneaky tricks and the capabilities of their armour had allowed them to wreak havoc on troops not trained to a high enough standard to play in this game. Prophet could hear their panic over their comms. The problem was that CELL didn't seem to be running out of personnel.

He had his suppressed Hammer II in his hand, killing opportunistically. He was using the stealth mode to move unseen through the carnage.

***

Psycho watched the suit energy in his Heads-Up Display. Every cannon round was agony, staggering him, sending him to the ground, breaking and rupturing things inside him. The energy bar was the countdown to his death. When lack of energy forced him out of armour mode, the cannon fire would tear him apart.

The APC trundled into view. *Well that's that, then,* Psycho thought, still firing the HMG at anyone dumb enough to shoot at him. To his surprise the APC turned its back to him. They're *going to debus!* he thought, exultantly, *that's madness!*

The turret on the APC turned to face him and the auto-cannon round took him in the chest. It lifted him off his feet and threw him back. He was astonished when he realised that he was still alive. Though living in pain.

He somehow managed to get up. The rear of the APC opened. He fired the HMG. The first two rounds killed the first CELL spec op soldier out of the armoured vehicle, then the weapon ran dry. Psycho threw it at the next soldier clambering out, with sufficient force to take him off his feet. The Londoner unslung his gauss rifle, put a quick burst into the one on the ground and then raised the weapon and started firing into the spec op team that was desperately, and foolishly, trying to debus from the APC.

Psycho noticed that one of them was holding a bizarre looking oversized weapon and trying to bring it to bear on him. Prophet appeared next to Psycho, and the Londoner started to turn to shoot the other nano-suited soldier before he realised what was happening.

A cannon round from the VTOL overhead just grazed Psycho's helmet. The force almost tore his head off. He hit the ground again. Prophet raised his gauss rifle and fired the weapon's underslung grenade launcher and then fired the entire magazine from the weapon at the VTOL's pilot. Hypersonic rounds outpaced the grenade and sparked off the VTOL's armoured windscreen. The armour-piercing solid shot made spider web cracks in the armoured glass. Then the grenade went off. The pilot was more startled than the VTOL was damaged, but he veered out of the way.

From the ground Psycho raised his gauss rifle and reached for the underslung grenade launcher's trigger.

'No!' Prophet screamed. Psycho fired the grenade launcher as the APC fired its main cannon. The APC round hit Prophet's gauss rifle and the weapon came apart in his hands while the huge round continued and hit him in the chest, just as he had re-activated armour mode. He was yanked off his feet and hit the ground, hard, and barely alive, despite the suit's systems. Psycho's grenade exploded in the back of the damaged APC. The spec ops team inside were now just so much red paint in the vehicle's interior.

'That was how we were going to escape,' Prophet muttered over the suit's comms as he tried to get up.

'Oh,' Psycho said, looking at the smoking interior of the APC. 'Yeah, that would have been a good idea.'

'Get in the APC,' Prophet said as he climbed to his feet. They were taking small arms fire again, from everywhere. The two remaining VTOLS were now overhead firing down around them.

***

Just a little closer, Amanda thought. The rest of her squad were dead. Shot down, taken out by grenades, caught under exploding VTOLS, had APCs roll over them. There was only her left. The shaven-headed African-American woman moved carefully and quietly through the rubble of the brothel. Her Jackal combat shotgun against her shoulder, ready to fire. She was moving as stealthily as she could, though the bulky special weapon slung over her back hampered her. She could make out movement from between the destroyed APCs that had been blown up when the fight started.

***

290

The missile was launched from a Sukhoi T-50 stealth fighter loaned to CELL by the Russian government. The T-50 then banked hard and kicked in its afterburners, trying to put as much distance between itself and the missile as possible.

The Circuit Breaker warhead in the guided missile detonated at one thousand feet above the township of Rovesky. Designed to recreate the electromagnetic pulse of a thirty-kiloton thermonuclear explosion, the burst of radiation fused every last piece of unshielded electronics in a thirty-mile radius. Even shielded electronics such as those in the CELL APCs were overloaded momentarily.

All the lights went out. The cobalt mine ceased work. All comms went down. That part of Siberia practically returned to a Stone Age level of technology in a moment.

***

Psycho didn't even have time to register the Aurora Borealis-style light show in the magnetosphere. He just hit the ground as all the suit's systems went down.

So reliant on the suit's fusion with his dead flesh, Prophet was dead before he hit the ground next to the Londoner.

***

To Amanda, standing amongst the rubble of the brothel, it seemed to happen very slowly. The two VTOLs almost looked graceful as their lights went off, the sky above them a shining fireworks display of electromagnetic radiation bouncing off the magnetosphere.

***

Psycho was still conscious. Locked in his dead suit. He saw the VTOLs fall out of his view. He couldn't even turn his head. He felt their impact through the ground. The fury at his helplessness overwhelmed him. He started screaming.

***

It had felt like sleep. It had felt welcoming, and cold. The ten thousand volts coursing through dead flesh, forcing sluggish systems in the suit's living technology back to life, felt less welcoming. It felt like fire surging through him. He was screaming.

He rolled onto his front and forced himself onto all fours. *Let me die!* he screamed silently at the suit. Just one moment of weakness, then he was taking fire again.

***

Short burst, correct aim, short burst, correct aim, repeat. Walk in on the target. The twelve-gauge solid shot slugs were impacting into the side of the moving armoured figure, knocking him over, battering him across the ground. She emptied the extended magazine of the automatic shotgun into him, ignoring the other armoured figure paralysed on the ground. She dropped the shotgun. She was appalled when he, it, the thing she'd seen far below St. Petersburg, stood up. She grabbed the weapon on her back and pulled it round in front of her. The armoured thing staggered towards her. She brought the weapon to her shoulder. It raised its hand as if reaching for her. She fired the netgun. The weighted high-tensile net, coated in industrial adhesive, spread open in mid-air, propelled by the four shotgun cartridges in each of the netgun's barrels.

The weapon's recoil staggered Amanda and she fell backwards over some of the rubble. She found herself staring numbly at the hand of a young woman sticking out of the rubble. She looked over at the armoured warrior that had killed so many of her friends. The net had entangled him. He was trying to move, trying to get the purchase to break it but he couldn't. As solutions went it had been around since the Stone Age. He fell over.

Amanda got up and drew the Hammer II from the holster at her hip. It was loaded with explosive rounds. She walked over to the armoured warrior's prone form. He stopped struggling when he felt the gun against his head.

'This is what it feels like to be human, motherfucker.' Amanda pulled the hammer back on the massive automatic. That was when the Spec Ops team turned up.

Weapons levelled at her. Screaming at her. She couldn't understand why they wouldn't let her pull the trigger. Empty the entire magazine at point blank range into his head. She relented. She spat on the armour.

'That's for Mikey,' she said and walked away.

***

It shouldn't have happened this way, the mission, too much was riding on the mission.

'What do you want done with them, boss?' the spec ops soldier asked the officer. Prophet was still wrapped in the adhesive-coated high-tensile wire. He could see Psycho. Power had obviously returned to Psycho's suit but they had him locked into heavy-duty restraints designed specifically for the nanosuits. Psycho was staring at Prophet, both of them being held on their knees, surrounded by a spec ops team with weapons at the ready. They were going to be transported in the APCs, the only vehicles with shielded electronics and therefore the only vehicles still working. More heavy-lift aircraft were being called in, as the ones at the mine's airfield were inoperative junk thanks to their fused avionics.

'That one is going to New York,' the officer said, pointing at Psycho. 'That one is going to the *Deepwinter* Facility,' she finished, pointing at Prophet.

Psycho was still staring at Prophet.

'We had a chance, Prophet. We had a chance.'

Enjoyed this book?

Then check out Gavin Smith's other high-octane SF thrillers.

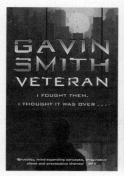  

VETERAN

Veteran is a fast paced, intricately plotted violent SF Thriller set in a dark future against the backdrop of a seemingly never ending war against an unknowable and implacable alien enemy.

WAR IN HEAVEN

Jakob Douglas, damaged soldier and unlikely hero, returns in another desperate, adrenalin-fueled adventure from Gavin Smith, author of the widely acclaimed Veteran.

AGE OF SCORPIO

We are machines, we are animals, we are hybrids. But some things never change. The Church knows we have kept our sins.

Published April 2013.